D1157068

CAPITOL

OFFENSE

Hill Kemp

This novel is a work of fiction. Although inspired by actual events, the names, characters, and incidents are the product of the author's imagination or are used fictitiously. Any resemblance to actual persons, living or dead, is coincidental.

For additional copies contact:
The Books
P.O. Box 26
Milam, TX 75959
www.capitoloffense.com

Copyright © 2003 Hill Kemp
ISBN # 1-878096-70-2

All rights reserved. This part and parts thereof may not be reproduced without written permission of the author, except for customary privileges extended to the press and other reviewing agencies.

Second Printing, 2004
Published by Best of East Texas Publishers
515 South First Street/PO Box 1647
Lufkin, Texas 75902
Telephone 936/634-7444/ FAX 936/634-7750

Dedication
To Margaret

Chapter 1

December, 1998

Dan Carb turned his dark blue Ford sedan in to the parking lot at the Angelina Grill in the deep East Texas town of Lufkin. As he cruised by the front door looking for a parking place, what he saw caused him to bring his car to a screeching stop.

"Shit. Would you look at that," he said to no one. In the handicapped parking space next to the front door was a shiny, black Ford Excursion with darkened windows. Dan didn't even have to look for the State Official "SO" plates identifying it as a Texas official vehicle. Everybody in the legislature knew that black SUV belonged to Lance Dunn, Governor Butch Grange's main enforcer.

Dan found a parking place around back of the building. The rambling structure took up nearly half of the city block and looked like the product of several unplanned expansions. As he stepped out into the warm December sunshine, Dan thought through several explanations. Sir Lance-a-lot's presence almost certainly meant the governor was already cranking up the hardball fundraising. Dan would have to tread carefully.

The early December meeting of the Lufkin Rotary Club was set up so Dan could mend some fences in this far eastern county of his district. Dan's reelection as State Representative over Jerry Pollock, a popular Lufkin city councilman, meant Lufkin had been split in the November election a month earlier. The public reason for Dan's being here was to lay out his plans for the January legislative session. The political reason was that he needed to give the Lufkin big guns a chance to get back on his side.

Paula Torry, Dan's legislative assistant, had reached him on his cell phone as he raced down Highway 7 through the tall pine forest from his ranch in Fairmount to Lufkin.

"Hi, Paula. I reviewed your notes for my Lufkin speech and they look great. I'm just getting into Lufkin."

"OK, Dan, but I've got a news flash for you. I got a copy of a letter from a Texas Utilities lobbyist. He's after the gov's staff to back a bill giving the big utilities ten billion in state funds to pay off their nucs in trade for deregulating the electric market."

"What the hell? Those greedy bastards built those plants over protests. And now they want to get paid for building them?"

"I know, Boss, but here's the bad news. There's a handwritten note on the memo recommending that the gov go along with it. Just thought you ought to know."

As he walked around to the front of the restaurant, Dan thought back to Paula's call and the battles between utilities and consumers he'd refereed as a member of and one-term as chairman of the State Affairs Committee in the Texas House. If the plan in that memo was why Lance-a-lot was here, he knew he'd better watch his ass.

"Hello, Mr. Representative. Welcome back to Lufkin." Bull Taylor, the mayor of Lufkin for the last twenty years, had stuck by Dan, even when a member of his city council had run against him. Bull was the key to getting Dan back on good terms with the Lufkin power brokers.

"Mr. Mayor. Nice to see you again."

As they shook hands, the mayor jerked his head toward the office behind the check out register. They stepped in and closed the door behind them. The cramped office seemed overfilled with Bull's bulk and Dan's six-foot-five height and broad shoulders.

"Look, Dan, I've got everybody here ready to mend fences and get on with it. But what the hell is Lance Dunn doing here? I thought getting my folks back on your side and your legislative plan were the only things on the agenda."

"I'm not sure, but I've got an idea what it's about. I think the big utilities have a plan to get a big wad out of the State Treasury in trade for deregulation."

"Damn, Dan. I guess that explains why that chesty woman that works for the Lieutenant Governor in the Senate is here too. Betsy something."

Dan's heart sank as his worst explanation for Lance's showing up got confirmed. "Damn. She just left the "Light Governor's" office and went to work on staff for the utilities' association. The fat's in the fire. The "gov" is already trying to line up big bucks for his presidential run and it looks like the utilities see it as a chance to make a killing at our expense."

"Well, if the gov is behind all these power brokers showing up out here in the piney woods, you'd better watch out what you say. They're probably getting lined up to storm your committee."

"Look, Bull, I'm just going to play it straight and not get into that fight now. Let's see if they bring it up."

"OK, Boy. Sounds like a shark pool to me. Just the kind of fight your daddy loved to get into."

Dan noticed that Bull was wearing a gray sport coat and red tie over blue jeans. "Bull, I'm not overdressed am I?"

Bull looked him over. "Just right, son. Nice blue coat and a pretty tie. You've even got your boots on. Like a cross between Gary Cooper and Rock Hudson. Perfect." Smiling, Bull slapped Dan on the back and they headed into the restaurant.

The Angelina Grill had been a Lufkin landmark for years with its red brick outside and lineup of mounted deer heads in the entry hall. The huge dining room was outfitted with a collapsible partition halfway down its length. For the Friday Rotary Club meeting the partition was closed. Bull and Dan walked past the public diners, who looked to Dan to be a mixture of truck drivers, tourists, and paper mill staff. Dan decided that most of the plates looked pretty unappetizing. He hoped their health certificate was up to date.

Dan Carb had gotten into politics only reluctantly. His father had been a politician in the House and then the Senate for nearly all of Dan's forty-seven years. Dan had grown up with his grandfather on the family cattle ranch on the east bank of the Trinity River. With his degree in agriculture and ranch management from Texas A&M, Dan settled at the ranch with his wife, Molly Ann, and their two daughters. His dad's drinking finally led to serious liver problems and he had to retire. At his dad's urging, Dan had run and been elected State Representative in his district when the incumbent was elected to his dad's Senate seat. Now here he was, probably heading into an electricity fight like the Carb family hadn't been in since his grandfather and LBJ organized a rural electrical cooperative in Houston and Madison counties in the forties.

"Hello there, folks. Good to see you again," Dan said, shaking hands around the group. Bull had started Dan off in a group of businessmen. They all looked like they wore their white shirts, ties, and sport coats with difficulty and would have been more comfortable in tee shirts and jeans. Dan was completely at home talking to total strangers as if they were long lost friends, and the conversation moved from the weather to the legislature, to football, and then to the lousy cattle prices. When it headed back to the weather, Dan excused himself to work the rest of the room.

This meeting, set as it was between the election in early November and the December 15th political contribution deadline, was the time for anyone who had not contributed to the winner's campaign to make up for their omission. Since there had been a local in the race, lots of people in Lufkin had given to Dan's opponent. By the time he'd worked the fourth group in the room Dan had been discreetly given seven envelopes containing checks. Known affectionately as "tickets on the late train," this late money always bothered Dan, but he smiled and thanked the contributors, again like they were old friends.

Bill Crandon, the vice-president of East Texas Paper, Lufkin's biggest employer, pulled Dan aside. "Dan, just a quick point. I see that we've got the governor's hatchet man and the utilities' newest lobbyist here. The Paper Association sent a fax around that those boys were going to make a play with Butch for the state to pick up the tab for their bad investments in nucs. You know we're big backers of Butch, but we can't let the utilities get away with robbery. When I make a bad investment at the mill, hell, I've got to eat it. It should be the same for them."

"I heard something about that too, Bill. Let's don't get too excited until we find out for sure."

"I just hope you've got the same fire in your belly that your dad had when it comes to thieving utilities."

"Oh, don't worry. I'm chairing the committee they'll have to come to. I'll keep 'em in line." Dan was tempted to look in the envelope Bill had handed him to see how bad the boys from the paper companies thought the problem was, but he knew he'd have to wait. If the Paper Association smelled a fight, the checks in the bulging envelope should be nice ones.

He finally located Dunn talking to a group in the corner of the room. Betsy Pertny, a long time capitol staffer in the Lieutenant Governor's office, was in the same group. He stayed away from them as long as he could, but couldn't completely ignore the governor's top staffer.

"Hi, Lance, what's got you out here in God's country? You lost?" Dan knew him to be a very tough but not unreasonable player.

Lance Dunn was way overdressed for this crowd, with a black suit and conservative tie. He smiled as he spoke to Dan.

"Hello, Mr. Chairman. When I heard you were speaking over here, I had to come by. I was down in Beaumont visiting some folks and we decided to take the long way back to Austin. Looks like you've got good supporters around here." The "we" was not wasted on Dan.

"Yeah, I did OK even with a local in the race."

"Hi, Betsy. I don't think I've ever seen you outside Austin. How ya' been?"

"Great, Dan. Oh, I love to get out and meet folks. We've been having great discussions." Dan noticed that Betsy seemed to know more about matching the dress for the occasion than Lance. She was wearing a nice green print dress and low heels and her only jewelry was a small gold necklace. Her brown hair was tied back in a ponytail. Betsy always made an impression on a group of men because of her nice figure. Most everyone in the group she'd been talking to seemed to be addressing her mid-chest.

Dan decided he'd better follow up on Lance's greeting. "Yeah, I hope folks will be just calling me "Mr. Chairman" this session instead of screaming it out like last time. You talk to Billy?"

"Yeah, Billy and I had a little sit down about the session after Thanksgiving. He told me you'd chair State Affairs again. You did a good job last time, Dan. Congratulations." Lance smoothed the sparse hair on his balding head.

"Well, I've tried to work hard. From what I hear, it still should be a lively committee this time." Dan grinned at both of them. "Plenty of fireworks, huh?"

Dan had learned from Speaker Billy Gibson that he again had the chairmanship only the week before. Dan had moved up fast in the legislature, both because of his dad's tutoring and the mentoring of his dad's best friend, Senator Andrew Giles from San Angelo. Giles and Senator Carb had been trench warriors in the redistricting battles between urban and rural legislators in the seventies. Giles acted like it was a major privilege to help Dan Carb, the son of the man he'd been so close to for so many years. It meant that Dan had gotten a vice-chair in only his second session and had moved up to chair of the heavy-duty State Affairs Committee in his third term.

"Well, Dan, you probably heard, I'm working for some of the investor-owned utilities, so I'll probably be seeing a lot of you this session." Betsy's soft Texas drawl gave her an air of ease and calm. Like a sleeping rattlesnake, Dan thought.

"That's great, Betsy. Hell, my dad always thought you were one of the best staffers in the 'Light Governor's' office. I'm sure we'll get along fine as long as you can keep those utility boys in line." Dan hoped they could keep up meaningless banter and not get into any serious questions about legislation. He decided that this wasn't friendly territory for the utilities, with the paper mill such a big influence. In Lufkin, when the paper mill brass spoke everybody listened.

Over the microphone came the call to take seats for lunch. "I'll catch you folks later," he told Betsy and Lance-a-lot. Dan breathed a sigh of relief and made his way to the front table.

The rest of the meeting was a blur for Dan. After the meal of canned beef and tired vegetables he gave a twenty-minute speech outlining some major issues due up in the January regular session, carefully avoiding utility issues. Paula Torry had done her homework and Dan was able to mention several ideas that would appeal to Lufkin. He was interrupted by applause a number of times.

After his speech, he worked the crowd, getting several more "late train" checks, before ducking out, managing to avoid both Betsy and Lance. Bull told him he'd hit just the right points and gotten good response.

As soon as Dan was on the highway out of Lufkin, he called Paula. "Nice work on the Lufkin speech. It went over big. Now, here's the bad news. Lance-a-lot was there and so was Betsy Pertny."

"Oh, God, Dan. They were out in Lufkin?"

"Lance said something about a meeting in Beaumont. I guess it was with Entergy. I'm betting Betsy's making the rounds of her new bosses at the utilities, so they were probably both down there. It says volumes if she's being squired around by the gov's hatchet man."

"All of us who pay electric bills had better get ready to fund that $10 billion. That's blatant of Butch and Lance."

"Paula, I think that Butch is going to be a real whore for money for his national campaign. This is just the beginning. But, look, it means that I've got a major fight in State Affairs. Have you had any luck finding me a committee staffer? I need somebody tough who'll do anything I ask them."

"OK, Dan, hold on to your hat. Or better yet, hold on to that steering wheel. You know that memo I told you about this morning? It had to have been slipped out of the gov's office."

"Yeah, that was a huge head's up for me, especially with Lance tracking me today."

"You know I don't usually bother you with how I get that kind of stuff. It's better if you don't know. But this time, it came from someone who might be that committee staffer you want. Randi Crendall has worked for Garza for the last three sessions and she's a real tough trooper. She did most of the work behind Garza's bill to give low-income ratepayers a break. That was a real piece of work. She came up to me at Starbucks this morning and gave me that memo. Said she thought we might find it interesting."

"Is she available? Do you think she could stand up to the pressure?"

"She didn't exactly say she was available, but getting that memo and then giving it to me was a gutsy thing to do. I think I should follow up to see what else she might have to say. With her utility experience, she's the best prospect I've found so far, and she's obviously not afraid to take risks."

"OK, Paula. Go ahead and talk to her. I'm coming to Austin Tuesday. If she sounds good to you, I'll meet her. Garza and I get along fine and I'm sure he'd understand if it's a step up for his staffer."

Dan's trip back from Lufkin took him through the Davy Crockett National Forest. Texas Highway 7 writhed over the red clay hills like a long black snake, in a tunnel with seventy-foot-high pine trees on both sides. His legislative district covered much of the East Texas forestland. It included his home county of Houston plus all or part of Anderson, Madison, Leon, Cherokee, Angelina, Hardin, and Tyler counties. He spent so much time driving over the scattered counties that he hardly had time for his ranch or his family.

The Carb ranch was located at the intersection of the Old San Antonio Road and the Trinity River. His great-great-great grandfather, Micah Carbach, as it was spelled back then, built a log cabin on a hill on the east side of the river in 1830 and cleared his Mexican Land Grant for crops and livestock. After the Comanches burned out his first and second cabins, he hauled stone from around Austin and built a stone house with a stone fence around it. From this fortress, "Firehead," as the Comanches called Dan's redheaded ancestor, successfully defended his home and established a safe haven for travelers on the famous road.

The ranch now occupied two thousand acres on both sides of the OSR. Since his grandfather died in 1983, Dan had lived on the ranch with his wife, Molly Ann, and their two daughters–Ruth, about to graduate from high school, and Mary, a freshman. Dan's mother, Judy, had lived in Madisonville until 1990 when Dan's father died of cirrhosis of the liver. She came to live on the ranch with them in the early nineties.

Dan thought again how lucky they were to have his mom living with them. Molly Ann had gone to Austin with Dan for his first three sessions and his trusted ranch manager, Ben Faust, and Dan's mom ran the ranch. The girls stayed home with their grandmother and went to school in Madisonville.

But two years ago Molly Ann started to develop pains in her arms. The condition worsened and she was diagnosed with Multiple Sclerosis last year. With Dan's daughters busy with school, his mom stayed home taking care of Molly Ann. Dan realized with a pang of sorrow that this would be the first session Molly Ann would not be with him in Austin. Her MS was mostly stabilized with medications, but she wasn't even able to get out of bed without help.

When Dan crested the last hill before home, he could see the outline of the Carb house at the top of the next rise. That sight always gave him a deep sense of wonder at himself as the keeper of the long Carb tradition. A tradition that featured maverick fights for nearly lost causes. He decided that the 1999 fight with the governor over the utilities' money grab, like all the times his father and grandfather had protected the local farmers and ranchers, would stand him squarely in that tradition. He just wished that Molly Ann could be there with him.

Chapter 2

The view from the undeveloped cul-de-sac that they'd found in the hills west of Austin was gorgeous on this clear Sunday night. Randi Crendall and Dave Treston frequently came up here to look at the city lights spanning the whole panorama. Dave had found a way around the chained off entrance, so they had the spot to themselves. At the center of the view, the lighted dome of the capitol building shone pink in the December chill.

"Hey, Dave, get me another beer too," Randi said over her shoulder. She had decided that it was time to let Dave in on her plans to jump jobs at the legislature, and another beer would help her courage. Randi wore a fuzzy, white sweater and denim jacket over red jeans. Her long blonde hair was loose and blowing in the cold breeze.

Dave brought the beers and joined her sitting on a rock ledge overlooking the city.

"Dave, I've got something to tell you that you can't tell anyone else about. You've got to promise me."

"OK, Randi, what are you up to now?" He sounded skeptical. In the dim light of the city glow Randi admired his thin features and neatly trimmed curly hair. She and Dave had met shortly after he took the job at the Legislative Council and they had dated off and on for the last four years. Dave had helped Randi curb her temper and get better accepted at the capitol.

"Well, I found a good use for that letter you got from the gov's office. I think it just may have done the trick for my new job."

"What the hell are you talking about, 'new job'? You've got a good job with Garza. Why mess with that?"

Randi drank deeply from her beer. When she spoke, her voice was high-pitched like a little girl. "Well, I've been a bad girl. I gave a copy of that letter to Paula Torry in Carb's office."

"Dammit, I hope you're making that up. You could get me in a mess of trouble if that letter gets in the wrong hands. What the hell is Paula going to do with it? Are you trying to get a job with Carb?" Dave took her arm and turned her to look straight at him.

Randi's reaction was quick. She knocked his hand off her arm and backhanded Dave across the face all in one swift move. "Don't you go grabbing me like that, Dave. You know I can't stand it. Besides, I'm not going to get you in trouble. I didn't let her know how I got it."

Dave wiped his face where she hit him. "Baby, sometimes you just don't make any sense. Damn. So what are you up to now?"

"I'm trying to get a job working on State Affairs this session. Dan Carb is chairing that committee."

"So? What's the big deal? You're dumping Garza to go work for State Affairs? You still haven't said why."

Randi looked out over the view. She knew she wasn't ready to tell Dave the reason. Hell, she wasn't even sure herself. She felt like the lizard on a checkerboard, not knowing which color to turn. "Dave, I just want to get to know Dan Carb better. I don't know. It just seems like something I need to do." Randi glanced sideways to see Dave's reaction.

"Randi, you don't go blowing a good job just for something to do. You'd better think about it."

"I have thought about it, Dave. I've got an interview with Carb next week, and if I get the offer I'm going to take it."

"Well, OK. You know Carb will talk to Garza before he offers you anything. Don't come bitching to me if Garza gets upset and you wind up out on your ass."

When Randi spoke, she was close to tears. "They wouldn't do that to me would they?" This time Randi grabbed Dave's arm and turned him toward her.

Dave shoved her hard, almost knocking her off the ledge. She screamed and held on to a bush to keep from falling.

"Shut up, dammit. You'll have the cops after us." Dave reached down and pulled her back up on the rock.

"Dave, you have to help me with this. I need to know you'll be there if I need help." Randi threw her arms around his neck and started to cry and wail.

"I don't know, Baby. You know I'll try to help you. But I don't want to mess up my job at the Council."

Randi wiped her tears and smiled at Dave. She stood up and unbuttoned her jacket, dropping it to the ground. Next she pulled the sweater off over her head and threw it onto the jacket. Her red bra was next. She unzipped

Dave's jacket, unbuttoned his shirt and hugged her bare breasts to his chest. "Come on, Davey. Let's go get in the back seat. It's cold out here." Randi could feel Dave's erection rubbing against her stomach. That's it, little guy, you just help me convince him.

Randi picked up her clothes and ran to the car. Dave was right behind her. By the time he got into the back seat, Randi had shed her jeans and panties and he fairly dived on top of her. She helped him as he frantically tore at his remaining clothes.

Randi started running her tongue up and down the inside of his thighs to his jubilant accompaniment. "You're not going to get to put this nice thingy of yours where you want to put it until you agree to help me with my new job."

"God, woman, you drive a tough bargain," Dave blurted between yelps. "OK, OK, I'll help. It'll probably get me in trouble, but I'll help."

The grunting and moaning of their lovemaking were muffled by the closed car and carried off on the strong northwest breeze. The car swayed on its shocks for over an hour.

"Hey, Davey, we really fogged up your windows. Let's go out naked and look at the city. Come on."

"Shit, it's cold out there. We'll catch pneumonia."

"Don't be such a wimp." Randi opened the car door and ran out to the ledge. Dave came running over, slapping his arms to try to keep warm.

"Dave, sometimes when I look out over Austin like this, I think I might like to fly out there over all those lights." She stood, arms raised over her head, her long blond hair blowing around her bare shoulders. "Austin, here's your little bird."

"Well, Miss Birdie, can we get in out of this damned cold? I've got goose bumps the size of marshmallows."

Later, in her apartment, Randi sat in front of her dressing table looking again at the picture of Dan Carb at the front mike on the House floor. Randi decided that Dan was a real hunk and that was why she wanted to work for him. When Randi went to bed, curled up with her stuffed tiger, she went to sleep fantasizing about curling up with Dan Carb.

Chapter 3

Dan's drive to Austin on Monday afternoon took him west along the OSR to Bastrop. He could take the four-lane US-290, which he crossed, but preferred to stay with the rural rolling hills of the backcountry on Highway 21. Just before he got to Bastrop he always looked forward to driving through the Lost Pines area as a taste of his home territory just before heading up to the stony hills in Austin.

Dan had spent much of the weekend working with Ben to get the cattle ready for the "blue norther" cold front that had come through in the wee hours of Sunday morning. Molly had had a rough weekend and Dan and his mom were worried that she'd have to go to the hospital. The last thing Dan needed was the call he got from Billy Gibson, the House Speaker, late Saturday night.

"Hey, Dan boy. I hope you're keeping warm in all this weather. Look, I got a call from Lance. He wants a little get-together at his house on Monday night. You, him, the governor, and me. Weren't you coming to town anyway?"

"Yeah, Billy, I'm due on Tuesday. Molly Ann is having some trouble, but if she's OK by Monday, I can get there Monday night. What's going on?"

"Oh, you know. Old Lance is just trying to get his ducks in a row before the session."

"OK, Billy, but if Molly's still having trouble you're liable to hear from me."

Dan had hung up the bedroom phone and looked over to Molly's bed. Her long brown hair was splayed across her pillow and her eyes were closed.

With a weak voice she said, "I heard you, Dan Carb. You can't go messing up your session and using me for an excuse."

"Molly, I thought you were asleep. Look, it's just the governor playing politics with the utility bill. If I go over there every time Butch gets a little nervous I'll wear out the highway and the truck."

Molly's smile was weak, but her dark eyes were shining as ever. "That wasn't Butch on the phone. It was Billy. And anyway, your mom and I can take care of things here. I'm doing a little better."

Dan marveled at Molly's strength through the adversity of MS. His wife of twenty years was probably still the stronger willed of the two of them.

With Molly doing better Monday afternoon, Dan had agreed to go but felt a growing sense of dread about what he was heading into as he got closer to the city. First, Lance in Lufkin and now an invite to his house to meet with the gov. Dan recalled the advice Senator Giles gave him for tight situations like this. *Go very carefully, the way porcupines make love.*

He skirted Austin to the west, past the new airport, and headed his crew cab truck toward the exclusive lakeside development in the glow of a bright, clear sunset. Dan drove his sedan to most campaign stops, but when he was just working he preferred the fire engine red, four-door Ford Lariat pick-up. By the time he drove into Lance's driveway, the sun was nearly down.

Being invited to Lance Dunn's house was a special privilege, but Dan had been there before and he didn't feel very special this time. He felt more like the sacrificial lamb on the menu with the Speaker, the Governor, and Lance-a-lot there. He hoped Billy hadn't sold out to the gov.

Lance's house, a one-story white brick mansion, was built in the shape of a triangle. The front entryway was at one point of the triangle and the back was a long, arched glass wall with a huge veranda looking west out over a grand view of the lake. Dan parked his pick-up in front of the four-car garage on the left next to Billy Gibson's Mercedes. A lighted, arched entryway led to elaborately carved double front doors.

Lance met Dan at the door, and as they walked toward the living room Lance said, "I'm glad you could make it on short notice. We just needed to put together a little strategy session to get Butch in the picture on some items coming up in the session."

"Oh, I was coming to town anyway. I just had to come a day early. Where's Billy?"

"He's out on the veranda with Nellie. Billy really likes the sunset from our veranda. Go on out. What're you drinking? I'll get it."

"I'll have a beer, thanks."

Dan headed across the living room. The huge room was outfitted in white. Over-stuffed chairs and sofas that could seat several dozen people were finished in white leather. Plush, white carpet covered the entire space, including the two steps up to the level of the glass wall and the veranda beyond. Dan had the urge to check to be sure his boots were clean.

Billy Gibson turned to greet Dan when he walked out into the chill night air. They shook hands.

"Hey, Dan boy, you just about missed one of the prettiest sunsets ever. Glad you could make it."

Billy Gibson had been elected Speaker in 1991 after five terms in the house. The popular West Texas rancher seemed to have a perpetual smile whenever he was seen in public. Dan knew a more intense, even somber Billy of countless bill negotiations and fights. Dan had supported him in all three of his previous terms, and now as a committee chair he was on "the Speaker's team." This meant he would need to find a way to get behind almost everything Billy was pushing. If that included the utilities' money grab, Dan was in trouble.

Billy Gibson was in his late fifties and had sandy blond hair, blue eyes, and a face that you just had to describe as pretty versus handsome. He didn't look feminine, but his looks were striking and attractive. Billy was sensitive about his five-foot, four-inch height. Whenever he was around anyone taller, like Dan, he always tried to conduct business sitting down. Billy was seated at a glass-topped table, holding his drink.

Dan spoke to Lance's wife Nellie. "Hello, Nellie. Enjoying this cold snap?" Nellie was a small woman with dark hair and eyes. She was wearing a long cocktail dress and a white fur jacket.

"Oh, Representative Carb. Yes, I always look forward to what little winter we have around here." She spoke very formally and with a decided Midwest accent. Nellie was not part of Lance's presence at the capitol, preferring the role of barely visible hostess to their many parties during the session.

"I guess Lance is getting your drink, Representative. I'll let you boys get on with business. Come see us again, Billy."

Dan felt comfortable in his suede leather sport coat as he sat down in a chair close to the other man.

Billy spoke first. "That cold front give you any trouble?"

"Well, I managed to get some hay out to my cattle before that freeze hit Sunday morning. Not that the market price makes them worth much, but at least I won't have to go to the trouble of burying them because they froze. I guess I'm doing all right."

"Yeah, we got down in the low teens Saturday night. I think mine did OK." Billy's ranch was north and west from Austin, close to Abilene. Dan knew to wait and let Billy bring up any political topics.

"Dan, my man, I thought you and Lance and I should talk a little about the session coming up to be sure everything's lined up." Dan nodded, waiting for him to get to the point. "Now you and I know that there's going to be a lot of attention on us this time because of what Butch is planning to do with his national run."

"Yeah, I guess the press will be making a big fuss."

"Right. And State Affairs is liable to get a lot of that fuss too. What with some of the bills you might have to deal with."

"Well, at least we don't have any big agencies in sunset review like last time."

"No, it's not that." Billy again showed his big toothy smile. "I think Butch wants to be sure that he's seen as big on deregulation, so he's pushing for something for the electrics. It may kick up a big fuss." Dan decided that Billy was trying to hold back some too. Maybe he wasn't committed yet.

"Big fuss, like what kind of fuss, Billy? Hell, we settled the Public Utility Commission and electrics last time. And Butch lined up with the big utilities to fight deregulation. What's he want to do now?"

Lance spoke up as he arrived with Dan's beer. He started off with a royal "we."

"We just want to set a good example by letting the marketplace rule versus some bunch of regulators that have never had to turn a profit in their lives." Lance set Dan's beer on the table in front of him and took one of the other chairs. "We think that the people and the market should determine the price and distribution of electrical power." Lance seemed to be warming to his subject and was sounding like a campaign flier. "The time for regulation of electric power in Texas is past."

When Dan spoke he tried to avoid sounding confrontational. "OK, Lance, I hear and agree with that in general. But if Texas is still an electrical island, split away from the national electric market because our four big utilities won't allow connections across the state line, what's in the market now to keep them from gouging Texas users simply because we can't play in the national market?"

As Lance started to speak, Nellie called from the door. "The governor's limo is just driving up. You should come on in. It's getting cold out there."

They pushed their chairs back and stood. Dan noticed that the sunset was now just a ruby red glow on the western horizon. The lights at the lake's edge curved around the shore like a string of pearls. He would have much preferred to just enjoy the view. Ah, but we get a private meeting with the great Butch. Shit!

When Lance escorted Butch into the living room, Dan and Billy had taken seats next to the fireplace that occupied one whole wall.

The gas log fire was turned up with a nice flame.

When Butch Grange entered a room he seemed to occupy the whole space. He was only five foot five, but with handsome good looks and bustling energy, he seemed a lot bigger. He had steely gray eyes and graying brown hair. Butch wore a dark gray suit with a royal blue tie. But Butch's strongest feature was his huge smile, perfected in years of being on TV selling cars.

"Gentlemen, gentlemen. Good to see you on this fine Texas winter night. I hope you and your families are doing well and that you're all prepared for our Lord's holiday, now just two weeks away." This all seemed to be said in one long exhale through a face-wide smile that looked surgically implanted.

"Hello, Governor," Billy strode over to shake hands. "Yeah, we're all doing fine. Old Lance here puts out a nice spread for company."

When Dan joined the greeting he was quickly aware that both the Speaker and Governor were about a foot shorter than him. "Hi, Governor. Billy's right. We're all doing great. Come on over by the fire and have a seat."

"All right, all right. Lance, bring me some of that branch water and let's set a spell. I'm anxious to hear what you boys think of my new plans."

When Lance came out with a tray of drinks he was followed by a woman Dan had never seen before. She wore her black hair in a pixie cut and she seemed to be taking in the whole room at once with dark eyes scanning everybody and everything. She carried a small leather briefcase.

"Gentlemen, let me introduce Ann Terrance. Ann, this is Speaker Gibson and this is Representative Carb, who chairs our State Affairs committee." As she shook hands with Billy and Dan, Lance continued with the introduction. "Ann is with the national committee that is helping the governor."

"Nice to meet you, gentlemen. You should ignore me and go on with your meeting. I'm just going to sit back and watch your governor in action." Her accent sounded like Pennsylvania to Dan, and she came across as strictly business. When their eyes met as they shook hands, Dan felt the distinct urge to protect himself.

Butch picked up on Lance's introduction. "Yeah, Ann here is working with my little ol' national committee. They're looking at me for a possible national run and she's here to observe me at work."

Ann took a seat on an unoccupied couch opposite Dan and Billy. Butch sat in a huge chair between the two rows of couches. Dan knew there was going to be pressure on him, and the presence of a stranger with that kind of charter made him wince.

Lance, standing near the fireplace, spoke up with more explanation. "Now you should know that Ann is only interested in observing Butch. Don't worry that she'll compromise the confidentiality of what any of us say. You should feel free to talk as if she wasn't here." Ann's expression showed she didn't like that last, but she kept quiet. She took out a note pad and poised a pen over it.

"Governor, we were just beginning to address the subject out on the veranda when you arrived. Your plan to deregulate electrical power in Texas squares completely with the free enterprise agenda you're so famous for. Dan, I think you were starting to ask a question when we got interrupted."

Dan was too smart for that trap. "Yeah, Governor, tell us some more about your plan to drop regulation. I thought that last session you weren't in favor of such a big step." The Public Utility Commission had come up before Dan's committee under the Texas sunset law, which meant that the legislature had to write a new bill authorizing the agency to keep it going.

"Well, uh, my boy, things change, you know. There are important forces moving us ever forward and we have to be ready to adapt with the change. Why I was telling Millie just the other night that what Texas needed was a lot more competition and a lot less go'ment." The way he talked about his wife, Millie, Dan always pictured her as sitting around waiting for one of the governor's pronouncements. Patented Butch bullshit, Dan thought.

"What the governor is saying," Lance said, "is that, with all the changes nationally in opening up electric markets, Texas should be at the forefront of deregulation and letting the market rule."

Dan looked to Billy, but he seemed to be lost in a study of the ice cubes in his Jack Daniels. "I know, Lance, but we looked at all that last session. We came to the conclusion that until Texas built electrical connections to the rest of the market it would be ratepayer suicide to deregulate. Our big utilities would just divide up the captive territory and charge whatever the traffic would bear."

Dan noticed that Ann started to respond to him, but she held back, instead making frantic notes on her pad.

Billy finally found his tongue. "You know, Dan's got a point there. We just went over all this electric stuff last session. Sunset gave us the ideal opportunity to change things and we pretty much left them alone. We'll look pretty silly coming right back and making big changes."

"Lance, what about that?" Butch asked, sounding genuinely lost.

"Look, Billy, this deal is pretty simple. There are a lot of other states that are dropping regulation and Texas can't afford to lag behind."

Dan saw an opportunity to help his own cause. "Well, if we handle it right and make sure we set up true competition, everybody should come out winners."

Lance started to say something to Dan, but Ann cut him off, striding into the center space in front of the fireplace. "Now, listen to me, gentlemen. Governor Grange has made it clear what he wants to do with the utility legislation. Your governor has spoken. You just have to do what it takes to make it happen. We don't need to hear any of this talk about the market or last session. Let's just get to the governor's agenda and make it happen." Her speech was delivered with crisp words and gestures that showed she was used to being in command. Damn strange way of just sitting and watching, Dan thought.

There was a few seconds of exchanged, stunned looks. Billy broke the silence.

"Now, look-a here, Little Lady. You just . . ."

She cut him off, slamming her notepad down on the floor. "Don't you address me as 'Little Lady.' My name is Ann Terrance. You can call me Miss Terrance or Ann but don't you dare call me Little Lady." Her eyes seemed to put off sparks.

Billy seemed ready to get in her face. With a look at Lance, he very visibly restrained himself. "OK, then, Miss Ann. It's clear you haven't been around Texas before. Let me explain a few things to you. First of all, the governor doesn't just get his way with his agenda in this state. The two branches of the legislature stand pretty well on their own. In fact, Texas has a weak-governor form of gov . . ."

"Stop," Ann screamed, cutting Billy off for the second time. "Everybody in this room better understand one damn thing right now. I never want to hear you utter the words 'weak governor' again – in private or public. That term simply has to leave your vocabulary. Governor Grange is a strong leader in Texas and will be a strong leader as president."

Billy shrugged, looking at Lance to step in. Butch seemed even more lost. Dan decided this was a pretty good show and wondered where it was going.

"Well, now, we just have to be sure of things before we head into action in the session," Lance said, making each word carefully. "Ann has a point that we need to be sure this all looks good for Butch. But Ann, you also need to know how the set-up works here in Texas. I assume that's partly why you're here."

Ann picked up her pad and sat back on the couch. "OK, I'm listening." She again sat with her pen poised over her pad. Her face was flushed from the outburst, and Dan noticed she took several deep breaths, trying to calm herself.

"Billy, you might want to give Ann some of the background you were referring to. It should help with her task." Lance still seemed tentative, glancing around at everyone's face. Dan had never heard Lance be so timid.

"Well, Miss Ann, the Texas Constitution was written just after the War Between the States—you folks call it the Civil War, I think. The federal government installed what Texans called a 'carpetbagger' governor and he ruled the state with an iron hand, running roughshod over all the other officials. As soon as the voters could they voted in a new legislature and convened a constitutional convention to write a new charter for the state. Those boys were really pissed, excuse my language, at that carpetbagger governor so they wrote the constitution to strip the governor of most all but ceremonial power. For a governor to do much of anything in Texas he or she has to make deals with the legislature. My job as Speaker of the House and the Lieutenant Governor over the Senate is where the real power resides. The governor can stop things with a veto, but can't really start much of anything officially. That's what I meant by that term you say we can't use anymore." Billy watched as Ann made frantic notes.

"Well, now, Billy it's not completely that bad. The governor has a 'bully pulpit' and exerts a lot of influence over state policy." Lance too was watching Ann write. The sight of Butch looking from speaker to speaker like someone watching a tennis match fascinated Dan. You'd think the topic of discussion was anything but the powers of his office.

Ann stood to speak again. This time she came to face Lance on the opposite side of the big fireplace. "Now, look, this quaint bit of Texas history may be interesting to some of you, but, Lance, you can't have people saying that kind of thing about Butch. Hell, that crap is poisonous."

"Well, like it or not, that is the way it is. There's nothing we can do about it. You can't rewrite history." Dan thought Lance had relocated his backbone.

"I damn sure can ignore it if it comes across like that. I can't put together the kind of national image Butch has to build starting with that kind of wimpy stuff."

Butch cleared his throat. "Hey, Nellie, could you bring me a another drink?" Nellie appeared and exchanged Butch's empty glass for a full one. She seemed to Dan to just appear from the door to the kitchen wing and disappear the same way.

Drink in hand, Butch seemed emboldened to join in the discussion. "Yeah, that's right, Old Billy here has a lot of stroke all right. In fact you could say he has his finger in every pie in Austin, Texas."

As the old joke was set up, Dan focused on Ann, writing on her pad.

"Heh, heh, at least every tart." Butch started chuckling at his joke, joined at first by Lance. Dan watched as the color drained from Ann's face and her expression turned white hot. She glared first at Butch, who didn't notice, and then at Lance, who quit laughing. Billy started his obligatory chuckle but managed a quick conversion to clearing his throat.

Butch finally realized that he was the only one in the room laughing and looked around confused. When he caught the expression on Ann's face he managed to inhale his laugh with what sounded almost like a burp.

Whatever Ann wrote in big letters on her pad got underlined three times. She simply smirked at the governor, right eyebrow raised, and waited.

In the pained silence that followed, Dan decided he was mixing in the big league, but figured to try his luck. "Lance, do you have anything specific by way of a proposal on the utility dereg? What you're talking about is a complete reversal by Butch and you'll have to get creative to bring that off."

"No, we're still drafting the plan. I don't think we can let it come across as a reversal of policy. Just dealing with new reality."

"Lance, you know that's bullshit." Dan was warming to the subject. "You know damn well that Butch was seen as the main force behind the utilities keeping competition out the last time. The consumer and independent power folks took a beating and they aren't going to forget who gave it to them."

"Well, Representative Carb, you'll just have to sell them on it. We need it for the party." Ann's explanation to Dan was delivered in matter-of-fact tones.

Billy grinned and winked at Dan. "Well, that's another thing you need to know about Texas, Miss Ann. When you say we need it for the party, which party do you mean? Dan and I and the majority of the House are Democrats. Is that the party you mean?" Billy looked like he could hardly keep from laughing.

From the look on Ann's face, Dan thought she was about to explode. "Lance, what the hell are you thinking? You mean these people are from the wrong party? What the hell are you doing setting up a meeting for Butch like this?"

"Well, Ann, that's the way we do things down here. You'll find that both parties in Texas are pretty conservative. And if we want to get anywhere with Butch's agenda, we'll have to work with both sides."

"Work with both sides, yes, but not for a strategy session aimed to shape the next president. Come on, Governor, this meeting is over. Lance, we need to talk. I'll call you in the morning." Her expression was stormy like that call might just burn up the phone lines. The top of Lance's bald head glowed more than the gas log fire.

Dan had never seen Lance so shaky and uncertain. This Yankee comes into his own house and turns him into a whipped puppy. This one bears watching.

Butch looked down at his nearly full drink, took a long sip and sat the glass down on an end table. "Well, it's been nice seeing you boys again. Have a good Christmas if I don't see you. And yu'all think about this electric stuff. I guarantee you we can do the deal." He shook hands around the room flashing his patented smile. Dan winced at the closing line from Butch's car commercial days.

When they had gone, Billy looked at Lance with a nod toward the front door and asked, "Damn, Boy, what the hell was that?"

"Oh, she's just getting used to how we do things down here is Texas. She'll come around."

Billy looked skeptical. Dan couldn't let this pass. "Well, Lance, she acts like she must bite the heads off twelve penny nails in her regular job. Does Butch know what he's getting himself into? She sounds like she's taking over."

"Now, Dan, don't read too much into this meeting. I'm still the main one the governor looks to and that's not going to change." The doubt in his tone completely undercut what he said.

Billy put his coat on and he and Dan said their goodbyes. Out in the driveway they stood and talked, leaning against Dan's truck. "Billy, the pins were pulled on about six grenades in there. We can't let that kind of shit run this session. We'll all look like the damn fools Butch and Lance were tonight."

"It did look a little stark, didn't it? Let's just see how this develops. I'm going to keep my powder dry and act like this didn't happen. You're in town tomorrow, aren't you? Come on over and let's see how this looks in the light of day."

Dan left the exclusive subdivision and drove toward the furnished apartment he rented in northwest Austin. He would need to talk to Paula Torry about the interview tomorrow, but could catch her at home tonight. "So Texas doesn't have a weak-governor system, huh? That'll be a trick."

Chapter 4

Butch's ride to the governor's mansion in the back seat of the chauffeured limo was not a memorable experience. Ann started in on him as soon as they left Lance's driveway.

"Governor, that was a disaster of a meeting. I don't even know where to begin."

"Now, Ann, you just have to get to know those boys. They're all right."

"It's not them I'm worried about. It's you. It's also Lance, setting up a meeting with the opposition."

Butch looked across the seat at the woman who was to be his tormentor for the next several months. For not the first time, he wondered if he hadn't gotten himself in over his head.

"And, Governor. That joke you told about tarts. It is beyond belief that someone looking to run for the highest office in the land would stoop to telling a crude boy's bathroom joke like that. You simply have to discipline yourself to never – I mean never, ever – say anything like that whatever the company. You just have to stop. Can you do that?"

Butch was reminded of Miss Maydee, his second grade teacher. He wondered if Ann would crack his knuckles with a ruler if he messed up again. He could feel his hands ache.

"Now, Miss Ann, I'm kinda new to all this. OK, I won't tell any more jokes if it will make you happy."

Butch looked out. They were heading into the center of Austin. The governor's mansion was just a few more blocks.

"It's not a matter of making me happy. It's a matter of you starting to act and sound like a president. And another thing, you didn't seem to be in charge of the discussion back there. That Representative Carb had a lot to say on an issue that you're supposed to be running with."

Butch didn't know how to respond. "Well, well .... Dan Carb has been around a long time. I knew his pappy, a senator, before he died. Yeah, them Carbs pretty well run East Texas."

Ann started to say something. She just turned and looked out the window.

Inside the enclosed entry at the back of the mansion, they stood on the brick-paved drive.

"Well, governor, they told me that I'd have a lot to learn about Texas. I guess I'm starting to understand that message. I'll make my first report to DC tonight and I'll see you in the morning. We have to go over that speech, right?"

"Oh, yeah. The speech. We'll get right on that tomorrow."

Butch sighed as he walked into the back door of the ornate mansion. What damned speech? He hoped this would get easier when he got into it.

Chapter 5

Dan worked in his apartment Tuesday morning, signing a pile of correspondence Paula had mailed him. He left for the capitol around noon. Austin had done a good job of maintaining views of the capitol building from most parts of the city. As he drove down the Mopac Expressway from northwest Austin he could see the capitol dome at several points.

A major point of Texas pride was that the pink dome of the capitol is actually taller than the national capitol in Washington, DC. As a committee chair, Dan rated an office in the capitol itself. The new annex, where most of the representatives were officed, was three floors built underground on the north side of the building. Dan's committee offices were in the annex but his office on the second floor of the capitol had a nice view looking out toward the University of Texas campus to the north.

He parked in the annex underground and headed for his office. Dan always admired the inside of the capitol building with its twenty-foot ceilings and intricate oak carvings. From the rotunda in the center, under the dome, wide hallways ran two hundred feet to the east and west under the House and Senate chambers. The emblems of the six nations whose flags had flown over the state surrounded the state seal in the middle of the marble rotunda floor. Texas deserved to be proud of such a majestic capitol. The railing on the wide stairway he climbed to the second floor was polished smooth by the thousands of hands that had passed in the century-plus life of the building. In contrast to times when the legislature was in session, the hallways were mostly empty and Dan could hear his footsteps echoing in the cavernous halls.

Later in the State Affairs Committee office, he and Paula ordered pizza and sat around reviewing paperwork and Randi Crendall's resume.

"Dan, look at the language in the versions of the bill I have highlighted.

You can see how Randi and Garza evolved the bill to try and get agreement."

"Yeah, Garza's filed version was pretty strong. The Utilities would never have gone for that. But when I look at the next several versions, they still managed to keep their basic protection for low-income ratepayers in place. You say Randi had a lot to do with that?"

"Right. Garza pretty well turned the negotiations over to her and she handled all the different players. Nice work, huh?" Paula Torry had worked for Dan for the last two sessions and the two were at ease together. Paula moved with a smooth grace that showed her daily tennis playing. A pretty, tall woman with reddish brown hair, blue eyes and a slim build, she was a hit with the guys on staff at the Capitol.

"Well, we're likely to have a bigger fight on our hands this time. But she shows some smarts and knows how to work the system. I'll see when I talk to her."

Chapter 6

Randi had gotten to the capitol at one on Tuesday afternoon, well ahead of her two o'clock appointment. She let herself into Representative Garza's empty office and spent the next hour going over her notes on index cards. She had researched every bill Dan Carb had ever filed, reviewed his votes on several controversial items and read his speeches in the House Journal. She had reminder notes on the cards. This was the most preparation she'd ever done for an interview.

Randi had dressed in a black pants suit with a white blouse and a small ribbon around her neck that she thought suggested a tie. She always used very light make-up plus a little liner around her green eyes. Her long, blond hair was pinned in a swirl at the back of her head.

At two, Randi walked into the State Affairs office. "Hi, Paula. Am I on time?"

"Perfect, Randi. Come on. Dan's waiting for you." Randi followed Paula to the closed door labeled "Chairman". She followed Paula in.

"Representative Carb, this is Randi Crendall. Randi, this is Dan."

Randi smiled and shook his hand. Paula excused herself and closed the door.

"Mr. Chairman. I've seen you around a lot and of course in State Affairs for our ratepayer bill last session. We were real pleased with that outcome."

"Have a seat, Randi. And call me Dan. Yeah, that was a good bill and it has helped a lot of people. I wasn't aware you had handled it for Garza."

"Oh, I stayed in the background. We had some difficult negotiations with the utilities, but managed to salvage most of what we wanted in the final bill."

Randi tried to calm her fast breathing. She decided that he was even more of a hunk from close up. Big shoulders and all that curly brown hair with red highlights. He also looked to her like he was dripping money. That suede leather sport coat probably cost a thousand or more. And the gold nugget ring. Randi didn't even have a guess at what that cost.

"Randi, from your resume it looks like you've worked several places here in the capitol. I don't see any committee staff experience, though."

"No, I haven't held a direct committee position, but I've dealt a lot with committee staff chasing Garza's bills. I think I can handle myself."

"Well, it looks like the session is going to start off hectic in State Affairs. There's going to be some controversial bills introduced and we're liable to wind up refereeing a big fight." Randi shifted in her chair and felt a little uncomfortable with Dan watching her like he was trying to track every nuance of her response.

"I'm not afraid of a fight. I usually try to steer around controversy if I can, but if that's the way it goes I can slug it out with the best of them."

"I agree. Sometimes you have to go to the mat for what you believe. Let's see, you live here in Austin. Did you grow up here?"

"Yeah, I was born and raised here and I live with my mom. Went to school here too. By the way, I'm taking classes in liberal arts at UT and I hope to go to law school some day. But don't worry about that though. That's what I work on when the lege is out." Dan nodded and looked back at her resume.

"So, Randi. I want to thank you for getting that memo to us. It has helped with things already. I don't know how you came by it and I don't want to know. But I have to know that if you go to work for me that you'll be able to keep confidences. I'm liable to be going out on a limb and I have to know that my staff is a hundred and fifty percent behind me."

Randi tensed at Dan's implication that she couldn't keep confidences. She had the sudden thought that she just might blow this interview. She knew she wasn't good enough to work for Dan and she was afraid he'd see through her confident act. But she had to smooth this over.

"I want to make this really clear. You can ask Garza about this. When I'm for you I'm completely for you. If I'm against you I'm just as strongly against you. You hire me and I'm yours." Randi leaned forward as she said the last, hoping she sounded genuine. Dan's broad smile gave her some comfort but she was still unsure how he was taking her.

"Well, Randi, I'm impressed with your credentials and the way you carry yourself. I'd like for you to visit briefly with Paula. If you go to work on State Affairs, you and Paula would be working closely together and I believe in coordinating things so there's no surprises or slip-ups. You'll find we're more like a family instead of just a staff. We all look out for each other. Oh, and don't worry, I'll square things with Garza if it's a go with us. Where are you going to be if we have more questions?"

Randi wanted to jump for joy. Dan was sounding positive. Steady, Girl.

"I'll be at my home number this afternoon. Mom and I take turns cleaning the apartment and this is my turn. And I plan to be in town for Christmas so call anytime."

When Dan shook hands with her, Randi looked at her small hand wrapped in his and smiled up at him. She decided that luck just might be with her.

Dan opened the door. "Paula, would you take a few minutes and tell Randi how we work things between you and the committee staff. Randi, thanks for coming by. We'll be back to you as soon as we can. We need to move fast."

"OK, Dan. I really appreciated the chance to talk. If you have any questions, you know where I'll be."

As Randi drove home she wondered again why she was doing this. It would be a slight move up, but she was happy with Garza. State Affairs sounded like it could be a big fight, not something she looked for but something she could handle. But just thinking about spending that much time close to Dan Carb made her start breathing hard again. Here's hoping he calls back.

Chapter 7

After the interview with Randi, Dan had met briefly with Paula to compare notes. Both of them were happy with what they had seen of Randi. Dan then headed right up to the Speaker's office on the second floor of the capitol at the back of the House Chamber.

"Come on in Dan boy," Billy Gibson said. " I've got just a few minutes before I have to head to the airport to get my son, flying in for Christmas."

"Yeah, I gotta' get back to the ranch. We've got a deer hunt planned with several of Molly Ann's relatives. I've got a nice crop of bucks this year."

"Hell, Boy, save me a nice one. Maybe we can go sometime before the session starts."

Dan admired the restored Speaker's office. The ceilings of the spacious office were twenty feet high and ornate carvings highlighted every corner. Billy's huge desk and the several chairs and couches hardly seemed to crowd the space.

Billy walked over and leaned against the tooled leather saddle on a stand beside his desk. "Dan, I've been thinking more about that meeting at Lance's last night. I know it sounded bad, but it doesn't have to be trouble as far as we're concerned. We just have to do our jobs and let Butch and his folks work out their situation."

Dan sat on the plush sofa facing Billy's desk. "Billy, I agree we just focus on what we have to do. But you know as well as I do that we all depend on Lance's thinking issues through to keep Butch straight. What showed up last night was two different people trying to steer Butch, but in different directions. Hell, I can work with Lance, but that fire-breathing yankee is another story."

"Yeah, she's something else, huh? But it's still the same old Butch. We've worked it out with him and Lance for the last three sessions." Billy's pleading tone began to worry Dan. And it didn't sound like Billy was calculating the volatile Ann into the mix.

Dan stood and walked over to look out at the front lawn of the capitol. "I know I can still run my committee and work with everybody I need to get the job done. But if Butch is being run in two different directions by two different sets of staff it makes it really dicey to keep him and us out of trouble. I mean, we'll have all kind of hell down on us if Butch starts to look as foolish as that threesome did last night."

"But, Dan, we can't do their jobs for them. Here's the bottom line with me. I can manage my business a whole lot better if I don't piss off Butch and the Republicans. As far as I can, I'm going to try to help them and still do what's right for the state. We'll have to help them a lot to bring off what Butch wants with the electrics."

"Now that's the part that worries me. I've got the electric co-ops and the paper companies on my case not to give the state treasury away to the big utilities. I think something can be worked out to look after everybody. But, dammit Billy, I'll have my hands full with that job. I can't be babysitting Butch's public relations program too."

Billy joined Dan watching the traffic on Eleventh Street in front of the Capitol. "I know, Son. It's obvious that Lance and that Miss Ann will have to work things out a damn sight better than they showed last night. And they'll do it too. Don't worry. I'm not going to put you and me and the House onto a train that's headed for a wreck. Let's just go along and do what it takes to give 'em what they want while staying out of trouble ourselves."

Dan studied Billy's face to try to figure out where he really stood on this. He knew that Billy's whole strategy as Speaker was to accommodate. Dan knew that he had to keep his own reaction to the utilities' money grab buried. With Billy in a mood to try and appease Butch, he'd have to devise a deep, hidden strategy. Dan felt a growing strain, knowing he'd eventually be taking on very powerful interests, probably including his good friend and Speaker of the House. This was going to be a long session and it hadn't even started yet.

"OK, Billy, that sounds like we wait and see what they propose and then work it, like always, to try and find the middle ground. I've done that before and I can do it again."

"Atta boy, Dan," Billy said smiling broadly, "I knew I could count on you. Lance said we should see a bill draft before New Years. I'll fax you something as soon as I see it." Billy stood facing Dan. "Now get on back to that wonderful family and your deer hunt. That sounds like a perfect Christmas to me."

"OK, Billy. What are you folks planning?"

"Well, my son is on leave from the Air Force and my married daughter is coming a couple days before Christmas with her husband and my two grandchildren. The old ranch will be alive with all kinds of celebrations."

They shook hands. "Well, I'm heading east this afternoon. Have a good holiday, Billy. I'll look for a copy of the bill draft."

Dan walked from the Speaker's office out onto the side aisle of the House Chamber. The cavernous chamber seemed even bigger in the muted light coming in from the side windows. The one hundred fifty carved oak desks with high-backed leather chairs stood in quiet solitude compared to the bustle Dan knew from the sessions. The third floor gallery seats, usually teeming with interested players and tourists, seemed to be just a dark mass behind the brass rail. Huge portraits of past Texas heroes hung around the walls of the chamber, standing guard over the empty hall. Dan walked down four steps and out into the foyer outside the House entrance door. Here, during the sessions, dozens of lobbyists, citizens, staffers, and Representatives swirled in a buzz that helped form the future of the law in Texas. Dan paused to enjoy the quiet of the empty space.

During his drive back to Fairmount, Dan was going over all that the last two days meant for him. Butch and the national run. Lance and Ann pulling a taffy-candy governor in different directions. Dan risking his political life to guard against the excesses of a national campaign thrust. He was almost home when he realized he had hardly paid any attention to the trip he usually enjoyed. As he drove through Madisonville just before sunset, the twinkling lights of the decorations and chilled shoppers carrying bulging bags finally freed him from his troubled thoughts. The Trinity River bridge and his pastures rising up in the fading western light welcomed him home.

Chapter 8

Austin at Christmas seemed to Randi almost like a different world. Most of the University of Texas students had gone home. The only people around the capitol were a few dedicated staffers and the capitol police, the "Squirrel Guards", the name given them by the capitol insiders.

Randi always loved the feel of the city at Christmas time. The natives remaining in town set a calmer, mellower tone in everything from shopping to clubs and just hanging out. But, Randi and her mom were in one of their non-speaking bouts the week before the Saturday holiday.

Dan Carb had called that Tuesday and offered Randi the State Affairs job at a nice raise. She had accepted and was going into the holiday feeling high. The fight with her mom over her working for Dan had gone on over several days and nights, but Randi was determined. The lively decorations around their two-bedroom apartment belied the strained truce between mother and daughter. She was glad to get out of the apartment with Dave on Thursday night.

"Now, Davey, I'm going to celebrate my new job and the holiday season and those iced margaritas are going to be going down freely." Randi and Dave were headed to their favorite club.

The Cactus 'N Angels club in north Austin was a popular spot for capitol staffers and the crowd was building when they got there. The club, in an old warehouse, had one main claim to fame. In the center of the huge room stood a live cactus garden with several large green cacti in wooden tubs, big boulders, gravel and an array of small bushes. Intense spotlights shown down from the high ceiling to try to keep the plants healthy. The other highlights of the center garden were several stuffed armadillos and rabbits. The rumor was that if you had enough to drink, the stuffed animals started to sing and dance.

Randi and Dave had danced to a couple of songs after their first two drinks, but settled at their table to talk and listen to the mix of country and rock from a local band.

"Dave, I think we'll have the perfect setup for the session. You'll know who's asking for what bill drafts from the Council and I'll be in the middle of everything State Affairs does."

Dave was peeling the label off his third beer and idly watching the dancers. "Yeah, OK, so we can see a lot of legislation that's coming and what's working in the committee, but what for? What is it you want to do, Randi?"

"Hell, just the usual trading. If you want to do favors for someone to get what you want, I can help you on the committee. But I'm going to need your help, too."

"What kind of help, Randi? I don't think you know why you wanted the job with Carb in the first place and now that you've got it, you're no better off."

"Well, I'm still trying to figure out my new boss. When I get that straight, I'll know better what I want to do and how you can help."

"Hell, it sounds to me like you just have the hots for him." Dave looked sheepishly at Randi.

"Now, come on, Dave. Look, I got a raise and whole lot more prestigious job. Anyway, Dan's married with kids. He's not going to pay any attention to little old Randi." As she said it, Randi knew that attention from Dan Carb was exactly what she wanted. He looked like a movie star and had money to throw away. She'd get to him somehow.

During a band break several people stopped by their table.

"Hey, Randi, congrats on the new job. Moving up in the world, huh?" Sue Linson worked for another representative on the same annex hall as Garza and she and Randi occasionally took their breaks together.

"Yeah, Sue. At least I hope it's moving up. By the way, Garza is looking for someone to replace me. If you got any ideas pass them along. My recommendation might help."

"OK. Thanks, Randi. I ordered you and Dave another round on me to help you celebrate your new job."

Randi and Dave lifted the newly delivered drinks in a toast. "Thanks, Sue. Here's to an easy session with no big fights." Randi's toast was a hit.

When she was working her way back to their table from the restroom after the band had restarted, Randi started to feel woozy and Dave got his worried look on.

"Hey, kid, you better take it easy. You've had a bunch of margaritas and we've only been here two hours. I'll have to drag you outta' here if you keep that up."

Randi's voice was high pitched and loud. "Now, Davey, this is my night to celebrate. I've got the job I've been angling for. My friends think it's great. I've got a nice raise. I'm thinking about finding my own place and leaving 'Dear Mother' on her own. And, Hell, Dave, it's Christmas. It time for good sh..cl..cheer. I'm just having a little trouble talking."

Randi tried to focus on the dance floor. The neon beer signs around the walls of the club were beginning to get fuzzy. She'd seen several other capitol staffers she knew. She was now having trouble recognizing the people dancing around the large room. The band was blasting loud music and the place was jumping. A pall of smoke hung just above the dancers' heads and Randi's vision was suffering from the steady flow of the tasty, green drinks. She thought she saw one of the stuffed rabbits wiggle its ears and wink at her.

She decided she should deal with something a little closer. "Hey, you see, Davey boy. When the session starts, you'll need to keep me ahead of the flow to State Affairs so I can show off for Mr. Chairman Dan."

"Shhhh. Randi, you'd better lower your voice. These walls have ears. And we'll talk about the session sometime when you don't have such a load on."

"But, Baby, I'm gonna' need your help. You'll help little Randi, won't you?" Randi tried to lean on Dave's shoulder, but missed. "Oops. You must have moved."

"Yeah, OK, kid. I think it's time to get you out of here. Yes, I'm going to help you. And you can probably even help me, but tonight's not the time to work all that out."

"But you're gonna' help. Right?" Randi was resting her head on his shoulder and fading fast. She became vaguely aware that she and Dave were walking unsteadily out of the club. Wasting away again in Margaritaville. The cold night air hit her face, waking her up.

"OK, now Dave, I'm awake. I'm going to celebrate tonight and to do that, we have to go somewhere and fuck." She stopped walking and stood as straight as she could to show Dave she was up to it. It was a valiant effort and she was struggling. She knew her fake calm sophistication that Dave had taught her was slipping badly.

"Let's just get in the car, Baby. We'll find somewhere."

"OK, just to let you know that however much I've had to drink, the celebration isn't complete until I get my holiday screw."

The last thing Randi remembered was getting into Dave's car. She woke up the next morning surrounded by her stuffed animals in her own bed with a very bad headache. She didn't remember getting home. She tried to remember where she and Dave had gone after they left Angels. It was no use.

"Damn. I hope I had a good time." But she worried that she'd made a mess of things with Dave. You little shit, going and getting stinking drunk again. Dave is probably ready to dump you. Worthless bitch.

At least it was a blessing that her mom was out and she didn't have to face another argument with her. Randi's breakfast was black coffee and a whole apple pie her mother had baked. It didn't cure her headache, but her stomach was so uncomfortable it helped her ignore her roaring head.

Chapter 9

The original stone Carb house faced west at the top of the hill overlooking the river and was built in a rectangle. There were two small bedrooms at one end and the rest of the house was a great room that included the kitchen area, a walk-in fireplace and a large area that was used for dining, visiting and for extra sleeping space for visitors.

Over the years, a large ell addition was added to the back of the house on the end away from the kitchen. With five bedrooms in the addition, the two original bedrooms were converted to a large dining room and the great room became an oversized living room with the kitchen in one corner.

Dan's daughters were out of school and they went with him on the Friday before Christmas to keep a family tradition, cutting a fresh tree from a neighbor's Christmas tree farm.

"Dad, are you sure this big tree will fit in the house?" Mary, his youngest asked. She was looking out the back window of the crew cab truck at the huge tree they'd just cut.

"Oh, yeah. The roof's plenty high. I just hope we don't mess up the limbs getting it through the door."

"All right, there's the house. It's time to start the singing. Jingle bells, jingle bells . ."

With all three of them singing at the top of their voices, Dan drove into the yard and stopped at the front door. His mom was standing on the small porch waving.

"Dan Carb. Don't you know that you Carbs can't carry a tune in a bucket? Not one of you is singing in the same key." Dan's mom was graying and beginning to bend forward a little, but she was still lively and full of humor.

"I know, I know, Mom, but it's the season. You just gotta sing to get in the spirit."

Ruth and Mary ran around the truck. "Grams, do you see our great tree? It's the biggest one we've ever had."

"I can see that, Ruth. We may have to break out a wall to get it in."

Dan grinned. "Oh, no. We'll take care of that, Mom. Just takes a little determination. We may not be able to sing, but we Carbs are big on determination."

Dan and the girls spent the afternoon decorating the tree next to the giant fireplace. Molly Ann's rolling hospital bed was in the great room and she gave the decorators a running commentary on how it was looking. The top of the tree nearly touched the rough hewn beams of the vaulted ceiling.

"More tinsel on your side, Mary. Get up on the ladder and get some near the top." Dan admired Molly Ann's spunk taking part in the decoration work. She and his mom had spent time getting Molly's long brown hair just right around her shoulders with bangs down to her eyebrows. But he was worried at how thin and frail she looked. He thought back to last Christmas when she could still walk around easily. Now she spent most of the time in that rolling bed. Dan noticed that she seemed to strain even more than usual just to see the decorations. He swore again at the tragedy of MS.

After their traditional seafood supper, the girls stacked the presents around the tree. With a roaring fire in the fireplace and the tall decorated tree the great room looked to Dan like a Christmas card.

"Dad, look at all these presents that got delivered for you today. The FEDEX driver said you got almost half his truckload. Here's one from Exxon. And another from some insurance company. This big red one is from Texas Utilities. It rattles and sounds like shelled pecans. Mmmmm. Pecan pies." Mary brought the package over to Dan.

"Yep, that's what it sounds like."

"Dad, do you have to do things for all these people that give you presents?"

"No, Love, they just send stuff so I'll remember who they are. I do what I think I need to, not necessarily what somebody else wants me to. And besides, some of those people want just the opposite of each other and there's no way to satisfy all of them."

"Well, you've got almost twenty presents addressed to Chairman Carb. You've even got one from the governor. He can get anything he wants, can't he. What's he want from you."

Ruth chimed in. "Well, old Governor Grange is planning to run for president. He probably wants Daddy to help him with that."

Molly Ann chimed in. "Yeah, it's something like that. Now look, your dad and I are going to call it a night. Don't you two stay up too late. We've got a big day tomorrow with all the relatives coming over for dinner. You'll have to help your Gram fix everything up. Goodnight, all."

Dan pushed his wife's bed down the wide hallway and into their bedroom.

He helped Molly Ann with her bathroom chores then put her back into her bed.

"You know, Mol, I've been thinking that this will be the first session when you're not with me in Austin. I'm going to miss you."

"Now, come on, Dan. You know your way around that process pretty well by now. I'd mostly just be in your way."

"Not so. You're my sanity when it gets crazy and you know how crazy it can get. Anyway, I know you have to stay here."

"I'll be with you in spirit, Hon. You know that. And you're going to have to call me all the time. I can stay in touch that way and I'll keep you straight." Molly Ann grinned and yawned.

Dan kissed her goodnight and went over to his desk. She was sound asleep in a few minutes. He'd spend another hour on state paperwork before retiring to his own bed, beside his wife's.

Christmas morning dawned clear and cold. Dan was out of bed, dressed and making coffee before six. He put on his fleece-lined jacket and got into one of the ranch jeeps for a look at the cattle.

Bouncing along the gravel paths, he drove past several pastures where cattle were gathered around big round bales of hay. Their collective breathing lifted a small plume of steam around the bale into the near freezing air.

The Carb ranch now spanned nearly two thousand acres with sections on both sides of Highway 21 for almost two miles of the eastern bank of the Trinity River. Most of the pastureland sloped steeply down to the river. The land away from the river was still wooded and that was also the section where the oil and gas wells were located.

The first drilling on the ranch came in the sixties and was brought on by one of the many dives in cattle prices. Now the dozen wells scattered through the woods on the eastern part of the ranch provided the Carbs with a sizable income. While Dan still kept several hundred head of cattle and insisted that the ranching not be a big money losing proposition, it was the mineral income that paid all the bills and kept the bank accounts full for him, his mom and his two sisters.

Dan's tour confirmed that the cattle had all made the night in good shape. He easily could have left this part of the work to Ben Faust but Dan liked the times he got to ride out over the fields. It was at least a taste of the life he'd prepared for when he went to Texas A&M.

The solitude of his jeep, his coffee and the ranch was such a contrast to his life as a State Representative. It was at holiday times like this that he got to enjoy his family in ways that were not even close to possible with the demands of his office. He knew painfully that his daughters were growing up with the same kind of absentee father he'd had. But he really paid attention to time with them on weekends and more when the legislature was out of session.

When he got back to the house, his mom was up fixing breakfast.

"Merry Christmas, Son. How'd the cattle do last night?"

"Oh, they're fine. A little cold, but not freezing at least. Anybody else up?"

"Merry Christmas, Daddy." Ruth and Mary ran into the great room lugging a three-foot square package wrapped in red paper and gold ribbon.

"Hey, you two. You've been scheming." Dan grinned as he took the package from them and placed it by the tree.

"Now you can't open it until everybody's here. Hi, Gram. Merry Christmas." Ruth hugged her grandmother and went over to pour coffee.

With Molly Ann's bed in the circle, the family opened presents after breakfast. The girls got mostly the clothes and computers they wanted and Dan's big surprise was a brass statue of a rider on a bucking bronco with only its front hooves touching the base. Something he'd admired on a shopping trip to Dallas.

"This is great. It will go right in the middle of my desk at the capitol to remind me of what's really important."

"What's that, Daddy? That the ranch is the most important thing in your life?"

"No. That no matter how rough the bucking gets, once you're there, you just have to hang on and ride it out."

The call from Billy Gibson came just as they'd opened the last of their presents. "Best of the holiday there, Dan boy. Old Santa treat you right?"

"You'll see my main present next time you come to my office. I got me a bronco statue that's as big as yours."

"All right, way to go. Look, Dan, I wanted to give you a heads up. I think Lance has been working on a draft of the electrical deregulation bill. The word I get is it'll probably be to me in a couple days. We should take some time to go over it. I'll fax it to you there as soon as I get it. We can try to get together."

"Hell, Billy, why don't you come on over here to talk about the bill and we can go get you that ten-pointer I saw day before yesterday."

"That's a deal. Is that airstrip over at Madisonville still workable?"

"Yep, it's in good shape. Just set it up and I'll come meet you at the plane. Nothing like firing a few rounds of 30.06 to get you in the mood to deal with utility legislation."

When Dan got back to the great room his mom asked, "You're not going to have to leave are you? We've got all that company coming for dinner."

"No, Mom. Billy's got something he's working on for the gov. He's probably going to fly over here between now and New Years. We'll do a little business and some deer hunting. Let him do the traveling around."

"You inherited some of your dad's smarts."

The phone rang again and this time Ruth answered it. "Daddy, it's the governor calling. You're getting all the attention." She handed Dan the portable phone. He walked back toward his office in the bedroom wing of the house.

"Hello, Governor. Happy Holidays to you."

"And the same to you Dan. I hope you and your family are doing OK this fine Christmas. I was just calling to let you know that I'm really looking forward to the session in January. I think that together we can do great things for Texas." Dan heard the old car salesman coming out, even over the phone.

"I'm sure of it too, Governor. I think great things may come out of the next six months. How is your family?"

"Oh, we're all doing great. Both of my daughters are here and my son is due. We're having as close to a family holiday as we get these days."

"I know what you mean. Billy told me that Lance expects to have a draft bill on electrics soon. We're ready to get to work on it."

"That's great, Boy. Yu'all just take that bill and fix it so everybody's on board and we'll do just fine. I'm glad to have your support." Dan thought that last was pushing it, but he kept quiet.

"OK, Governor. I'll be seeing you soon, I'm sure. In the mean time, Happy New Year to you and yours."

"And the same to you, Dan. Bye now."

They didn't even let Christmas Day pass before they started in on him. But he was determined not to let those calls ruin this time with Molly Ann and the family.

Dan brushed away their questions about the call from Butch and instead got everyone interested in roasting pecans in the fireplace coals. This tradition dated back for several generations and was a regular ritual. The smell of pecans roasting filled the room and everyone began singing carols again. With Gram's and Molly Ann's voices added it sounded a bit more harmonized.

Soon Dan, Ruth, Mary and his mom were all in the kitchen preparing the turkey and fixings while Molly Ann supervised from her bed. Dan decided that this was what the season was all about.

Chapter 10

Butch and Millie had decided that they would spend this Christmas in the Governor's Mansion since this might be their last chance to do so. They had traditionally spent the holiday with Butch's family in San Antonio. But this time a photographer was coming to the mansion and there were big plans afoot for family holiday photos.

Butch had made the six phone calls on the list Ann gave him by ten o'clock. When he came down the spiral staircase on Christmas morning, Millie and his daughters, Allison and Dedra, and his son Butch, Jr. were already sitting around the tall tree, slumped down in their chairs. The staff had laid out an extravagant breakfast and Butch helped himself to a plate full of eggs, sausage and potatoes.

"Merry Christmas, all. Everybody looks great this fine morning."

"Yes, Dear, we're all just fine. Right, children?"

There was chorus of grunts.

"Now, that doesn't sound like a very happy greeting. What's going on?"

Butch, Jr., the eldest spoke first. "Well, Dad, I know that spending Christmas Day here in Austin was a big deal for you, but I'd rather be down in San Antonio with my cousins. They're probably having a great time by now."

"Now, now, Junior. You can make a little sacrifice just this once." Millie's tone sounded like she was talking to a little child.

"Oh, come on, Mom. I'm thirty years old. I know what I want and what I don't want."

Butch decided that his daughters, both college students, didn't look any happier.

"We had to sleep in the Sam Houston bed last night. Daddy, when are you going to get a new mattress for that bed? That one's too hard," Dedra the youngest said. "And now, there's some reporter coming to cover Daddy having a traditional Christmas in the mansion. We don't have to enjoy it. We just have to do it."

Allison said, "Damn, are we going to have to pose for pictures? I should have fixed my hair."

Millie frowned at her. "Don't worry about your hair, Allison. You look just fine. Junior, you need to go put on a tie."

"A tie? Why put on a tie, Dad? It's Christmas for goodness sakes."

"Now, Junior. You know as well as I do that when the picture winds up in all the papers you'll want to look nice. Think what it'll do for business."

"OK. I'll go up and get a tie. Let's just try to get it over with as soon as we can."

The reporter and photographer from the Dallas paper showed up just as the family was beginning to open presents. Butch's press secretary organized everyone into the poses she wanted. After pictures of them opening presents they had to go out to the columned front porch of the mansion to pose for a family picture. There were also photos of Butch and Millie in front of the Christmas tree in the high ceilinged living room.

Butch reflected on how nice it was not having Ann Terrance around to aggravate him. She'd gone back to Pennsylvania for Christmas and wouldn't be back until the day after New Years. With his family gathered around him, Butch thought for the thousandth time how nice this felt and how he was really messing with things with this presidential venture. The governor's job let him be the out front spokesman, the thing he was good at. The way his damned national committee was starting to make demands and sending him four-inch thick briefing books, the run for president was ninety percent hassle and very little enjoyment.

Sacrifice, sacrifice. That's what somebody had said.

Chapter 11

Dan had called Senator Giles on New Years Day to wish him happy holidays and try and set up a meeting. With the session only two weeks away, Dan had to get some things worked through and his trusted mentor was the only person Dan knew it was safe to talk to about what he was heading into.

Giles lived in San Angelo in West Texas but was playing in a celebrity golf tournament in San Antonio during the first week of the new year. He and Dan set up a meeting at his hotel on Wednesday, the morning of his golf tournament. Since Dan was meeting with Randi in Austin on Thursday, he drove to San Antonio with plans to go up to Austin that afternoon.

Billy Gibson's trip to Dan's ranch had been a mixed pleasure for Dan. Billy bagged a nice ten-point buck from a stand in the eastern part of Dan's ranch. He was proud and already making plans to add a mounted head to his office.

Going over the governor's utility bill the night before, however, had been rough for Dan. The bill draft was well designed to wrap the money grab in a lot of high-sounding language that hid its true result. It was obvious that Lance and the governor had gotten to Billy since they'd last talked. Billy was fully behind the proposal, providing additional rationale for supporting it. Dan's mood was gloomy as he drove the last miles into San Antonio.

The lobby of the Grande Rio hotel reflected San Antonio's blend of traditional US and Hispanic holiday traditions. Two bright piñatas, a donkey and a Santa Claus, hung on either side of a twenty-foot, decorated Christmas tree in front of the huge windows looking out on the famous Riverwalk.

The senator answered Dan's knock on the door. "Come on in, Son. Best of the holiday to you. How was your trip?"

"Just fine, Andy. I hope you and your family had a good Christmas."

"Oh, yeah. Pretty much the regular thing with all the family around us. How's Molly Ann doing?"

Dan sighed deeply. "She just seems to get weaker and weaker with every passing day. I mean, she was still trying to take part this time, but, Andy, she can hardly get out of bed. I'm worried sick about her. But enough of my struggles. What time are you due on the golf course? I don't want to mess up your schedule."

"I've got a couple hours. You said on the phone that you needed some advice. From your tone, you sounded like your dad when he had the bit in his teeth over something. What's up?" They had been standing at the glass door leading to the balcony outside the hotel room.

The Senator hardly looked his seventy-five years. With a big mop of gray hair and deeply tanned face, he looked like he would be a natural on a golf course. Dan knew that Andy's tan came from all the hours he spent on his ranch west of San Angelo. His spry movements showed the good shape he was in. Dan decided he'd better get down to the business.

"Well, here's the deal. Butch and his national campaign staff have cooked up a scheme to deregulate the big electric companies. It involves the utilities getting a huge pile of state money in trade for letting competition in. I'm sure there's a big wad of campaign contributions involved too, but of course we won't see that for a while. Andy, from the bill draft Billy showed me, they plan to give them ten billion dollars and spread it over every rate-payer in the state, even the ones the big guys don't serve. It'll come out of the state treasury."

"Damn, Dan. That sounds ludicrous. Are you sure that's what they're planning?"

"No doubt about it. And Lance Dunn was squiring Betsy Pertny, the utilities' newest lobbyist, around to meet her new bosses. Hell, they even showed up in Lufkin when I was giving a speech."

"I'd heard that Betsy had jumped ship. So Lance is already working the deal."

"Yeah, and he set up a meeting for me, Billy and Butch at his house just before Christmas. Butch brought this yankee from his national committee. I can tell you, Andy, you'd better watch out for this Ann Terrance. She's a one-woman assault tank and she'll be pulling Butch's strings this session. Hell, Old Lance acted like limp lettuce around her."

"Bullshit. Lance? In his own house?"

"I've never seen the likes of it. Anyway, you know that my daddy and granddaddy would turn over in their graves if I let those big utilities get away with this. From the chair of State Affairs I'm probably the only one to stop them. Billy was holding off at first, but I think he's on board with Butch now. They must have got to him somehow." Dan and Andy walked out onto the balcony. From six floors up they could see a long view of the Riverwalk with tourists, shoppers and strolling mariachis walking below. The flow of crowded riverboats looked like a parade with their festive decorations.

"But, Dan, if you take on Butch and the whole damned Republican establishment, you're really risking it. What's their justification for the ten billion?"

"They are going to claim that the utilities were ordered by the PUC to build all those expensive nuclear power plants. They can't compete with independent power with the debt from those plants so they want the state to pay them off."

Andy was shivering from the early January chill, so they went back into his room and sat in overstuffed chairs facing the fireplace. "Dan, as much as I disagree with it, their argument makes a certain amount of sense. That might be enough to sell the idea to the voters."

"But, Andy, here's the truth of the matter. The PUC finally ordered them to build the nuclear plants, but only after a fight with the consumer groups and the utilities spending millions in legal costs and lobbying to force the PUC to give them the order. Look, nuclear plants were the answer to the utility manager's dreams. The regulated utilities operate on a guaranteed rate of return on investment. Their energy cost to produce power gets passed through directly to consumers. The only way they make money is on investment."

"So how did the nuclear plants help that?"

"Well, a nuclear plant costs more than three times what conventional power plants do, the nucs power cost is mostly capital investment. The energy cost for nucs is almost nothing. You see, the utilities got to sell power at almost the same price, but their profit on the deal more than doubled. That's why they lobbied so hard to get them."

"You mean that they lobbied the PUC to let them build the plants, made all the extra money off the regulatory formula and now they want more money to take the plants off their hands?" Andy was getting red in the face.

"Exactly. It's a clear case of 'have your cake and eat it too'. Don't you see, that's why I have to stop them? But I can't openly oppose it because of all they have lined up behind them. Andy, I'm going to have to come up with a dead certain poison pill. One that I can trigger late in the session and even Billy won't be able to stop it. That's why I need your help. But first, don't you think this is the kind of taxpayer ripoff I should stop?"

"Dan, the way you say it's structured, they'll get some of their payoff from my constituents and they never had anything to do with those damned nucs in the first place. Boy, if your dad was here. He'd be sharpening up his battle-ax, too. You know you'll be risking your political life if you do this. Butch is becoming the darling of the Republican presidential race and there are some heavy-duty players in the mix. Are you ready to take that on?"

"I don't know any other way. I'll do what I can to hide what I'm doing, but Billy will figure it out eventually, I'm sure."

"OK, Dan. If you're sure, you know you'll have my backing on it. Now if you want to set the bill up to kill it, you'll have to do it several different ways to be sure you get it. In committee you can show a quorum when one wasn't present. That's fairly reliable but it points to you and you'll have to get another member to go along with you. Probably not recommended for this."

"Right, I don't want any other member to get caught in this if it blows up."

"The next most reliable way is to use the seventy-two hour rule in the Calendars Committee during the last days of the session. As committee chair you can have Calendars delay placement of the bill before the House by telling the Calendars chairman there is some hold up by the people who want the bill. It doesn't take much to go over the limit of seventy-two hours in Calendars and that's a sure killer."

"So I come up with some excuse to delay the bill after Calendars has it. Then I plant that delay with old Rieger, he springs it during the last two days of the session and the bill is dead. Right?" Representative Rieger had been elected to the Legislature for ten consecutive terms from a sure district in Dallas. He only filed bills for his principal backer, a big Dallas insurance company. But he was the House watchdog for adherence to the rules. Rieger poured over the flow on legislation and was famous for knocking bills off the floor for technical rules violations. Of course, for Dan, that made him perfect to kill the utility money grab.

"Right. Now this Calendars move isn't one Rieger is likely to catch in the late session rush of bills. You'll just have to plant the facts with him at the right time. You wait until the last minute and then sit back and watch Rieger work. He's good."

"Andy, I don't think I'll have much trouble coming up with a delay if Butch is still being pulled in different directions by both Lance and that yankee. They'll make my job easy. OK. I know what I have to do."

"Now, Dan, you and I will have to stay close on this during the session. If I see anything from the Senate side that would get in your way I'll let you know."

"Don't worry. I'll probably be bugging you the whole time. This is important and risky. I don't dare fail."

"All right, Son. I've got to get on out to that Country Club. I'm not much of a golfer, but they're depending on me for the opening ceremony. You take care of that wonderful family and say a special hello to your mom."

"Oh, yeah, I almost forgot. Mom said to tell you congratulations on making it to the new millennium. She stays real busy with the ranch and the girls but I know she misses dad."

"Well, Dan, your dad was one of the finest men that ever served in Austin and I'm proud to say you're following right in his footsteps. I just hope I'm around to see you move up to the Senate."

"OK, Andy. Well, enjoy your time in San Antonio. I've got to get up to Austin to meet with my new State Affairs staffer. She's gonna' have her hands full with this mess." This wasn't the first time Andy had mentioned the Senate, but Dan never had felt much enthusiasm about it. But if everything went right it might happen some day. Dan knew that any Senate possibility depended on him not getting his ass kicked for messing with Butch's big plan.

Since his meeting with Randi wasn't until the next day, Dan considered staying the night in San Antonio. The holiday festivities were a great temptation. But he headed up I-35 to Austin. He'd find a chance to bring the girls to San Antonio sometime so they could enjoy it too.

Chapter 12

Ann Terrance had returned to Austin the Monday after New Years and Butch had spent the last three days in national issue briefings. It was slowly starting to make sense to him, but Ann was a tough teacher and Butch was feeling pushed too hard. The meeting with Lance and the group of utility executives was a welcome relief. He'd finally get to do something he was good at.

Butch and Lance were being driven through Austin in a big, black limo. "Now, look, Lance, I want to be sure we've got this deal settled before we get into the session. Are you sure everything's lined up?"

"Don't worry, Governor. I've talked personally to every person who's going to be there tonight. Everybody is signed on and ready to go. Billy is ready to assign House Bill One to this legislation as soon as the House opens. He's gone over it with Carb and it's a go. We've got Jim Clower, the top Republican in the House, as the sponsor and he's got a bipartisan list of co-sponsors that should mean smooth sailing. And Betsy Pertny, who will be at the dinner tonight, has the Senate all lined up too. It should be a cake walk."

The limo pulled into the parking garage of the downtown Austin office building where the utility companies had rented the entire top floor club for the night. The elevator ride up twenty-five floors gave Butch time to look over the notes of his remarks. He knew his speech was just for show. The main business tonight was letting the utility executives know the way was paved for their bill and get them lined up behind Butch's presidential campaign. Good old Lance sure knew how to work this system.

As they walked into the plush club room, Jim Counce, the Chairman of Houston Lighting and Power, shouted out, "And here is the Honorable Governor and soon to be President Butch Grange." The room rippled with the kind of applause people make with a drink in one hand.

"Gentlemen, Gentlemen and you too, Ma'am. It's good of all of you to come to town for this little get-together." Butch admired the low-cut bodice of Betsy Pertny's dress as she handed him his drink. The rest were all men who were the top executives of the major investor-owned utilities in the state. In addition, Sam Turpin, the chief utility lobbyist was there. Butch and Sam were occasional golfing partners, but Butch had only met the others in the room a few times.

Sam spoke raising his voice. "Governor, we want to welcome you on behalf of the power industry in Texas and say how pleased we are to be working with you on matters so important to the people of the state." The rest of the dozen people had gathered in a circle as Sam was speaking. "I raise a toast to the great Governor of Texas and the next president of the United States."

"Hear, Hear."

"Well, folks, I thank you for your kind words. I just hope that I can live up to it all. Millie and I are humbled by all the attention we're getting. I think that there are big things ahead for Texas and for this nation if we can keep on our path of free enterprise and better government. I know that all of you share that vision and I look forward to a fruitful legislative session. When we do this deregulation deal, we will be accomplishing something for Texas akin to the victory at San Jacinto." Butch wondered if Lance still thought that last line was too much. Oh, well. It would be impossible to mess up with these boys.

Butch was seated for dinner at the head of the long, candle-lit table. Lance was on his right and Sam on his left. The prime rib meal was served by waiters who were almost invisible as they worked.

Lance was finishing his dessert. "Butch, Sam and I have been rechecking the draft legislation and we're pretty confident we've got it where we want it. Right, Sam?"

"Yep. It's a fine piece of work all right. We've been working the members already and it's looking good. Billy is going to designate it as House Bill One to show his commitment to it. We've got the funding mechanism built right in to the open market language so it's part of the whole thing."

"Well, I figured you boys would look after your part of the deal. What about my part?" Butch signaled the waiter to refill his wine glass again.

Lance looked pained, put his hand on Butch's arm and spoke in hushed tones. "Butch, we can't talk about that here. Sam, let's go over and show Butch the view." The three men stood and walked over to the floor-to-ceiling windows that looked out onto downtown Austin and the capitol. The downtown buildings had been limited in height and design to preserve the capitol views from around town. Their twenty-fifth floor view showed a grand panorama.

Sam looked over his shoulder to be sure there was nobody within earshot. "Governor, you know we'll come through with the whole deal. There just can't be a quid pro quo connection to the deregulation bill." The rest of the people were still at the table, glancing only occasionally at the group at the window.

"OK, OK. I know there can't appear to be a connection. But, generally speaking, what does the other side of the deal look like?"

"Here's the way it works. Now you can't breathe a word of this. We'll do it with the "Thirteen Eighty-Eight" method. The federal campaign contribution limit is a thousand dollars from one individual. We've got about fifteen hundred utility employees plus another five hundred spouses in mind to each give you a thousand dollar contribution."

"Good. That's a cool two million that I need badly to kick start my campaign. But what's this 'Thirteen Eighty-Eight' business?"

"Oh, that's based on the income tax rate. If you take the one thousand, plus twenty-eight percent tax on that plus tax on the tax and so forth you come up with thirteen hundred eighty eight dollars and eighty eight cents bonus from the company for our folks to give you the contribution at zero cost to them personally. That's the bonus we'll give them and if their wives give too, they get twice that. Anyway that's why we call it the Thirteen Eighty Eight method."

"Now, Governor, you have to forget what you just heard." Lance looked worried. "Sam, you just manage all that and we'll look after things on the legislative side."

Butch looked out over the lighted scene and thought how easy political deals were compared to the thousands of automobile deals he'd made. No haggling, no fussing. Just get the players lined up and be sure everybody gets taken care of. Old Lance looked awfully nervous. He'd better calm him down.

"Don't worry, Lance. I'll keep my trap shut. Sam, when do you think this money can start flowing? I need to lease a plane and pay for staff." Lance looked worse rather than calmer.

"My folks need some comfort that the legislation is moving without any big opposition. I'd say we could start some of the early givers by middle February. March first at the latest."

"Damn, Governor. We can't be talking about this kind of stuff. Even if it's safe, we shouldn't be covering this." Lance rubbed his hands nervously over his hairless head.

"Calm down, Lance. Sam, let's you and me set up to play golf around the first of February. We can have a little chit chat where it's safe. Although, Lance, I can't think of a safer crowd than this one."

"It's not that it's not safe. You just shouldn't ever talk about this to anybody, even us."

Butch looked at Lance with a sly grin. "Lance, you're starting to sound like our little Miss Ann. Have you been taking lessons? Heh, heh, just kidding. Let's wrap this up and get out of here."

Butch thought Lance was still brooding as they rode back to the mansion in the limo.

"Come on, Boy. Those were our friends back there. I just wanted to get some idea of what we're getting for our ten bil."

"I know, Butch, but I still worry. If even any hint of this ever got out it would ruin you. There are some things you just trust to the system and never ask about."

"I've done a lot of deals in my time, Lance. I've never done one blind and I don't plan to start now."

Back at the mansion, one of his staff members showed him two thick briefing books from Ann Terrance. There was a note on top outlining the meeting for the next day and requesting that he review the books beforehand. Feeling a little high from the night's wine, Butch left the books on the entry table and headed upstairs for the night. That crap would keep.

Chapter 13

Dan and Paula Torry spent Wednesday afternoon going over Paula's work to clear their active files of last session's bills and correspondence to make room for the onslaught of paper already beginning for the session now a week away. They had done this several times before and Dan only had to make minor changes.

Dan and Paula worked through the Legislative Council requests on several bills that Dan was going to file. Two were on ranching and would be going to the Agriculture committee where Dan was a regular. He expected no problems.

When they got to Dan's next bill, Paula got a pained expression on her face. "Dan, are you going to make a third run at the oil well clean-up bill? We had to work like hell just to get a committee named on it last time."

"I know, Paula, but I've got to try. East Texas is splotched all over with good land ruined by sloppy oil wells left behind. I've got a meeting set up with the oil boy's lobbyist and I'm going to try and make this version a little better for them."

"Good luck. They sure wouldn't give an inch last time. Let me know what you come up with. I've got to get whatever we're running with to the Legislative Council soon."

Dan had called home that night and got word that the girls were ready to start school the next day and things at the ranch were in good shape. Molly Ann's doctor appointment in Madisonville was set for Thursday and his mom would take her in.

Dan was in his committee office Thursday morning when Randi arrived for their ten o'clock meeting.

"Dan, I've spent some time with Paula and I've been going over the committee filing system from last session. I think I understand things pretty well. Do you want any changes from last time?"

"Not much. The only thing I'm sure about so far that's going to be really big is House Bill One on electric deregulation. You just as well reserve a whole file drawer for that one."

"Another big electric fight, huh? I thought y'all took care of that last time."

Dan grinned. "Yeah, we thought so, too. The gov has changed his mind, but, don't tell anybody," Dan said, laughing. "He's now fully behind open competition and deregulation. He's got the Speaker on board so HB-1 is going to be one of the high profile events of the session and State Affairs will be the main stage."

"Well, that's what everybody else wanted last time, if I remember right. Won't it be smooth sailing?"

"I've never known anything having to do with utilities to have smooth sailing. I mean the bill you worked on for Garza should have been easy last time but you saw how complicated it got. HB-1 is a bill drafted by the utilities themselves so look out for the independent power folks and the consumer lobby to take it apart piece by piece looking for the hidden goodies."

Dan was happy with the ease with which he and Randi were working. She had been in the office on her own initiative, spending time getting to know how State Affairs was organized. Dan hadn't had to spend a lot of time explaining. Mostly he just answered Randi's questions. A good choice so far. He also liked her relaxed style of dress for the working session. Nice jeans with a plush pink tee shirt. Muted perfume, too.

"Oh, I see. I'll work up a list of the usual players for you to check over so we can be on the lookout for them. So, Dan, what's your take on the bill so far?"

Dan hoped his smirk didn't reveal too much. "It's complicated but it seems to open up the market like the independents wanted last time. There's some tricky financing language in the draft I saw. That'll probably draw some of the controversy. The way Billy is pushing this I won't have much wiggle room to change it a lot. The wheels are greased for it in the Senate, too."

"So are we going to hold hearings on it early? It sounds like it's on the fast track."

"I think the gov and the utilities would like it on the fast track, but I don't plan to push it too fast. There're a lot of folks who will need to sign on before that deal is done."

Dan found himself admiring Randi for more than just what she knew. She had a nice figure that filled her tee shirt and slacks well and she moved with a smooth grace that was somehow sexy. He also noticed that Randi's face got flushed when the two of them were close, like when they were going over a document. Randi always stuck close to business, but Dan found he was admiring her looks and style. Dan tried to remember the last time he and Molly Ann had had sex. Damn, boy, keep you mind on the business at hand.

"OK, Randi, now lets talk about how the committee sessions themselves are set up. Especially with the potential battle over HB-1, I want you and I to be in complete control over how the committee works, what goes down in the meeting, how we deal with problems and work issues between meetings." They spent the next hour detailing the paper and agenda flow Dan wanted. Randi again showed quick understanding and offered several good suggestions. They also talked through the likely members of the committee. Randi's familiarity with the long-time members showed and she told Dan she'd keep a file on each committee member in her secure cabinet. By the time Dan was ready to leave, Randi already had files set up on the pre-filed bills likely to come to the committee and had revised all the committee documents on the computer to reflect the new session.

Dan headed back to Fairmount confident in his readiness for the session. He'd have to check early on with Andy to be sure his poison pill plan was tracking too. A few days to get the ranch and family matters in order then dive into the six-month ordeal of the session. He breathed a big sigh as he drove through the ranch gate.

Chapter 14

Randi felt good after her session with Dan. Things were working out just right in her view. And she knew Dan liked what he saw of her. Now though, Randi dreaded going home to let her mom know that she was moving out to her own apartment. They were still barely talking over her mom's objection to Randi working for Dan Carb and this wasn't going to make it any better.

Her mother was sitting at the dining table in the apartment wearing an old, plaid bathrobe and flip-flops. Her brown hair was in tangles as if she'd just gotten out of bed. "Randi, you're doing this to make my life more miserable. You know we've had just enough money to pay rent on only one apartment. We just can't make it paying rent on two."

"We can't make it? You aren't interested in us. You're only interested in how you are going to make it. Anyway, my new job at State Affairs is working out fine. I can tell that Dan really likes what he sees. You haven't gotten another job at the capitol because you're just lazy. You'd rather be a three-day-a-week Kelly girl instead of working for a living."

"Dammit, Randi, that's not fair. I work hard at what I do. And another thing. What's this shit about Dan Carb liking you? You'd better not be swishing your ass for Dan Carb." Her mom slapped her hand down on the table where she was sitting, spilling the ashtray all over the tabletop. "I absolutely forbid you from starting anything with him!"

"Hah. You abso-fucking-lutely what? Look, Mother Dear, you long ago gave up any say in what I do, where I go or who I fuck for that matter. Where the hell do you come off forbidding me? I think Dan Carb is a nice hunk and he likes little Randi. You just take your 'forbid' and stick it where the sun don't shine." Randi was throwing clothes into a big toilet paper box that was sitting on the couch.

She watched as her mom went to the cabinet and poured herself an ice tea glass of bourbon and tossed in a couple ice cubes. Randi knew that was a sure sign this was getting serious.

"Randi, look at me. I need you to promise me. Please. Don't you ever try anything personal with Dan. You need to stay away from him." Randi was surprised at the pleading tone.

"What's the deal? Is it because he's married? Hell, that never seems to bother you. That old banker you've been dating sure isn't single."

"Randi, Randi. I can't explain it. You just have to stay away from Dan."

"And what if I don't? I think you're just jealous because I've got a shot at a good looker and you're stuck with old baldy."

Randi wasn't prepared for what came next. Her mom grabbed the corner of the toilet paper box, spilled her clothes onto the floor and spilled half her drink on the couch. "Randi Crendall, you just don't get it. You can't date Dan Carb and that's that. You just can't do it."

Randi slapped her mother hard and then reached down to pick up the spilled box. The kick in her behind sent Randi sprawling onto the hard floor.

When Randi stood up she grabbed for her mother's hair and the two of them went round and round pulling each other's hair and screaming. Their downstairs neighbor's pounding on his ceiling finally got their attention and they separated. Randi, sweating and covered with bourbon, was still seething mad.

Half crying she said, "You bitch. You damned dirty bitch. I'll show you who I can and can't date. I'll have Dan Carb in bed before the damned session's over and you'll just have to lump it."

Randi starting throwing her clothes into the box, keeping a close eye on her mother. She watched her refill her drink then head off to her bedroom. When her mother returned she had a stack of papers in her hand.

"Randi, I have something to tell you. Come over here and sit at the table." Randi marveled at her level tone. She decided that the booze must be calming her down.

"You've already told me six times that I can't have Dan Carb. Are you just going to tell me again?"

"No. This time I'm going to explain why."

Randi was intrigued. "That'll be a trick." She went over and sat at the table opposite her mother.

"Randi, this isn't going to be easy for me. Try to be patient and understand." She took a big swig from her drink, her hands shaking. "You know that I've told you all your life that your daddy ran off and left us when you were little."

"Yeah. He went off to South America, if I remember right. What's that got to do with anything?"

"W-well, that's not quite the whole story. When I worked in the legislature I started off in the House working for Dan Carb, Senior and I moved over to the Senate when he was elected there." Randi took in a surprised deep breath. Dan Carb, Senior?

Her mother continued. "Well, while he was still in the House, Dan, Senior and I . . well we had a thing going. We'd worked together a long time and had gotten to know each other well. He always told me I was more like family than staff."

Randi felt a knot forming in her stomach. Family not staff sounded familiar. "Go on. Go on. What about Dan, Senior and your thing?"

Her mother's effort to light a cigarette almost didn't come off with her hands shaking wildly.

"Randi, your daddy didn't exactly go off to South America." She blinked, struggling to get her words out. "Your daddy was . . .he was . .he was Dan, Senior. We had an affair and you were the result. There, I've said it."

Randi gasped, almost choking. "You're full of shit. You're just making that up. What the hell are you up to? Dan, Senior is no more my daddy than Elvis is." She said it with conviction that she wished she really felt inside. Randi had never seen her mother like this and was having trouble reading her.

"Randi, I'm telling you the truth. Look here." She held out the stack of papers she'd brought from the bedroom. "Your daddy set up a dummy corporation and sent a thousand dollars every month to help raise you. We couldn't do anything to hurt his name. He was too big in the government. These are copies of the monthly checks."

Randi took several of the sheets. They were copies of checks made out to Norma Crendall. There appeared to be one check from The Madison Development Company every month for a lot of years. The stack of copies was over an inch thick.

Randi looked from the copies to her mother and back to the copies.

When she spoke she was forming her words carefully, one at a time. "Do you mean to tell me that you've lied to me all my life? My real daddy was right over there at the capitol and you didn't tell me?"

"Now, Randi. Don't you see? If I'd told you, you'd have just blown the whole thing, ruined the senator's reputation and lost us the thousand a month. I just couldn't tell you. And now. Now he's dead so it wouldn't do any good anyway."

Randi's rage was beginning to blur her vision. She felt like every muscle in her body was tense to the point of breaking. "Goddammit. I've spent my whole life without a father and you're talking about a fucking political reputation and a lousy thousand a month. You're a worse low life than I thought. And talking about the thousand a month, where the hell was that when I was wearing my underwear until it was all shreds and holes? Damn you. God damn you. How dare you deny me my own father and then talk like this?"

Randi stood and began pacing the room. She had just taken the gut punch of a lifetime. She wanted to scream. She sat back down at the table across from her mother, staring at her intently.

"OK, one more time. You tell me one more time."

"Randi, I'm sorry. I had an affair with Dan, Senior and you were born about three years after we started. He was up and coming and couldn't afford the scandal so he took care of me with the money and I continued to work for him. We broke off the affair. So you see, you can't get in bed with Dan Carb. He's your brother."

Oh, shit, Randi thought. Dan's my brother. I'm jammed all around.

Randi stood up and grabbed the edge of the table, picked it up and dumped table, contents and all, onto her mother. The chair and table hit the floor with a loud thud and her mother shouted out then lay on the floor crying.

"This is the end of us, Mother. This rips anything we had left and throws it in the shitcan. I'm moving the fuck out of here and you'll never see me again. How could you do this to me? What did I do to deserve not having a family and living dirt poor while the damned Carbs were state heroes, dripping with money? I've got some heavy duty thinking to do. But I can tell you one thing for sure. You and all your protecting the Carbs precious reputation at my expense is done for. I'm going to get even for my whole life of suffering and there's going to be hell to pay." Randi finished the speech in a hiss.

When her mother spoke Randi could hardly hear her over the sobs. "You ....you were supposed to be ....to be my ticket to marriage. B-but, he wouldn't do it. I loved him too much to hurt him. Ohhhh, arrrgh." She lay on the floor in a crumpled heap with her chair on top of her.

"So my life is just a cheap soap opera that turned out bad. Thanks a bunch, Mother Dear. I'll come get the rest of my stuff and you'll never see me again if I have anything to do with it." Randi grabbed the partly filled box and stormed out the door, slamming it loudly behind her. Her glare at the downstairs neighbor standing in his doorway sent him scurrying back into his apartment.

Randi and Dave moved her things Saturday morning while her mother sat in the living room smoking cigarettes and drinking bourbon from the bottle. Dave made a few efforts at conversation with her mother as he hauled boxes and furniture out. Randi told him it was useless and soon both of them were mutely marching out the door with arms loaded.

With Randi all set up in her new apartment, she and Dave had dinner there and talked about the session. She was glad for something to get her mind off the fight with her mom and the realization that she'd grown up in the same town with her father and never even known him. Randi fought hard to keep her feelings under control.

"Oh, Dan is sure easy to work with. I really impressed him knowing about that list of pre-filed bills you gave me. He thinks I'm a genius."

"Good, Randi. You sound like you're settling down a bit. Try and make a go of it. You know that in every job you have at the capitol you are on trial for any future work. You have to be careful and don't piss anybody off, especially your boss."

"I've got him wrapped around my little finger. I really surprised him with the work I'd already done. We're off to a good start. He likes what he sees, too."

Dave spent Saturday night at Randi's and they had sex for the first time in a bed instead of a car or on the ground. Dave left around noon Sunday and Randi spent the rest of the day straightening out her belongings. Her collection of stuffed animals soon lined the built-in bookshelves in the bedroom.

She also admired the view out the living room window where she could just barely see the statue on top of the capitol dome over the low buildings downtown. The front door of the apartment opened into the living room and there was a small dinette area in one corner. The efficiency kitchen had a pass-through window into the dining area. A short hall with closets on both sides led to the one bedroom across the entire back of the apartment. There were no windows in the bedroom and the small bathroom was carved out of one corner.

She went to bed thinking again about how differently she viewed Dan Carb and her job at State Affairs. She knew that if she watched herself and played her cards right she could do just fine and go a long way toward getting even. But Randi also knew she faced another sleepless night alone, full of rage and cursing. The picture of Dan Carb on her mirror now had deep scratches all across it and he was barely recognizable.

Chapter 15

Dan had called a meeting with Randi and Paula for his capitol office on Monday afternoon before the session opening on the second Tuesday in January. Randi was still frazzled from the blow up with her mother, but she was determined to keep her cool and not show Dan a hint of what she knew.

Randi dressed up in her best black pants suit with a nice jacket and peach colored blouse. She and Paula waited in the outer office while Dan finished a session with two other Representatives.

"Hi, you two," Dan said from his office door. "Come on in. This shouldn't take too long."

Dan was wearing his suede sport coat over brown slacks and, Randi noticed, a new pair of rattlesnake skin cowboy boots. She figured the boots must have cost a couple thousand. It must be nice to be able to wear ten thousand dollars so casually. Randi silently cursed herself and tried to smile broadly at Dan.

This was the first time she'd seen him since she found out he was her brother. As he sat down in the huge chair behind his desk it was like Randi was seeing two different people. The hunk she'd been warming up to for the last month and the secret brother with all the money and power she now hated with a passion.

Paula pointed to the molded statue of a bronc rider waving one arm high and hanging on to the reins with the other as his horse landed on its front feet. "Heh, Dan, that's new. It looks great."

"Yeah, that's what my daughters gave me for Christmas. It's like the one Billy has on his desk, but I think this one is a little bigger." He grinned as he admired the statue.

"Gosh, Dan, they must have been saving their allowance for a long time." Randi could hardly believe she could make light of something that must have cost over five thousand. The thought of money oozing from all corners of the office had Randi's teeth clenched hard. She knew she needed to relax. Steady, girl.

"Sure, right, Randi. I guess Molly Ann must've helped out some. Anyway, I'm proud of it and can't wait to show it to Billy. Now, let's do a quick review of tomorrow's plan. Billy's going to announce HB-1 on electric dereg tomorrow afternoon and immediately refer it to State Affairs."

Randi looked at a steno pad of notes. "OK, Dan, we've got the State Affairs system all ready for that. I've got the files prepared and we'll be able to sprint when it hits. What if the press wants information on it?"

"Just tell the press that it's too early for any comments because the committee members haven't had a chance to analyze the bill. And, Randi, don't assume that this bill will necessarily be on the fast track. It's very complex and we'll have to bring a lot of people on board before we're done."

Randi was surprised by Dan's saying again that the bill wasn't on the fast track. In her experience any bill that got HB-1 designation was automatically on the fast track. She'd have to watch how Dan handled this.

Paula and Dan got into a discussion about some of Dan's agriculture bills and it gave Randi a chance to look around the room. Dan's political clout showed in the pictures of him shaking hands with governors, senators and congressmen. When she got to the large photograph directly behind Dan's desk, Randi sucked in her breath. It was a picture of Dan, Senior standing on the senate floor making a speech, gesturing with one hand and holding his microphone with the other. That handsome, distinguished man looking so powerful and in command was her father. Randi turned her head away from Dan and Paula and wiped the tears that had come unbidden to her eyes. She knew she had to stop that thinking. She forced herself to focus on what Paula was saying.

"Well, I think you might be carrying more bills than you can handle if the electrics fight really blows up. Don't you think so, Randi?"

Randi tried to recall what they'd been talking about. She hadn't been listening. She decided to wing it. "I don't know, Paula. He's got big shoulders." Randi grinned widely. "Seriously, Paula, I think you and I can monitor the situation and if war breaks out in State Affairs, Dan can always let some of his own lower priority bills go. Dan, what do you think?"

Dan seemed distracted and didn't respond right away. When he did he wasn't well focused. "Yeah. Right. Well, I've got someone on my case to pass every one of those ag bills. We'll just have to hope the 'war' Randi mentioned doesn't happen." Dan took out his planner and made several clicks. "Oh, I've got to get going. I'm due at a big party for a bunch of bigwigs and I've still got to go to the apartment and get in my tux. But before I go there's one thing I want to highlight to both of you. Randi you're new to the office but as I mentioned, we operate very closely here like a family, not like the usual staff and boss bit. When the going gets rough, and it's liable to be really rough this session, both of you need to know you have instant access to me any time and that I'm as committed to protecting you from the craziness as I am to getting the legislation done."

Randi didn't hear anything Dan said after he said 'like a family'. That's how her mother had said Dan, Senior had put it. Now that she remembered, Dan had said that to her in the interview. Randi looked at Dan and saw in him the full embodiment of all the things she'd been denied. He had a daddy, he had a home, a family, money to burn. Randi had to fight the urge to scream and throw her chair at Dan. His calm, smiling manner only served to make it seem he was making fun of her. She pictured him like her photo at home with slashes across his face, torn and mutilated. Randi realized she was gripping the arms on her chair so hard her knuckles were white.

Dan had stood up. He was saying something and looking at his big gold Rolex watch. More damned money. Randi had to get hold of herself.

"So, you two get a good night's sleep tonight. Tomorrow starts one helluva session and we need to be on the top of our game." Dan gathered up some papers and put them into his briefcase. An alligator skin briefcase.

Randi hoped she managed to sound casual. "Oh, sure, we'll get rested and be ready to run. And, Dan, you shouldn't party too long. You need to be on top of it, too."

"Don't worry. This is one of those events where all I have to do is make an appearance. A couple drinks and dinner and I'll be outta' there."

Randi didn't know how she'd managed to get to her car. She had declined Paula's invitation to go out for a beer, pleading a need to get her apartment cleaned up. Randi drove out of the underground parking and finally stopped in the parking lot of a closed auto parts store next to I-35. With no one around she screamed as loud as she could. "That pompous, filthy rich asshole! A five thousand dollar present from his kids! The fucking outfit he was wearing probably cost my salary for the whole damned session." She cried and pounded on the steering wheel. "It's not the fuck fair! He got it all and I got the shaft! Damn." It was as though something had burned a hole in Randi's brain. She could only think of one thing. It was the Carbs that set her up to get screwed by this life and it would be the Carbs that would get the payback. And as nice as he was and as much a hunk as he was, Dan Carb was the one she could get to. Randi swore to herself that she would do anything it took to make Dan Carb wish he'd never been born with that famous last name. Little Randi is going to get even.

Chapter 16

The legislative session started right on its constitutionally designated time at noon the next day. The usual pomp and ceremony were made more dramatic with the presence of the satellite trucks and the throng of reporters from the national and international press covering Butch Grange and his now certain run for the presidency. House Bill 1 got sent to Dan's committee right on plan.

Billy Gibson followed the traditional pattern for the five-month session. Roughly the first third was devoted to filing of bills. By March 1 more than four thousand separate pieces of legislation had been filed by the one hundred and fifty State Representatives and thirty-one Senators. The middle third of the session was primarily for committee hearings leaving the final third for floor action on major bills. The House met each week, Monday through Thursday, but much of the early session floor action was ceremony and congratulatory resolutions.

Dan used the early weeks of the session to get his committee organized and let people begin to understand the major bills before them. The State Affairs committee had received about five hundred referrals by mid-March, but most of those were destined for dead-end sub-committees, never to be heard from again.

Having had a dozen or more committee meetings, Dan and Randi had worked out a regular operation. Randi was now known by all the groups whose bills were before the committee and was doing a lot of the coordination on her own. Dan decided that she was even better than he'd at first thought, because she seemed to have good instincts on what to check with him and what to handle herself.

When it came time for the first real hearing on HB-1, the electric deregulation bill, Dan and Randi set aside an afternoon for the planning two weeks ahead of the hearing.

"Randi, when you met with those folks from Consumers Union did they tell you how many amendments they had in mind on the dereg bill?" When Randi leaned over to hand him a list of possible amendments she'd worked up, Dan noticed for the first time that she was wearing a blouse that was cut low at the front. Nice.

"They wouldn't be pinned down on that. They are working with Jones and Blackson to put their stuff on. With both of them from safe, liberal districts, I think the consumer folks feel they have it covered."

"What issues are they on?"

"Their biggest issue is the compensation language. From what they told me, any plan to give the utilities ten billion dollars for building nuclear plants that they clearly never should have built in the first place was, in their terms, 'Dead on Arrival.' They also have a suspicion that this bill will somehow erode environmental regulations on power plants, but they couldn't show me the part of the bill that does that."

"I know the utilities and environmental people are working the committee members hard. What about independent power? I haven't heard much from them."

Randi pulled out a file of business cards and leaned way over the desk pointing out the cards and the notes she's made on each one. Dan was having trouble keeping his eyes off the front of her blouse. "Those guys came by and left me their cards, but haven't really said or done anything about the bill. Dan, I get the impression they're sitting back, letting the consumers and utilities beat on each other, planning to step in to get what they want out of the spoils." Dan felt his pulse racing as she sat back down.

"All right, Randi. I've been meaning to tell you that you have really stepped in and are doing great work. I've been getting praise for you from the members since our first meetings. It's going to get rougher soon and I'm just glad we could work together first and get things organized." Dan hadn't noticed before she was that well built.

"Thanks, Dan. I think I chased around a bit early on, but now things are moving just like we want. Here's hoping this dereg fight doesn't get to fists." Randi smiled and put up both fists playfully at Dan.

Dan equally playfully put up his arms in defense. "Surely we can keep them mostly sane and civil. So we will be ready for the April 6th hearing with all the paper sequenced and ready. Just keep me posted as you get any sure amendments."

Dan decided that he couldn't have done much better than Randi given the fight that was shaping up. She showed that she'd learned from her experience and he should be able to focus on his own agenda and let Randi look after the committee workings.

Chapter 17

Press conference. Press conference. Butch had heard so dammed much about the press conference that by the Thursday before Good Friday in early April he was sick of the whole topic.

Ann Terrance had insisted that Butch hold a press conference to showcase his free enterprise agenda and come down strongly in favor the HB-1 due up for a key committee battle next week. Lance had argued just as strongly that the governor shouldn't meddle into the legislative process this early. He would risk being publicly out on a piece of legislation whose fate was by no means sure. With the press scheduled in the capitol at ten that morning, there was one final strategy session.

Ann was in her command mode. "Lance, you just don't understand how important this is to the national picture. Yes, Butch needs to stay clean and let the legislative process work, but I need him to come out strong on this. His critics in the party are already saying he's waffling on open markets and we need to stake out clear ground on this." Ann Terrance had by now become a regular fixture in the capitol, following Butch like his shadow everywhere he went.

"Look, he can say all he wants to in general terms about free enterprise, but if he gets too specific about the particular bill, there's liable to be hell to pay."

Butch listened as Lance and Ann continued the arguments they had been making for two weeks. Butch had always thought that Lance was strong as an advisor, but Ann had cranked up the level several notches. Lance lately had begun to struggle to oppose Ann's ideas.

"Governor, what do you think about this?" Lance's question had a pleading tone.

"Well, I think we should do . . I think we should make it clear that we want to make a deal and move Texas forward in free and open markets. What are y'all arguing about anyway?"

"You see, Lance. That's what I mean when I say his opponents say he's waffling. I say we have to come down hard behind this legislation. Take a stand." Ann took a document with a speech in large type on two pages and handed a copy to Lance and Butch. "This is what I think the governor should say. I've reviewed this with the national committee and they are unanimous on this."

Lance looked over the document and his bald head began to turn red and sweat beads formed on his forehead. "Well, this surely puts Butch squarely behind the legislation. Remember, Ann, he doesn't have any standing in the legislature in this state. His words can only sway public opinion, which the legislature will surely take into account, but they vote their districts and the outcome is not certain. The consumers and independent power people have been working hard to make major changes to the bill and the votes on the committee are close on several of their amendments. But if you have to have it, go ahead."

"Well, Lance, you've sure got yourself in position to say 'I told you so' if this fails. What are you doing to make sure it doesn't fail?" Ann spoke with her hands on her hips.

"Now look, dammit, you just arrived in this state a few months ago. We've been here all our lives. Don't go implying I'm not trying to get this bill passed. You don't even know how to start helping this to really pass. I'm doing my part." Lance was clearly pissed at Ann.

"All right, calm down, Lance. Governor, are you ready to go before the press with this speech?"

Butch looked over the words again. He hated to hear his long-time friend Lance run over like this, but this seemed to be the way this campaign was going. He didn't have a lot of choice.

"I'm ready. I'll give it my best and hope I don't get asked too many questions."

"Don't worry about that. I've already set it up so you can make the speech and Lance here will stay close by to answer any technical questions about the bill." Lance looked like he wasn't very enthusiastic about that assignment.

"Right, I'll be there the whole time, Governor."

When Butch walked into the press conference with Ann and Lance the room was packed. The addition of more than a dozen press organizations to those that normally covered the capitol meant a big crowd at an event such as this. Butch noticed that Dan Carb was at the back of the room, leaning against the wall in one corner.

"Ladies and Gentlemen. This is a pivotal time for Texas. We are launching into a new era of opening up markets and unprecedented progress in making electrical power more affordable and reliable. There is a key hearing set for next Tuesday in the State Affairs committee and I am fully committed to getting a bill out of this legislative session that will push my free enterprise agenda forward." Butch noticed that Dan Carb quietly slipped out of the room. When he had read the rest of the speech there was a barrage of questions.

"Yes, I'm committed to deregulation of not only the electric market but of all the markets. This country has moved beyond the usefulness of regulators. We're in a new era." Ann had given Butch several key responses on this and she'd planted that question with one of the national reporters she knew.

To a question about the bill's provision for compensation for the utilities as part of deregulation, Lance answered.

"If we are to have a fully free market, all the players have to start on an even foot. We can't have those players who have been regulated be penalized just because they have supplied power for all these years under regulation. We must see that the market starts off evenly then let market forces determine who survives and who does not."

They fielded a few more question, mostly answered by Lance and ended the press conference. Ann was jubilant over the result.

"Butch, you did great out there. You came across as sure and certain. That'll give your detractors pause before questioning your commitment to free markets. Didn't you think it went well, Lance?"

"Oh, I think it went well all right. I just hope that the legislators don't think the Butch is messing in their business and do something we don't want. I'll get a sense of that when I talk to them next week. I've been talking to the sponsors and the committee members. I don't think we have any trouble brewing, but nothing is ever for sure when the legislature is in session. That's a quote from a former speaker. That's just the way it is here in Austin."

"Well, Lance, I plan to be at that committee meeting on Tuesday just to be sure nothing goes wrong."

"Ann, you better be careful doing that. You don't know the people or what you're getting into."

"Look, Lance, I've been around legislators all my professional life. I know how to handle these situations. Don't worry about a thing. What about having Butch show up at the hearing?"

"That would be highly out of order, Ann. I wouldn't advise it."

"Oh, come on Lance. I wouldn't get in the way. It sounds like a good way for me to nudge those boys along to make a deal." Turning to Ann, "Yeah, Ann, I'd like to be there. That's Tuesday night, right?"

"Yeah. A seven o'clock hearing. OK, Lance?"

"OK, I guess. I'll be there for sure. I plan to spend Monday talking to our votes on the committee to get a pulse of the situation. I'll have a good read for us by Monday night."

Butch rubbed his hands together. "OK, OK, it's all arranged. I hope you two have a happy Easter. After all, Easter is the time for new beginnings. That's probably good luck for us."

Butch still got the idea that Lance was unhappy about all this. But Lance had been wrong on several things that Ann wanted to do lately. Like today's press conference. He guessed it just came from all that national experience Ann had.

Chapter 18

Dan went from the governor's press conference directly to Billy Gibson's office. Billy's door was closed, but Dan was determined to wait. Butch was letting his presidential campaign get in the way of good sense and Billy would have to try to put a stop to it.

When the door to the Speaker's office finally opened, a young woman, who looked to be in her twenties stepped out. Dan recognized her as a new addition to the Speaker's staff he'd met only last week. The well-proportioned young woman was a law student from Texas Tech if he remembered correctly. Her face was flushed and her long black hair was splayed on both shoulders. She was straightening her skirt and blouse. Dan noticed that she'd missed a button on her blouse and there was a pink lace bra showing through the opening.

"Hello, Mr. Chairman. Nice to see you again."

"Yes, Cindy. Nice seeing you too."

Billy was walking out from behind his desk when Dan came in. They two men shook hands and Billy pointed to one of his couches. Dan thought how it was almost an erotic experience shaking hands with Billy with what he'd just been busy doing. On that basis, it was probably an erotic experience shaking hands with Billy lots of times.

"Mr. Speaker, I just came from Butch's press conference," Dan said. "He came down big time in favor of HB-1. I think he might be making a big mistake. Several of my members are chafing over that utility compensation and the consumers and the independent power folks are pushing hard."

"Well, Dan, my boy, this isn't really a surprise is it? We knew from the get go that would be a tough part of the bill. Have you been talking to your committee members?"

"Sure I have. Most of them are fine with the overall dereg part but several of them have been getting district heat on the financial package. The opponents have pulled out all the stops to get that cut out."

Billy looked pained. "Well, that is as much an integral part of the bill as any other part. Dan, you're going to have to get tougher on the committee. We can't have them cutting up a bill that's got all that muscle lined up behind it, now can we? Look, I'll talk to them myself if I need to." Dan could see that Billy was tied to the bill passage as strongly as Butch was. Dan could feel his chest muscles tighten.

"I'll take another shot at it. I'll let you know if I need your help. Billy, we're getting pushed out on the same limb Butch is out on. I don't mind telling you it makes me nervous."

"Dan, boy, we'll be all right. Just keep this train on the track and we'll do fine. By the way, you're invited to come down to the valley for a dove hunt next weekend. I'm going to be there and several other committee chairs. We'll shoot a few white wings, play a little poker and get a taste of the valley life. You're on board, aren't you?"

"Sounds fine to me. I haven't been white wing hunting in a while. Whose ticket is it?"

"Oh, just some of the boys I've been working with. I've told them there's strictly no lobbying bills while we're down there. Just a chance to unwind and have a good time part way through the session. They all understand that. It's just a chance for fun. We'll get on their plane right after we adjourn next Thursday, which is Speaker's Day. We'll see our old friends here during the day and then have a nice three day weekend in the valley."

"Sounds great, Billy. I'll bring my gear when I come back after Easter. Well, I'm off today for home. My girls are out of school for spring break and we've got plans."

They shook hands and Dan went out to his desk at the back of the House Chamber. He picked up the direct phone to his office. "Paula, come on down to the State Affairs office. You and Randi and I have to get together before I leave town."

Dan outlined what the governor had done on HB-1 in his press conference. It meant that the Tuesday night hearing would likely be turned into a circus. Their plan for controlling the show was still the same, but extra attention would have to be paid because it was going to draw the national press horde. Dan told Paula to be in the room to back Randi up if things started to get out of hand.

Dan reflected how his two key staffers had taken the news in stride and sounded ready for anything. They'd worked out a partnership that operated seamlessly. At least some things could give comfort in the midst of a storm.

Dan admired the few early dogwoods showing on his trip home. He wondered again if he wasn't getting too old for this legislator's job. How the hell had dad done this into his sixties?

Chapter 19

Dave's trip home to Dallas for a family gathering over Easter left Randi with a weekend alone for the first time in her new apartment. By Saturday night it was beginning to get to her. She'd even considered calling her mother, but just thinking about that made her so angry she found herself pacing the living room floor.

Randi was still trying to read where Dan Carb was on dereg. She knew that the Speaker had been getting weekly updates from Dan on the bill's progress. Randi had been preparing summaries for Dan for those meetings. She thought he had some problems with the bill but he was going right along with the process to move it to a hearing and a committee vote. She would have to dig deeper to find out what bothered him.

One thing she'd found out for sure was that if she wore a low cut blouse, Dan couldn't take his eyes off her. Poor bastard, with his wife sick, he's probably horny as hell. Yeah, come on, big boy.

Randi was also interested in her own feelings about Dan. Their working together over the session so far had shown Dan to be a level-headed, caring person. Randi almost found herself beginning to like him. But then he'd say or do something that would remind her of all the money he and his family had and she'd be right back where she started. The mighty, powerful rich and the struggling white trash. Just stay on track, girl.

Randi thought about going out to the Cactus 'N Angels but decided she didn't want to be there alone. Just asking for trouble if she got drunk without Dave there to look after her. The video rental store down the street provided a copy of her favorite movie, "Thelma and Louise."

Back at the apartment, she put on shorts, a tee shirt, white bobby socks and braided her hair in pigtails. By eleven she had a double batch of microwave popcorn popped along with a large pitcher of iced margaritas and settled down on the couch to watch the movie. She always cheered the wayward pair encouraging them to avoid their mistakes.

She sipped margarita and munched popcorn while she shouted encouragement to Thelma dealing with her abusive husband. "Yeah, listen to that asshole. He doesn't give a shit. Well, we don't either. Just haul ass outta here. If you don't leave him, he'll leave you."

"That's it Thelma, take that fucking gun. With all those no good bastards out there you're gonna need it. Leave that motherfucker behind, Yeah." Randi poured her second drink and stood up, pacing, yelling at the screen. "Let's hit the road."

Raising her glass in a toast to Louise, she said, "Wahoo, this is a wild club. Just like Angels. I'm up to my ass in 'see-date' too. Pour those damned margaritas, Louise." Randi poured herself another drink.

"Shit, Thelma, I'm feeling dizzy too. Watch out for that son of a bitch, Thelma. He's got that slimy look in his eyes. No Thelma, don't go out there. Shit." Randi sat back on the couch staring at the screen like she was in a trance. She could feel herself getting high. "Uh, oh. Here goes trouble." She stood, yelling at the TV.

"Damn, slug the bastard, Thelma. Don't let him slap you around like that. Goddammit, that's what those bastards did to me behind the gym. Stop him, Louise." Randi jumped back from the TV as the man abusing Thelma suddenly turned into Dan Carb. "Kill that bastard, Louise. That's it Louise, stuff the gun right up his ass. Yeah, yeah. Shoot his dick off. Right there in the dick. Oh, well, that hole in his chest should teach him better than thinking with his pecker. We showed that summa bitsssh." She decided she'd better get something to eat before she got too drunk.

Randi went over to the kitchen and mixed another pitcher. Still watching the movie she heated six hot dogs and toasted the buns. She slathered mustard on the buns came back and sat watching in fascination.

"Come on now, girls. Get your damned act together. Wait till Louise gets her money and get the hell to Mexico. Oops, here's my song." Randi stood and started shakily dancing around the room, singing off key along with the sound track. "That lonesome highway, so many miles to go. We can never know about tomorrow, still we choose which way to go, we are standing at the crossroads." She fell down, spilling her drink onto the carpet. "Shit, waste of good margarita." She refilled her glass and sat on the couch again, feeling drowsy.

She awoke and stared at the TV. Damn, I must have dozed off. "Look at Thelma up there on that store security tape. You go girl. Show 'em your gun and tell them bastards exactly what to do. Lay back down, motherfucker. That's it."

That was the last scene Randi remembered seeing. Try to keep it together girls. Randy mused aloud, "The way big Dan was looking down my blouse that other day, I bet I could get him over here. Yeah, work on a bill or something. Show him a little more skin. Hee, hee. See if I could get him on tape jumping in the sack with little Randi. Hmmmm. You bitch. You rotten little whore. You're more interested in the sex than the tape. Yeah. Drag him down a few notches." She lay over on the couch, spilling the popcorn off onto the floor. With her head resting partway in the bowl, Randi was out of it. Thelma and Louise went flying off the cliff as Randi, sound asleep, rolled off the couch onto the floor at one thirty in the morning.

She finally woke up around two Sunday afternoon. The first thing she noticed was a sick feeling in her stomach. The TV had a blank screen and was roaring a scratchy sound. She found the remote on the floor among spilled popcorn and couch cushions.

"Take that, you noisy bastard." The remote plunged the living room into silence and darkness with the only light that leaking around the closed curtains. Randi turned on the lamp at the end of the couch and looked around the room. "What a fucking mess. My stomach feels horrible." A welling sense of nausea sent her racing to the bathroom.

After several minutes on her knees at the toilet she stood to squint at herself in the bathroom mirror. "Ugly slut. You look worse than what you just flushed. No wonder you get left all alone." Her hair was a tangled mass and her tee shirt was soaked where she didn't quite make to the toilet in time. "Arrrgh. Gotta' get cleaned up. If Dave comes back to this, I'll really be in the shit." She rubbed her aching temples.

Starting with a shower and fresh clothes, Randi slowly began picking up the mess in the living room. It took her twenty minutes to get the spilled mustard out of the carpet. The vacuum got the popcorn a lot easier. She sprinkled carpet freshener around to kill the sour smell. By the time she'd finished she was exhausted, took three aspirins, and headed for bed.

Her headache was pounding her pulse rate as Randi tried to find a comfortable sleeping position. Half asleep, she remembered the idea of getting a video of Dan Carb having sex with her. It was enticing if she could bring it off. She still wondered if it was the idea of sex or getting the video was what was so interesting. She'd look for a camera on Monday.

In the dream she had she was chasing Dan through the capitol hitting him with a horsewhip. Every time she'd hit him, another piece of his clothes would fly off. Finally, completely naked he wound up on his knees in the center aisle of the House with all the other reps watching. Randi just kept slashing him with the whip, making bloody streaks all over him and laughing when he cried out.

Chapter 20

Dan's three-day break for Easter was more hectic than he preferred. First there was a crisis with two cows stuck in mud at one of the stock ponds on the ranch. He and Ben spent all day and into the night Friday before the two hapless cattle were finally freed. Saturday was spent at a series of meetings with groups in Crockett in the morning and the afternoon in Centerville discussing Dan's proposed legislation to help ranchers deal with the federal agricultural regulations. These sessions were critical for Dan's own legislative package and he was looking for articulate speakers to use as committee witnesses for his bills.

Finally on Easter Sunday he was able to spend some time with his family. Dan took his daughters to the services at the Lutheran Church in Crockett on Sunday morning while his mom stayed home to be with Molly Ann and prepared the traditional ham and vegetables for lunch. The girls were all decked out in new Easter dresses and he was struck with how they were starting to look less like little girls and more like young women. People grow up awfully fast these days, he thought as they rode back to the ranch. What ever happened to enjoying being young?

Dan and Molly Ann were relaxing and talking after lunch. "Why is this session so different than the last three, Dan?" Molly asked. The girls were in their rooms writing themes they'd been assigned before spring break.

"Well, there's several things, but the biggest is that Butch is running for president and he's putting all kinds of pressures on everything. I mean just the mob of reporters from all over everywhere is enough to drive you crazy."

"But, Dan, you're showing a lot more strain than I've ever seen in you. You're always hectic during the middle of the session. But this is different with you. What's going on that has you so nervous?"

Dan marveled at Molly Ann's ability to see through him. They were in their bedroom with Molly Ann propped up on pillows in her hospital bed.

Her long brown hair was brushed and fell softly on both shoulders. Her eyes were as dark and shiny as ever. And as for her mind. Dan couldn't believe that Molly Ann could see through his façade to what was going on with him. It was time to fess up.

"Mol, you're too much. OK, here's the story. Butch is pushing a bill to let competition into the electric market in trade for ten billion dollars in the utility's pockets. They claim it's for paying off their expensive nuclear plants."

"You don't mean he's going to reward the utilities for doing what almost everybody said was wrong, do you?"

"That's exactly what it is. And the ten billion comes out of the state treasury so everybody pays, even if their utility didn't join in the nuclear mess. It's highway robbery and I'm sure that Butch is getting a lot of contributions to his national campaign from it, but the train is on the track now. Even Billy is on board and twisting my arm."

Molly Ann frowned, looking at her folded hands. "Well, Dan Carb, you can't let that happen. You couldn't live with yourself. Just what are you going to do about it?"

"What any Carb would do. I'm going to stop it. And that gets back to your first question. That's what's got me nervous and a little uptight. Hell, Butch has an army of national advisors, led by this woman from Pennsylvania who is like a cross between a wildcat and a bulldozer." Dan reached out and covered Molly Ann's hands with his. "Mol, Andy is helping me to set up a poison pill for this money grab. I'm starting to put it in place now. When this hits at the end of the session, all hell is going to break loose. Billy will kill me. I sure wish you could be there with me."

Molly Ann stared out the window at the hills behind the house. When she spoke her voice was firm and sure. "Dan, it sounds like you know what you have to do and you're doing it. You know that no matter what, this family is nine hundred percent behind you. Look at it this way, if it all blows up, you'll get to come home and stay with us. Would that be so bad?"

Dan grinned and leaned over and kissed her gently. "No, Ma'am, that's not bad at all. I don't know if Austin could survive without at least one Carb there, but I can't let them get away with this robbery. I'm going to try to protect myself, but the bottom line is I'm going to stop this. Even if it costs me my seat in the House, I'm determined they won't get away with this."

"Your grandfather would be proud. But, Dan, I didn't know all this was going on. Look, you should be calling me more often. I may not be able to be there with you, but we can at least talk it out. You shouldn't be carrying all this just on your shoulders."

"Mol, I didn't want to put any of this stuff off on you. You have enough to worry about."

"Dan Carb, don't you patronize me. My body may not be with it any more, but I'm still as committed to this service as you are. You can't leave me out."

Dan was thrilled at again hearing the dedicated partner he had known for all his time in office. "As usual, you're right on, Mol. OK, from now on, you'll be the third plotter with Andy and me. We've got three different ways working to kill this bill at the last minute. Now, with all the reporters, it'll make the national news, but that doesn't slow me down at all."

Dan decided that his talk with Molly Ann fit right in with what he and the girls had heard from the preacher in Crockett. He felt new life well up in his efforts and the promise that whatever happened he would come out all right. He could face the upcoming turmoil with renewed vigor and certainty.

Dan's appointment Monday morning with Addus Fendley meant he had to leave the ranch earlier than usual. Fendley had been the family attorney in Madisonville as long as Dan could remember.

Dan was at Fendley's office at nine-thirty to sign papers having to do with the family business. Addus Fendley was in his seventies, about the same age as Dan's dad would have been. Dan had seen his wizened face twice every year since he'd become the de facto head of the family. Today there was a sheaf of papers to sign.

"So, Addus, how is the business coming along? Still lots of money coming in?"

The attorney looked at Dan over his half lens glasses and frowned. "Sure, Son, the royalties are still coming in nicely. It would be good if you would take a look at these deals the oil companies are offering more often. I try to do my best, but I don't get around as much as I used to."

Dan had a pen, signing the stack of papers he'd been given. "I'm sure you're doing just great. Anyway, I don't know anywhere near as much as you do. Dad never told me much about the oil business. I guess all these papers are necessary." Dan looked at the next document. "What the hell is the Madison Development Company, anyway?"

Addus ruffled through the papers for his own copy. "Oh, that. Now, that's just a set up to take care of some of the oil business. Just some fees to cover regular expenses."

"Well, a thousand dollars a month should cover a lot of expenses. What exactly do we get for a thousand a month?" Addus' phone rang and he got into a conversation with someone about a filing before the Railroad Commission. Dan went on signing the documents.

When he'd finished signing all of them, he stacked them neatly and handed them across the desk to Fendley.

The old lawyer sat listening with the phone held with his shoulder and looked over the signed pages. He shook his head to Dan's unspoken question if there was more to sign.

Dan looked at his watch and gestured he had to leave. Addus shook Dan's hand and waved him on.

Dan did want to ask what happened to all this when the elderly lawyer retired, but he didn't want to get into that now. Addus never did tell him what the Madison Development Company was. Oh, well, he had to get to Austin for the noon opening of the session.

Chapter 21

Butch, Ann and a few of his national entourage had flown to Denver for a gigantic Easter service at a natural amphitheater that was carved into the red, rocky foothills west of the city. He was getting used to the leased Lear jet and the ease of making meetings all over the country. Easier than covering Texas in an election, Butch thought.

The meeting was a gathering of a number of independent Christian churches and Reverend Wright, with his hand on Butch's shoulder, introduced him to the crowd numbering in the thousands as the front-runner for the Republican presidential nomination. He had gotten a noisy standing ovation from the crowd on bleacher seats that seemed to Butch to go up five hundred feet above the stage. The rock walls made the cheering even louder.

For lunch on Monday they met at an exclusive country club southeast of the city. Ann Terrance had arranged for all the independent ministers of the area to be there along with representatives of four national lobbying groups for those same churches.

Butch looked around at the crowd. "I want you gentlemen and ladies to know that when I'm elected president of the United States that you'll have a God-fearing man in the White House." There was nice applause from the fifteen people around the table. "Yeah, Millie and I have been regular church goers for all of our lives. We've always believed that you're a Christian first before all your other titles." The line that Ann had worked up for him was going over well with this group and he smiled at her sitting at his right.

Butch tried to remember the other main point Ann had drilled into him on the plane. What was it now? He looked at Ann and she pulled at her right ear lobe. Oh, yeah. "Now you're going to be hearing from some of the other Republican candidates that they are the real believers and you should be backing them. Just remember that I was the first to stand before you and I'm going to be the one standing on that podium accepting the nomination."

When Butch sat down after his remarks, Reverend Wright stood and spoke for the group. "Governor Grange, you've made a fine impression on us and our members. We'll be getting the word out in our churches that we've already made our pick. But tell us, Governor, how do your prospects look in the rest of the country?"

"Oh, we're doing real good, Reverend. Real good, right, Ann?" Butch hoped Ann had something on this.

"The Governor is right. Our initial polling is showing us leading in all the early numbers and we're the first to be working nationally. It can only go up from here." Several of the ministers nodded approval. "Further, we are putting together state organizations and expect to have those in place in the key primary states by the end of summer." Ann looked at Beth Johns from RCT, the Real Christians Together. "Beth, we want to coordinate with your organization drives, too."

"Right, Ann. We're on track now to have believers running precinct, district and state conventions all over the country. By the fall we should have over seventy-five percent of the Republican precincts nationally run by our people." There were appreciative murmurs around the table.

"That sounds great. We will be working closely with you to tie in our state organizations. And of course we'll be in contact with you as we develop positions on the issues to be sure we're in lock step." That last brought applause.

Butch marveled at the way Ann stepped right in and took charge of these technical discussions. She was so much more a political strategist than Lance ever was. Butch wondered how he'd ever done without her. By now he and Ann had spent enough time together that he didn't have to worry about her getting on his case. They had worked out little signals to help him when he was speaking publicly, he'd cleaned up his language and he was making fewer and fewer mistakes.

They were in the Lear heading back to Austin. "Well, Miss Ann, I think this is looking more and more like a deal. Those Bible thumpers really ate up what I had to say."

"Now, Butch, don't call them Bible thumpers. Those are the people most likely to deliver the nomination to you. You remember that better term we came up with?"

"Oh, yeah. Believers. Hey, that's what they called themselves. Believers. Can they really organize three-fourths of the precincts with their folks?"

"I guess so. They have been getting more and more organized every election. I think they run training sessions for precinct operations all over the country. I've heard they're spending a lot of money and effort on it."

"Well, I'm glad they're on our side. Do they control a lot of votes?"

"Not as many as you'd think from the way they drive our agenda. Their interest seems to be to put their people in all the key positions so they can name the winner and control the platform. It's all good and well if they're with you, but if you don't dance to their tune they'll turn on you in a minute. That's why I had you rehearse everything you said to them. You really have to walk on eggs as far as their issues go."

Butch settled in to nap the rest of the way to Austin. He knew there was a big hearing on his electric deregulation coming up this week and he was depending on that to help pay for this expensive airplane and those mounting staff costs. His daddy had given him a few hundred thousand out of the business as a starter, but he'd have to start getting some real money soon. Two thousand utility managers at a thousand a clip should prime the pump.

Chapter 22

The Monday afternoon House session was mostly a waste of time for Dan. He spent nearly all of the time on his desk phone checking on Lance-a-lot's lobbying efforts on the electric dereg bill. Butch was so desperate he didn't seem to mind ruining Lance's reputation to get this bill passed. Dan had watched as Ann Terrance had replaced Lance pulling Butch's strings and how it made Butch a different person. Lance was being a good trooper and working where he could do some good. Butch's desperation about the electric dereg bill made Dan's plan all the more risky. Oh, well, in for a dime in for a dollar.

Dan had set up a late night meeting with Paula and Randi to check last minute signals on the dereg committee hearing. They met in his State Affairs office and Randi led off, handing thick files to both Paula and Dan.

"Here are the amendments that I have so far. Dan, I'm afraid your deadline of six o'clock tonight for amendments got blown. There are at least another five more I know of and maybe more. Should I try to hold them to the deadline?"

"No, we can't really do that. I just wanted to control the circus a little. Just let 'em come."

Paula was looking over the thick sheaf of amendments. "Well, from what I see here there are at least twenty big fights looming. Dan, we're liable to be there all night."

"That reminds me. Let's be sure that the caterers are ready to keep the committee fed and coffeed as long as it takes."

"Already done," Randi said. "This mess has been shaping up for a week. I knew we'd have to cover the food."

Dan scanned through the amendment file. "OK, here's another kicker. The governor is going to be there and that means that whole damned flock of reporters will be jammed into the room. I doubt that they'll last very far into the night, but we'll have to start off with them."

"Dan, I've already lined up the overflow room with TV's. I figure there's no way we can avoid that."

"Good, Randi. Paula, this girl is taking this on like she's been there before."

Paula grinned at Randi. "Well, she's a good pupil too. Really sounds like you've got it wired, Randi."

Randi blushed and closed the open files in front of her. "Just hold your compliments until we actually bring this off. We still have to cope with three hundred people in a room designed for seventy five and not get anybody's nose out of joint, including the mighty Butch."

Dan smiled at both of them. "Well, I tilted at the windmill of trying to lay down rules for that national press mob. That was a wasted eff . . ." The phone on Dan's desk rang in the two ring pattern of his private line.

"Hello." Dan flashed his eyes upward then back at his two staffers. Paula gestured that they could leave him in private, but Dan shook his head 'no'.

"Yeah, I know. But I've already taken care of that." Pause. "Well that's the second one. The first one is already done, the second will be tomorrow night." Pause. "What? No, I don't think so. I think old crazy Butch will give us plenty of reasons for three. I'm already starting to hear the signals." Dan listened for a long time.

When Dan finished the call, he looked at his watch. "Look, I've got to go meet someone. Is there anything we're missing for tomorrow night?" Paula turned both hands palm up.

"Dan, the only thing I can think of is any more last minute amendments. Like you said, there's not much we can do about those." Randi was gathering her stuff to go.

"Well, thanks for staying so late, especially with another late one tomorrow night."

Dan thought that Randi's bloodshot eyes and tired expressions showed she'd had a rough weekend, but she smiled and said she was ready to go the distance.

Chapter 23

Randi and Dave met for drinks at a club on Sixth Street.

"Well, Davie, you've been giving me hell about why I went to work for Dan Carb. The reason has changed, but I think I'm finally ready to explain it to you."

"Hell, Randi, the session's only got two months to go. Are you just now figuring out why you jumped jobs?" Dave had apparently had a calmer Easter break than Randi had. Randi thought, hell, that bastard had all his family around him and I was the only one that was abandoned.

"Dave, don't be a smart ass. Look, finish your beer and let's go over to my place. We've got some heavy duty things to wrestle with."

"That's the best offer I've had all night. Let's get to it." He put his hand on her bottom as they both stood.

"Now, dammit, I wasn't talking about going to bed. Just wait until you hear what I have to say. This is really better than sex." Dave gave her a skeptical look as they headed out of the club.

"Hey, Randi, when did you go on the wagon?" Dave pointed to Randi's water bottle as they sat down on her couch.

She grimaced at him. "I'm still getting over my movie party Saturday night. My head is hurting so bad, I can't even put powder on my face." Randi managed a crooked smile. She was struggling with where to start. She sat facing him, leaning against the couch arm.

"Now, look, Dave. I'm going to tell you some things that are damned important. You have to swear that this conversation will go no further. I'm going to be getting into some serious shit. Are you sure you can keep it secret?"

"Damn, Baby, what's all this cloak and dagger? Hell it's just a job, isn't it?"

"No, it's a helluva' lot more than that. OK. Here goes." She paused. "Dave, Dan Carb is my half brother."

"Wh, what? What the hell are you talking about?" Dave was leaning toward her.

"It's true. My old lady was working for Dan Senior when he was still in the House. She was bedding down with old man Carb and got pregnant with me. Dave, that's why my old lady was so dead set against me working for Dan. We had a big knock down, drag out back in January and she finally told me she'd hid who my daddy was all these years. It's the big Carb family secret. Carb sent her hush money for years. It's still coming even though old daddy is dead and I've got copies of a bunch of the checks to prove it." Randi tried to figure out how Dave was taking all this. He didn't look like he believed her yet.

"You mean you're actually his sister. Does he know?"

"No, he damn well doesn't. I plan to use that fact and turn it over to the press to ruin his and his daddy's reputation. I want to stomp his ass into the ground. He's the damned millionaire while I had to scrape the bottom of the barrel all my life. Well, I'm going to get even. I'm going to smear the Carb name all over this town."

"Randi, you're serious aren't you? Hell, I thought you were making it up, but you're not. Do you know what you're doing taking on a rep with his power around here?"

"Dave, all his power rests on his reputation and that's what I'm going to burn. Look, it's not just my being his sister. I've got more plans. And I need your help."

"Ohhhh, I don't know. It sounds like you're heading into deep shit."

"Dammit, Dave, that's why I'm asking you so seriously. This is sure not just a game or a prank. I'm dead serious and if you're not on board, I'll go it alone. Just make up your mind." Randi knew this risked Dave's help, but she couldn't have him half in and half out.

Dave got up and started pacing around the room. "Randi, those guys play hardball over something like this. He'll just say you're lying. You'll wind up a laughing stock."

"That's partly why I'm planning to get him two other ways. But I have to know you're with me before I go into those. Come on, Dave, I want you to help me. I'll be the one taking the heat. I just need you with me to help me set it up."

"OK, Randi. This is your craziest idea in a long line of crazy ideas, but what the hell. I'll help as long as I can stay out of the line of fire. What is it you have in mind?"

It was Randi's turn to get up and pace while Dave sat on the couch.

"One thing I've learned about Carb is that his wife is sick with MS and can't even get herself out of bed. She's an invalid. I've worn some pretty skimpy clothes around Dan a couple times and he can't keep his eyes off me. The bastard probably hasn't been laid in over a year from what I can find out."

"Randi. Randi. Just what the hell are you heading for?" Dave had a strained look on his face.

"I think that if I can get him over here to work on some kind of made up idea about the lege, I can get him in bed with me. I've been looking at those tiny new video cameras. I get him all steamed up, bring him back to my bedroom and make a nice little film of him in there." Randi gestured with her thumb toward her bedroom.

"Good God, woman. You're really into this, aren't you? You mean you'd go to bed with your own brother just to video him?"

"He's no more like a brother to me than anybody else. He's just the guy that's got all the money and power and I'm determined that he's going to pay for all my pain." Randi stopped pacing and looked at Dave. He was looking a little trapped. "Dave, you said you were with me. You still on board?"

"Sure, sure. But what the hell do you want me to do? Hold the camera?"

"Dave, be serious. No I can handle all that. It's the third way, in the legislature, I need your help with."

"Fuck, Randi. There's more? OK, OK. Go on. You're some kind of maniac."

"The third way I plan to get him is less certain now, but I'm working on it and I'll definitely need your help. I'm almost sure Dan Carb has something up his sleeve on that big electric dereg bill that the governor and all the Republicans are on. He's plotting with somebody. He had this mysterious phone call the other night about 'one, two and three'. I'm going to get to the bottom of that and if I can I'm going to throw a monkey wrench into his plot to get him in trouble with the Speaker and the Governor."

Dave bowed his head and rested his face in his hands. Speaking toward the floor, he said, "God damn, Randi, you've got a real hard on about this guy, don't you? You're talking about getting into a high stakes legislative battle. We're both liable to get scorched if you start a big fire like that. Hell, why don't you just kill him?"

"Oh, no, killing him would let him get off too easy. I want him and every son-of-a-bitch named Carb in the State of Texas to wish they were dead. That's a lot worse. And don't worry, Dave, I'm just going to let Dan get his little secret plot underway and I'll leak the plot out before he can spring it. That's why I need your help. I don't know yet what he's up to, but from the council, you may be able to help me figure it out. He's being all kind of secretive about it. I'll get to the bottom of it though."

"How can you be so sure that if he's hiding this plot that you can find out what he's up to?"

"I'll do it. Don't worry about that. At least part of his plot is going down tomorrow night – or actually tonight. Damn, it's three in the morning. I've got that big show in State Affairs tomorrow night. I'd better get some sleep. Anyway I am in the thick of all the battles around that bill and I'm watching Dan's every move. I should know more after that hearing." Randi walked over to where Dave was sitting on the couch. "So, Davie, are you in this with little Randi?"

Dave stood and put his arms around her. "Randi, when you talk about this you scare me a little, but sure I'm with you. You'll probably get both of us run out of Austin forever, but what the hell? There are some jobs up in Dallas."

"Now, don't be so glum. It'll all work out. And I'll take the heat when it comes."

After Dave left, Randi took all her stuffed animals off the bedroom shelves and put them into her bed. "You're the only friends I really have. You never leave me and you're always ready to comfort me. And you don't give me a ration of shit. Just stay with me through this one, too." With her favorite stuffed tiger in her arms Randi went into fitful sleep. This time in her dreams she was being chased nude all over the capitol.

Chapter 24

At seven fifteen Monday night, when Butch and Ann arrived at the State Affairs committee room in the Capitol Annex there was already a big crowd milling around in the hallways. Butch's State Trooper escorts had to clear the way for them to get through.

At the front entrance there was an even tighter knot of people all jostling to get into the main committee room. Butch recognized Paula Torry from Dan Carb's office trying to sort through who got into the room and who had to watch on TV in an adjoining room.

As soon as the reporters in the crowd saw Butch, they formed a circle around him, shining bright camera lights on him and started asking questions.

"Governor, how much importance do you put on the bill being heard here tonight?"

"Gentlemen, this is one of the most important pieces of legislation to come before this state in a long time. We are poised to become the leading edge of competition and deregulation in this country and this bill is the vehicle of that change."

"What are the chances the legislature will actually pass the bill? It's got a long way to go, Governor." This question came from an *Austin American Statesman* reporter who had been reporting on the legislature for his paper for years.

"Well, from the people we've been talking to everyone seems to understand the gravity and pressing need for this bill. I'm sure the legislative process will run its course and I fully expect to be able to sign this bill into law. Texas needs it in the worst way."

Ann started to push her way out of the circle, leading Butch toward the committee room door. The shouted question came from behind them and Butch couldn't catch who asked it.

"Governor, isn't it true that it's you and the utility supporters of your national campaign that need this bill in the worst way? Isn't Texas going to suffer from it?"

Ann turned to scowl into the crowd of reporters, but couldn't seem to catch who had asked the question. She said, "Sorry folks. The governor needs to get in to hear the committee deliberations. No more questions." To Butch she hissed, "Who the hell was that? Did you recognize the voice?"

"No, but don't worry about it. I think the national boys had their cameras off by then."

"I sure as hell hope so."

They went in and sat next to Lance Dunn in their reserved seats at the front of the audience. The room was full with people standing around the walls. Butch could see the committee members were not all there yet, but Carb seemed to be getting ready to begin.

"Hey, Lance, how is it looking?"

"Governor, I think we've got the votes we need to stop the bad amendments. But there are a lot of them. We've had to spend a lot of chits getting the commitments on this, but I think we're there."

Ann leaned toward Lance and said, "You don't sound very certain. Do you have the votes nailed down or not?"

"Ann, I've worked the members of this committee for the last three weeks. House Bill One brings up a lot of issues that are critical to these guys' re-election and they have some tough votes to cast. I think we have enough votes to stop bad amendments. It's going to be close and the only uncertainty is if there is a seven-seven split on an amendment and Dan Carb has to break the tie, it could get iffy." Lance spoke barely above a whisper.

"You mean we don't have Carb nailed down? Damn, Lance, he's the chair and you don't have his vote for sure? What the hell have you been doing?"

Butch started to get uncomfortable with an argument coming up in such a public place. He looked around and a number of people were staring at the three of them.

"Now, you two, keep it down. Don't let those cameras catch you fighting." Butch smiled broadly at the bank of cameras at the side of the audience seats.

Lance was clearly pissed. He hissed, "Look, Ann you've picked a fine time to get interested in the details. You don't even know what you're asking about. Just trust me. I've got the votes we can get and I think we have enough that Dan shouldn't have to break any ties. At this point, we can only watch and see what happens with the committee. We need to be quiet now. It looks like Carb is ready to go."

Chapter 25

Dan still was missing two of his fourteen committee members, but decided to go ahead with the meeting. He looked down the table at the committee he had been trying to knit together for the session so far. Billy had stacked it with a number of members whose districts were served by the four big utilities. There were three members from the Dallas area served by Texas Utilities. Four more were from Houston, Reliant's territory, but one of them was Jones, the African American who was offering the consumer's amendments. The rest of the committee was a mix of people from across the state, mostly from rural areas and small towns.

The make-up of the committee pretty well represented the House split of Democrats and Republicans, nine and six. As far as Dan had it figured out, all six Republicans would toe the line of the bill the way it was drafted. There were at least two others who had been lobbied heavily by people from their district to not change the bill and four others that were swing votes, depending on which amendment was up. Jones from inner city Houston and Blackson, one of the few true liberals in the Texas house, from El Paso, were going to be pushing the amendments to undo the bill.

To Dan's reckoning there were at least eight or nine votes to stop most all of the amendments, but as heavy as the lobbying had been on this bill, there was no way of telling. He noticed that Lance-a-lot established body language contact with all the members he was tracking. Dan had also seen Sam Turpin, the head lobbyist for the utilities, huddled with several of the members as the crowd was settling in.

Dan looked around at Randi, seated directly behind him, and raised his eyebrows in the unstated 'ready' question. She looked at the pile of paperwork stacked on the chair next to her and nodded to Dan.

Dan banged his gavel on the table and said, "The State Affairs Committee will come to order. I want to acknowledge the presence of the Honorable Governor Butch Grange." Butch stood and waved to the crowd. There was scattered applause mixed with an undercurrent of mutterings. Dan proceeded with roll call and read the listing of the several bills that had been posted for the meeting.

"Now, because of the widespread interest, we are going to begin with House Bill One on electrical deregulation. Members, the bill is before us and Representative Clower, the sponsor, is prepared to present his bill."

Chapter 26

Randi logged the two late representatives in when they arrived, together, around eight o'clock. It was Jones and Blackson and it appeared they were together doing whatever made them late. She figured they didn't need to hear the Republican Clower's presentation and were probably scheming to get their amendments on.

After the main bill presentation Dan opened the floor for any amendments. Randi moved into action and by ten o'clock they had been through the first twelve pre-filed amendments. Dan waved her over to talk.

"Randi, how many more do we have before we get to the big one on the compensation?"

"Five more. Why?"

"Since they've only been able to add two minor amendments, I'm looking for some of them to be withdrawn. The writing is pretty well on the wall on this one. We may not have to be here all night after all. We'll see."

"OK, Dan. I'm going to get Paula back here. I need to go use the restroom."

"OK, I'd better listen to this next amendment."

Chapter 27

Ann leaned over to talk to Butch. "Looks like it's going according to plan. Carb has this bunch all in line. How long do you want to stay?"

Butch had had more than his fill an hour before, but felt he should make his priority for the bill known. As Lance told them, some of the amendment votes were close but it was going right along and nothing bad had made it onto the bill. He wanted to know when they'd get to the money amendment from that damned Jones.

"There's one more amendment I'd like to stay for. It has to do with the money. I want to be sure that one goes our way. Can you find out where it is and try to get it moved up? Lance, any ideas?"

Ann spoke up. "I've got an idea. I'll be right back." Butch watched her go out of the room, following Carb's little blonde staffer.

Chapter 28

Randi started to head for the staff restroom but decided it was too far away. She'd just pop in the public ladies room. Her head was killing her and she needed to pee something fierce because of all the water she was drinking. She still hadn't been able to catch Dan doing anything suspicious. He was being open and handling the process by the book.

She was standing at the mirror trying to get her lipstick to go on straight when the door opened and the woman from the governor's staff Dan called the wildcat came in.

"Hello, I'm Ann Terrance, from the governor's office." She offered a handshake to Randi. Randi shook her hand, wondering what this was all about.

"Oh, yes. I've seen you around. I'm Randi Crendall, from Chairman Carb's committee staff." Randi went back to applying her lipstick.

"Yes, I know. Look, the Governor has a busy schedule and we want you to move one of the amendments up in the sequence. I think it's from that Representative Jones and it's about the compensation."

"Well, I'm sorry, ma'am, but the Chairman has worked out the order of the amendments. That one is only about five away."

"You don't understand, young lady. The governor wants that amendment next and I'm giving you an order."

Randi glanced sideways. "You're giving me a what? Oh, maybe you don't understand. I take my orders from Dan Carb."

"Now look here. You just get with it and do what I say or I'll have your hide on my office wall."

Randi concentrated on getting the last touch of her lipstick exactly right. This woman was something else. Maybe that's why Dan called her wildcat.

"Look, lady, I don't know where you come off with that kind of talk. The sequence of those amendments is the result of a complicated negotiation among thirty or forty people and it's not going to be changed on the fly just because you and the governor want to go do whatever it is you do in the middle of the night. Why don't you just take your 'tough bitch' act somewhere where it plays? 'Cause it damn sure doesn't play here."

Randi was holding her lipstick in her left hand applying it to her upper lip when Ann grabbed her arm to spin her around. The lipstick made a bright red streak across her cheek. As the spin brought her around to face Ann, Randi balled up her right fist, planted her feet and just kept on coming. Her right fist caught Ann's left eye just at the top of her cheekbone. There was a loud smack and Ann let out a yelp. She staggered back several steps and banged against the paper towel dispenser.

"You hit me. I'm bleeding." Ann was looking incredulously at the hand she'd just put to her eye.

Randi looked at her own hand. Her Hopi good fortune ring on her right middle finger showed a drop of blood. Randi went over and grabbed both lapels of Ann's jacket and shook her. "Look, I told you to lay off and I mean it. You keep your fucking hands off me or that eye will be the least of your troubles." Randi's tone was raging and her eyes were fierce.

Ann started to faint and leaned over on the counter to catch herself. She looked at her eye in the mirror. "Damn, I'm liable to have a black eye." Her voice was high, a bit hysterical.

Randi finished wiping the lipstick off her cheek and washed her hands. "Consider yourself lucky. You look like you'll live. Next time don't go grabbing unless you're ready to take the consequences." Randi opened the restroom door and headed down the hall to the committee room.

Chapter 29

The committee bogged down on an amendment about power plant pollution so Paula didn't have to handle any paper work while Randi was out. Dan noticed she came back in and relieved Paula, sitting directly behind him again. She touched his shoulder during a long speech by the sponsor of the next amendment.

"Dan, I thought you might want to know that your 'wildcat' caught me in the ladies room just now. It seems Butch wants to move the money amendment up so they can get out of here. I told her it wasn't going to happen since this was a complicated negotiation, but she wanted to insist."

"Well, that one has a way of insisting." Dan grinned at Randi. "You look a little flush. You OK?"

"Oh, yeah, I'm fine. I think your little wildcat might have lost a whisker or two."

Dan raised his eyebrows. "Trouble?"

"Nah, I handled it. She's just got a little souvenir of her stay in Texas."

It was about fifteen minutes later when Dan saw Ann return to her seat next to Butch. Dan noticed that her left eye looked puffy and she had a pained expression on her face. He at first thought the daggers she was staring were meant for him until he realized it was Randi sitting behind him that Ann was glaring at. Dan wanted badly to turn and look at Randi but he didn't dare. For the remaining hour that Butch and Ann were there, Dan watched Ann's left eye swell completely shut with a bright red bruise glowing below it. He had to quit looking at her to keep from grinning at her obvious discomfort.

Chapter 30

Ann told Butch that the amendment was just a few more away. He didn't like the news, but kept his pretended attention on the proceedings. Butch decided that this had to be the dumbest activity that a group of grown men could get themselves into. All the endless speechmaking and wrangling only to have another eight to six vote and move on to the next one. Why the hell didn't they do them all at once?

When the money amendment finally came up, there were several more people testifying on it than the previous amendments. A bunch of liberals if you ask me, Butch thought. Grand theft, indeed. But in the end the same eight voted to dump the amendment and the same six voted for it.

Butch and Ann left the room followed by the few reporters who had lasted until after midnight. They were mostly locals. The national press corps had gone hours before.

"Well, Miss Ann, we've got our money past its first hurdle." Butch turned his wide smile toward Ann as they walked. "Hey, what happened to your face? It looks like you got a bump."

"Don't worry. I'm all right. Just slipped. Yes, the money is on the way. But that damn process is enough to drive you crazy. Butch, I'm wondering if spending the whole night there was all that good after all. Let's see what the national press makes of this. It went on so long I think you might get some flak for wasting so much time on a dull proceeding."

"Well, I was plenty bored and hell it's after midnight. We did waste a lot of time listening to those liberals and all their insulting amendments. You'd think those guys would get the idea. They're not going to get in on the deal talking like that."

Chapter 31

Several committee members pulled their amendments around three in the morning so the list shortened and Dan gaveled the meeting closed at three-thirty. All the members looked like they had taken a beating. Ties had long been abandoned, sleeves rolled up and trips to the private, members-only break room were taking longer and longer.

The committee voted to send the amended bill to a sub-committee to work out any interference between the approved amendments. In the end, only five of the more than thirty amendments got put on the bill. None made any substantial change, so Dan wouldn't have any serious explaining to Billy.

With Randi and Paula picking up their papers, Dan signed the committee report and purposely dated his signature with Monday's date. Just a little thing that hopefully nobody would notice, but enough of a flaw for Rieger if it was needed. Number two.

Back in the committee office Dan said goodnight to Paula and Randi. Randi said she had a few things to put away and would see them tomorrow. Dan really felt the strain of the previous nine hours and had trouble staying awake for the drive to his apartment.

Chapter 32

Randi poured over the committee documents for another half hour. She was just about ready to put them away when she noticed it. Dan had misdated his signature. The date he used was the day before the committee meeting. Randi's thoughts were spinning. That's what he's up to. He's going along with the bill, but putting in little glitches to use to kill it. Ooooh, this is good. And he told whoever that was on the phone that this was number two. I've got to find out what number one is and keep on the lookout for number three. Yes, Dan Carb, just keep on feeding little Randi. You'll go down even harder when you get caught messing with the gov's plans.

When she got home, she called Dave's apartment. The answer she got was a groggy grunt.

"Dave, wake up, wake up. I found out what Dan is doing to the dereg bill. I caught him at it tonight."

"Randi? Randi, is that you?" Dave still sounded half asleep. "Shit, it's four in the morning. Can't this wait?"

"Oh, all right, be a spoil sport. I just wanted to let you know I caught him. Go back to sleep. We can talk tomorrow."

"G-naa . . ."

Randi decided he may never have been awake because she heard the phone clatter and crash before Dave managed to hang it up. Its OK, Dave, you just sleep. I've got what I wanted. She mixed herself a single margarita and toasted to the top of the capitol building out her window. Here's to blowing that top off when Dan Carb goes up in smoke.

Chapter 33

Dan was so wiped out the next day he didn't even make it to the capitol until five in the afternoon. He gave Billy a brief picture of the HB-1 hearing and how it had gone. Dan checked out the sub-committee he had in mind for the bill. Billy thought it was risky to put Blackson on the sub-committee even if the other two were sure utility votes, but Dan convinced him that with all the division and close votes in committee they'd lose floor votes if they stacked the sub-committee.

Thursday the former members were all over the capitol for Speaker's Day. Not much official business went on. Dan did see Ann Terrance when he went over to the Senate to talk to Andy Giles. Ann was wearing an eye patch and Dan decided that it was more honest because it made her look as fierce as she really was. Andy told Dan that Ann's explanation for the patch was that she'd had some minor eye surgery.

Thursday at six in the evening Dan drove to the back entrance of the Austin Airport. He had a duffel bag packed with hunting clothes and gear plus his 12-guage, automatic shotgun and several boxes of shells. He couldn't shake the impression that this was going to be more pressure on him and the dereg bill, but he decided that he was going to enjoy dove hunting along the Rio Grande and not let the rest of it bother him.

The first person to greet him when he walked into the private waiting lounge was Sam Turpin. He was decked out in kakis and a camouflage vest. That sets it up plainly, he thought.

Sam extended his hand, "Mr. Chairman, Mr. Chairman. Glad to see you could make it."

"Hi, Sam. I guess we're going to be spending the weekend with you guys, huh?"

"Yep, we're going to go down to the valley and go after those elusive little birds. By the way, I haven't seen you since the hearing the other night.

I thought you and your staff did a masterful job with all that ton of amendments and all."

"Thanks, Sam." Dan grinned big. "We aim to please. When are we scheduled to take off? Do I have time to make a quick call?"

"Sure, go ahead. Billy is due any time and the rest of the guys are already out looking over the plane. There's only going to be six of us. Can I get you a drink?"

"No thanks. I'll wait."

Dan checked in with Paula at his capitol office to be sure that the bill he had up before the Agriculture Committee had gotten posted for Tuesday. All was in order so Dan hung up and headed out to the plane. They had already stowed his gear.

"Hey, Dan boy, wait for me," Billy called out from the lounge door and joined Dan walking to the twin-engine plane.

"Hi, Boss. I was wondering what happened to you." They continued to the plane.

On the flight to MacAllen, Dan was introduced to Sam's brother Kevin from Beaumont and Orel Hanston, a manager from Reliant. The sixth person was Representative George Kerr, an old-timer from Tyler who chaired the Committee on County Affairs. George tended to operate in the backwater of the legislature, rarely taking to a microphone on the House floor, rarely seen as strongly backing anything in particular. But he and Billy had been close ever since Billy had been elected to the house.

Sam was acting at host and during the flight he told them about the weekend plans. "Now, Kevin and Orel and I commit there'll be no lobbying on this trip. Just good hunting, good food and fun. Right, Billy?"

"That's right, Sam. We leave all the session behind and chase those birds. I get enough lobbying in Austin to last me. George, Dan and I don't need any this weekend."

After Sam repeated his no lobbying pledge three times more and Billy twice, Dan figured that he would be the focus of any move Sam and his friends had in mind. With Billy in the chorus with Sam and George not particularly for or against anything, Dan was the logical target.

They arrived at the hunting lodge about ten thirty and ate a late supper of thick, grilled steak, potatoes and refried beans. There was an open bar with all kinds of drinks. The lodge consisted of the main building where meals and gatherings were held, a motel-styled building with individual sleeping rooms and baths and an open utility building where the staff would clean and prepare the birds that were killed. All the buildings were made of stucco with red metal roofs.

With everybody tired from the trip they were all in bed by midnight.

The elderly Hispanic woman who looked after the sleeping rooms knocked on Dan's door at five announcing breakfast and coffee.

"Well, boys, they say that there's plenty of birds around this year." Sam was making announcements over their huge breakfast of eggs, bacon, sausage, beef fajitas and fried potatoes. "We'll be going out in pairs each with a local guide to help us spot birds. Billy, you'll be with George. Kevin and Orel will be another pair and Dan and I will be the third. We can go whenever y'all finish eating. The guides will pack drinks and snacks for us. All you'll need is your gun. Does anybody need shells?"

Dan and Sam headed out with their guide, a twenty something, short Hispanic man who's English was limited. They walked down a dirt road with fifteen-foot high mesquite trees forming a barely visible archway in the semi-darkness. Sam seemed to know the area and spent most of the walk talking to the guide about where they would hunt.

As they walked, Dan reflected on his family's tradition with hunting and guns. Dan still had on display over the fireplace in the great room at home the long rifle his great-great-great grandfather used warding off Comanches from his home in the 1830's. It was an article of faith that any Carb boy got his first hunting gun when he turned ten and was taught how to shoot by either his father or older brother. Actually, Dan's grandfather had taught him and they had hunted birds and squirrels all through Dan's grade school years. He'd moved up to deer hunting as a teenager. Hunting just seemed like a natural part of life.

The shotgun he carried today was one he'd gotten recently and it was still shiny like new. Dove hunting had always been easy for Dan. He loved to work out the lead for birds zooming around at sixty miles an hour from all angles.

The guide turned off the road and the three of them emerged into an area where the trees had been cleared and there was five-foot brush as far as Dan could see.

"OK, Senores, this is the spot." The guide placed the two hunters fifty yards apart with a view toward the big opening. The sunrise was just beginning to lighten the sky to Dan's left.

The first flight of birds came at Dan flying along the tree line behind him to his left. "Bamm. Bamm."

"Good shooting, Senor. You got three with two shots."

"Hey, Dan. Save me a few." Sam had fired at the flight as they scattered from Dan's shots, but didn't hit anything.

By nine o'clock Dan had reached his limit and was mostly just enjoying the view and being outdoors. He was surprised that Sam hadn't mentioned anything about the dereg bill. Maybe he meant it when he said no lobbying. Naaah, just biding his time.

During the walk back to the lodge at mid-morning Sam commented again on how well the hearing had gone.

"Well, Sam, as you know, Randi is new on my staff and I was hoping you could tell me how she performed from your point of view."

"She acted like a seasoned pro as far as we could tell, Dan. She had all her paper work ready and was helpful in getting the information we needed. And that hearing with all the potential for blow-ups. I thought between your chairing and her support it came off like a dream. You know it could have turned into a free-for-all real easy."

"I'm glad to hear that. I thought she was doing well too. I think I might give her a raise."

After lunch, Dan passed on the afternoon hunt in favor of the old Zane Grey novel he'd brought. He napped and read and was really starting to relax. The happy hour started at six and they sat down to another huge meal of grilled chicken halves just as the sun was going down.

"All right, guys, tonight we get to find out who can play poker." Sam had set up a round table with six chairs, several decks of cards and boxes of chips. "Everybody starts off with a thousand dollars of chips and we'll see who is still standing when we get done. By the way, the game is draw poker."

Everybody sat down with their drink and stacked their red, white and blue chips. Dan was drinking beer, his favorite, and Billy had started with Jack Daniels before supper.

It was a friendly game and Dan won a few hands and was up about three hundred dollars in chips by nine. George had lost most of his chips and left to go to bed. After that, the game somehow took on a different character. Dan continued to draw and play as well as he could, but Sam, his brother Kevin and Orel, the Reliant manager, who had been small winners up until then started to lose almost every hand. They were betting big on poor hands.

Soon Kevin and Sam were out of the game and Billy and Dan sat with big piles of chips. It was obvious to Dan that there were some stupid bets being made and he began to wonder if this wasn't a rigged game. By midnight he and Billy had most of the chips and they decided to call the game. Dan had just over three thousand in chips and Billy had around twenty-five hundred.

"Well, I guess that's why you boys are running the legislature and the rest of us are just working for a living," Sam said as he stood. "Isn't legislating and playing poker somehow kin, Billy?"

"I suppose it is in a lot of ways. You just have to be a shrewd judge of character and keep your mind on the game all the time." They all bid each other good night in the hall and headed to their rooms.

Dan tried to read his book again, but couldn't get his mind off that crazy poker game. What the hell were Sam and his guys up to? Oh, well, tomorrow's another day.

The Saturday hunt went much the same as Friday's had gone. But when Dan and Sam were walking back from hunting in the morning, Sam made his move.

"Dan, you know that hearing went really well for us. None of the amendments that got on are a big problem. In fact, the votes were better than we expected." They were walking along the dirt road, shotguns over their shoulders.

Dan nodded, "From what I got from my members, the lobbying was hot and heavy. You guys pulled out all the stops and so did the other side. So you thought the votes would be closer than they were?"

"Yep. The fact that we got eight to six on the compensation surprised us. And Dan, we've been doing some more calculations. That compensation is actually low for our costs."

Damn greedy bastards. Ten billion in state tax dollars isn't enough. Dan almost stumbled over a rock in the road. "Sam, how can that be low? That's a big chunk of cash. If you go trying to raise that you're liable to lose several committee votes. Those boys had enough trouble selling it at ten."

Sam walked several steps before responding. "I know it sounds like a lot of money, but we're in a high stakes game with our new competitors. If we can't go in as strong as possible, we won't be able to compete. That's why we have to have it raised to thirteen-five. It's a whole new world for us, Dan."

"Well, you've got a helluva sales job on your hands. Those folks made tough votes they'll have trouble defending in the next election just to give you ten billion."

"We know that and we're going to remember our friends. But we figure we can lose one more vote on the compensation and we've still got your tie breaker vote if it's needed." Sam glanced at Dan. His last comment ended with an up tone like a question. Slimy, raw greed.

"Sam, why are you breaking your no lobbying pledge? And another thing, why is another three and a half billion so damned important since you already have ten? Is it based on your needs or the votes you figure you can get?"

He didn't hesitate. "Oh, don't doubt it, it's based on our need. None of the rest of our competitors is going in with anywhere near the debt we'll have. And we've got a committee member ready to run with the amendment for thirteen point five billion."

They were almost back to the lodge. Dan wanted to point out that they had dozens of power plants as a result of that debt and the dominant position in the market. But that, of course, was too logical. "Sam, let's just see how the sub-committee and then the full committee take to this idea. We can talk about a tie vote if it comes up." Sam got a worried look on his face but said nothing.

When Dan walked into his room to clean up for lunch, there was a thick envelope on the pillow of his made bed. His name and "your winnings" were hand written on the outside. Inside he counted three thousand four hundred and fifty dollars. The exact amount total of his chips from last night's poker game. So it was a rigged game. And this is supposed to be my winnings. Damn blatant of them. Not an illegal political contribution, just poker winnings. He'd decide what to do with it later.

With Sam cranking up the pressure to increase the money grab Dan really had to watch his step. He needed to maintain public appearance of support to avoid bringing down the wrath, but it made his poison pills that much more critical. Thanks to Andy he already had two in place. Hey, wait, this change might give him reason to delay the bill in the Calendars committee. It just might be the key to getting the third pill in place.

By the last hunt Saturday afternoon, Dan and Billy each had a big ice chest of cleaned birds packed in dry ice and sealed to go on the plane. The others had gotten a few birds and collected them in a chest for George. Old George was in his seventies and apparently his aim wasn't any too good.

After supper Saturday night, Orel disappeared for about an hour and when he returned to the main building he was with three young Hispanic women, each wearing a print dress and flip flops. With all six men standing around in a circle in front of the bar, the women started asking one or another to dance. A boom box blared country rock.

Dan danced first with the tallest of the three. Her hair was shoulder length and showed a slightly lighter color than the typical Hispanic black. She had gray-green eyes and was thin compared to the other girls. The other two were shorter and plumper and had the round face and dark eyes Dan was more used to seeing in Hispanic women. All of them were good dancers and they made the rounds of all the men. Even old George seemed to enjoy the dancing.

Then Orel, who seemed to be recreation director for the evening, put on a CD with a brash samba rhythm and the girls started to dance solo in the middle of the circle. The tall woman was dancing, facing Billy and she raised her skirt up to her waist, showing bright red bikini panties. The other two followed suit and soon the woman dancing in front of Dan was writhing her bare hips right up against the front of his jeans. She was short and smelled of cheap perfume, but Dan could feel himself getting aroused as she rubbed on him.

Sam, Kevin and Orel had moved over and taken seats at the bar watching as the women performed with the three representatives. Dan decided that Sam was going all out to get his billions. It gave the scene an ugly sense for Dan.

Billy had been dancing with the tall woman, his hands on her buttocks. They seemed to be getting along fine until the woman suddenly stopped dancing.

"No, Senor, I'm sorry, I won't do that," she said in a heavy accent.

"Now, come on little lady. We're just here to have a little fun." Billy was grinning at her.

She looked in Dan's direction and jerked her head. Dan's dancing partner walked over to face Billy and Dan found himself dancing with the tall one again.

"What's your name?"

"Senor, it does not matter what is my name. Let's just dance." Her expression was sultry but with a sad tone to it.

Dan noticed that Billy headed out the door toward the sleeping rooms with his new dancing partner. George, who had been dancing with the same short woman all the while, came over closer to Dan.

"You know, son, I spent a lot of money on a Viagra prescription and my wife won't come near me. She says it's not natural. No use wasting all that good Viagra." He and his partner headed out the door toward his room.

Dan started to feel obvious the only one still dancing with their three hosts at the bar alternately watching and talking among themselves.

"Lets go," he said. "My room is over here." Dan lead her out the door and moved toward the sleeping building. He stopped in the open area between buildings and pointed to her left hand. "That band of lighter skin on your left ring finger. What's that about?"

"Don't concern yourself, Senor. That is from a ring I wear sometimes."

"A wedding ring I'll bet." She looked down and then off into the dark distance.

"I do what I have to do, Senor. But I would not do what your friend, Billy, wanted. He wanted me to do sex on him with my mouth. That I will not do. But we can go to your room and you can do with me what you want. I need the money." She still was not looking at him.

Dan figured that as desperate as Sam was acting about the thirteen and a half billion, that he'd stoop to anything to get it. His room was probably rigged with a camera and Sam planned a little back-up if he needed Dan's tie-breaker vote. Damned scum. This is about as ugly as Dan had seen it.

The money. That's it, Dan thought. "Wait here. I'll be right back." He ran to his room. He couldn't resist looking around to see where a camera might be hidden, but didn't see anything. He retrieved the fat envelope of bills from the small table beside his bed.

Back outside, he said to her, "Let's take a walk. You live down this way?"

"Yes, Senor, but we cannot go to my house." She was looking panicked.

"Don't worry, we're just taking a short walk."

When they were safely out of the lodge compound, Dan stopped. "Ma'am, I don't know what those guys pay you for coming down here and doing this. I've got an envelope here I'd like you to take. Maybe it'll help you out."

"But, but, I'm . ." She took the envelope and opened it. In the partial light she seemed to know it was money but looked questioningly at Dan.

"Ma'am, there's over three thousand dollars there and I want you to keep it. Use it for your family."

Dan had to catch her as she almost fainted. "But, but, Senor, I could never . . What do you want me to do with this? Oh, I know what you want. You want me to do oral sex too." She was starting to cry.

"No. No. That's not what this is about. That's some more of their dirty money. You just take it and feed your family with it. I'm glad to have a decent way to get rid of it. I have only one request. Try to use some of that money to learn something and get a good job. Not one where you have to sell yourself like this."

She looked down at the envelope then back at Dan. "Senor, the others called you Dan. Is that from Daniel in the bible?"

"Well, as a matter of fact, it is. All the men in my family have biblical names. Why?"

"Senor Dan, you are a great man. I promise you that I will take this money and get my kids and my husband what they need and I will then go to the community college. I have always wanted to learn about the computers and this will let me do that." She came close to Dan, put her arms around his neck and kissed him softly. She stepped back, looking up at Dan. "This was only my third time doing this. It is an ugly business, but I have to feed my children. My husband is hurt and not working. But you, Senor, you have given me freedom from this. Are you sure you want to give this big pile of money to me?"

"Yes. I don't want any of it. You take it all."

"You are kind and generous. Muchas Gracias. Thank you."

She turned and continued down the road in the dark. She stopped and turned one time, looking back at Dan. She was barely visible in the dim light from the compound. Then she disappeared into the darkness.

Dan was shaken by his next thought. He had never had even the slightest notion of using a gun on another person in anger, but into his mind flashed the idea to getting his shotgun and going after Orel and Sam. Arrrrrgh. This shit will tear you all to pieces.

When Dan got back to his room he could hear laughing and low voices from Billy and George's rooms down the hall. As Dan read himself to sleep with Zane Grey, he hoped that Sam enjoyed his video of him reading alone in bed. Serve the bastard right.

Chapter 34

The April twenty-first celebration of San Jacinto Day, honoring the defeat of the Mexican General Santa Ana, was a lot of ceremony and speeches about the Texas revolution. With Dan's long family history in Texas he was properly proud of the state's founding as a nation, but he was always bothered by how the capitol itself was two-faced about this.

While there are a number of monuments and statues in front of the capitol honoring the war with Mexico, the grandest and largest number of statues along the great walk sloping down to Eleventh Street honor Texas role in the Confederacy. In fact by Dan's reckoning the front of the Texas capitol had at least twice as much about the Confederacy as it did about the Revolution. But the state holiday and all the speechmaking were full of Goliad and the Alamo and San Jacinto. The holiday meant not much legislative business got done so Dan used it to catch up on committee business. He and Randi were in Dan's committee office to review progress on all the State Affairs bills.

"Randi, as you know, I'm impressed with your work so far. I've gotten all kinds of compliments on you."

"Thanks, Dan. Everybody's been nice and of course Paula's been a great help, too."

"Well, I think most of the credit goes to you. Anyway, I'm giving you a raise and making it effective March fifteenth. You'll see a difference and the catch up in your next check."

"Gosh, thanks, Boss. I didn't expect that. I really appreciate it, Dan."

"OK, now for you to earn that new salary, did the sub-committee actually do anything or just meet to argue?"

"Well, they talked about a lot of things, but Blackson kept arguing that the sub-committee couldn't break new ground. He said that they had to stay within the original bill and the amendments that were added. No,

Dan, they didn't do any bill writing, but they are getting closer on understanding the rules they are operating under. I guess that's progress."

"Damn. It may have been a mistake putting Blackson on that sub. Billy warned me, but I wanted to keep some balance in it. OK. Do they have any idea of schedule? April is almost gone and we're under pressure from the gov to get that bill moving. Another month of session may sound like a lot, but with all the fight over that one, it needs all the time it can get. I'll talk to the members."

"Dan, I've bent over backwards giving them everything they need to get going. I don't know . ." The phone rang and Randi answered it.

"May I tell him who's calling?" She covered the phone as said, "He wouldn't tell me anything but 'Andy'."

"It's OK. I'll take it. Could you go get me some coffee?"

"Sure. I'll be right back."

When Randi went out to her desk she noticed that the call was on the main State Affairs line, not Dan's private line. She was in the office alone and from the way Dan reacted to that call, it might be the one she'd been looking for. She had a slight bout of guilt after Dan's nice speech and her raise in pay, but it didn't last long.

Randi carefully lifted the receiver from her desk phone, holding the button down on the phone. She slowly let the button up and heard Dan speaking.

". . .use that to cover it up. That way it'll look perfectly natural."

"But, Dan, won't Billy be looking at that too? As much pressure as Butch is putting on this dereg bill, Billy will probably have it on constant monitoring when it gets to the Calendars Committee."

"No, Andy, I've not given him any reason to suspect a thing. Anyway by the time we get that late in the session he'll have plenty to keep him busy. No, I think that the utility's greed for three and a half billion more will give me just the cover I need for number three. And the seventy-two hour rule in Calendars is ironclad."

Randi slowly depressed the phone button, hung up the phone, ran out into the hall and spun around on one foot, driving her fist up into the air. "Bingo. Bing-fucking-go. I got it!" She almost ran over one of the pages pushing a cart loaded with papers.

"Sorry, I just got the best news of the whole session," she said over her shoulder as she raced down the hall toward the cafeteria.

"I hope you don't break you neck over all this good news," he yelled.

Chapter 35

Butch watched Lance pace back and forth in the living room of the Governor's Mansion. Lance was sweating even though the air-conditioned room was comfortably cool.

"Now, Lance, don't have a hissy. Those boys just want to have a little talk. What the hell does it matter where we talk?"

"Governor, I think I know why Sam and his CEO's are coming over here. They are going to ask you to start putting pressure to raise their compensation under the deregulation. You know last time, when we were at the club, the discussions ranged into areas that made me nervous. Now here they come again, but this time with your staff around. I don't like it."

Butch looked out the window. "Well, boy, here they come. We'll just have to be careful."

When Sam Turpin came into the room, he had the top executives of three of the four big utilities with him. They sat in a tight circle on two facing eighteenth century couches. Butch decided that Lance was rubbing his balding head so much he would lose the few tufts of hair he had left.

"Now, boys, Lance here thinks we need to be careful about what we talk about here. After all this is official state property. We wouldn't want any questions that our discussion is above board."

"Of course, Governor. We just need to lay out some changes to our plans. Everything on the up and up." Sam Turpin was typically the only one who spoke in sessions like this. The others sat looking around nervously.

Sam handed Lance and Butch each a legal sized piece of paper. Butch looked at it and asked Lance, "What's this, Lance?"

Sam started to explain, but Lance cut him off. "I can read it, Sam. Governor, this is an amendment to HB-1, the electric deregulation bill, that's now in sub-committee in the House. This amendment would raise the compensation to the utilities from ten billion to thirteen and a half billion. Is that the bottom line, Sam?"

"Well, that's the money impact. You can see that it contains specific language that commits us to help see to it that the state has adequate supplies of electricity no matter how the market goes. That's a big commitment from us in exchange for compensation that is closer to our true costs."

"Sam, you mean you're wanting to increase the deal after it's already going?" Butch's question seemed to catch Sam by surprise. "I thought we had a deal."

"We do have a deal, governor." Sam looked agitatedly toward the hallway. "But, but . ."

Lance stood up. "Now, Sam, don't get off onto the wrong track. Let's look at the legislative side. You just barely got the ten billion through State Affairs. Do you have any hope of even getting committee approval of a higher number? And what about the floor vote? The consumers and independent power folks have been hitting home with a lot of House members since they lost in committee."

"We've got our own polling numbers going, Lance. We feel like we can get the votes when it comes down to it. We've had our supervisors and union members calling their reps and we think we can prevail on this. We will need to have you and Butch put pressure on too, but it looks like we can bring it off."

Butch stood to speak this time. "Now, Sam, you're already asking a lot. It's like Lance said, we've been getting a lot of calls from the other side. It sounds like they're liable to make this a big public fight. I can't afford to have the legislature in an ugly fight with all the national press boys around. I've got my national image to consider. I can't go risking that when there's nothing in return." He was proud he'd remembered Ann's lecturing on image. Butch wondered why Lance looked so pained.

"Governor, could you take a walk outside with me? I think I could use some air," Sam said with a look toward Lance.

"Sounds good. You boys just make yourself comfortable and have some more coffee. Lance and Sam and I'll be right back."

They walked out the back door and headed over to the octagon shaped gazebo in the mansion side yard. Butch decided that it was such a pleasant May morning they might want to move the whole meeting outside.

Lance spoke first. "Dammit, Sam, I don't like this at all. We shouldn't even be having this conversation, especially here at the mansion."

Butch patted Lance's arm. "Now, now, Lance. We just have to be sure how the deal looks. You didn't want him talking in front of the staff. Out here there's nobody around but us chickens." He grinned widely and looked expectantly at Sam.

"Governor, we need that additional money badly and we're willing to make good on our side of the deal. We have identified another group of utility employees who can contribute. That means another three million in contributions, but we have to have some assurance on the added compensation."

"Shit, Sam, you're really pushing your luck." Lance was sweating more profusely. "And don't go linking it directly like that. Even just among us. I don't like it."

Butch snorted, "Hell, Lance, shut up. This is the part of the deal I want to know about. You're not the one spending big bucks all over the country. I've got to have money for that. Sam, that extra three mil sounds good, but I need some money now. As part of this new deal, can you start the first two mil coming in now while we work on the next three?"

Lance put his palms to his forehead and looked away.

Some people just don't know how to do a deal, Butch thought.

"Sure governor, we can get some to the top people started. After all you did your part to help us get it through the first hearing. I'll have my guys make the calls and get that money flowing right away. Do we have a deal on our amendment?"

"Lance, do you think it can pass at thirteen plus?" Butch asked.

"Hell, Governor, the House members I talked to were straining to do ten. I don't know. I think it's starting to get into the ugly range. But what the hell, we can try if you say to." Lance sounded like this was getting him down.

Butch rubbed his chin and looked out at a knot of tourists gathered around a tour guide at the front fence of the mansion. He knew that Ann was pressuring him for a bigger plane and more national staff and the national contributors were still holding out to see how his other fundraising did. His daddy's start-up stake was beginning to run low.

"We'll do it. You just start that money flowing as soon as you can get it. I'm sure three million will get me what I need. I think it's a deal."

Chapter 36

By the second weekend in May, the word had leaked out around the capitol that the utilities were going for even bigger compensation. It was hard to maintain any office routine since the regulars on both sides of HB-1 had taken up vigil outside the State Affairs committee office and Dan's capitol office. Randi and Dan were both under constant onslaught by advocates trying to push their views prior to the upcoming hearing.

The prior Friday Dan told Randi that he was planning to come in earlier Monday so they could have a strategy session on the hearing. Randi suggested that they work at her apartment since nobody knew where she lived. Dan agreed and on Monday morning he approached Austin from the south, avoiding the capitol and his own apartment, just in case.

Randi's apartment complex on Oltorf, south of Town Lake, was tan brick with two-story buildings grouped around courtyards. The outside décor used the same desert gardening as Dan's apartment with yucca plants, cacti and lots of stones.

He climbed the steps to the second floor balcony. There was a nice view of the courtyard and to his surprise he could just see the top of the capitol building over downtown.

"Hi, Dan, come on in. You're right on time." Randi answered his knock and opened the door wearing loose fitting green shorts and a matching top, not the business dress Dan was used to.

"Hi, Randi. Say, I don't think I've ever seen you with your hair down. It looks nice that way."

"Oh, I never go out with it like this. I guess maybe I should." She pointed to the couch and the pile of papers and files on a coffee table. "We're all set up over here. I hope I brought all the paperwork we'll need."

"You don't quite look dressed for the capitol either with that blue tee shirt. Maybe if we went in like this that crowd wouldn't recognize us." Dan sat on the couch and Randi headed for the kitchen. "Dan, I've got a fresh pot of coffee. Want some?"

"Sure. I probably could use a jolt of caffeine to get me ready to tackle all this."

When Randi brought the coffee and settled on the couch, Dan noticed that the top button on her shirt was open and the next only half buttoned. He didn't think she had a bra on under the shirt.

Randi pointed to a notepad, "Here's the file of notes I made on the sub-committee meetings. As you can see it took them a while to get going, but they have made enough progress that one or two more meetings should do it. You must have talked to them because the fighting subsided and they got down to serious trading."

"Yeah, Blackson is smart enough to know when to back off. He's even made some headway on some of the bill provisions he wanted. The serious fly in the ointment is the utility's push for more big bucks."

Randi reached over to the coffee table to pick up a file on the utility's new amendment. When she did the next button of her shirt opened. When she sat back down, Dan had a view of her right breast and the bright pink circle near its tip. He sucked in his breath and tried to focus on the paper Randi was handing him.

"Yeah, Dan, here's the latest edition of their amendment for thirteen plus billion."

Dan hoped his breathing didn't sound as loud to Randi as it did to him. He wiggled to get more comfortable on the couch and tried to concentrate on the amendment to stop the involuntary erection he was beginning to feel. "OK, the money is still the same, but haven't they changed the service commitment language? It looks like they're backing off that part of the deal." His tight jeans were beginning to feel uncomfortable with the swelling. *I should try looking at her face.*

"Dan, this is the fourth version of that amendment I've seen and every one changes that service language. You'll have to get the Legislative Council lawyers to try and sort out the different versions. They just don't make sense to me."

Looking at Randi's face, Dan noticed for the first time how the green outfit made her eyes even deeper green. The effect of her shoulder length hair and beautiful eyes wasn't much help for his problem. He looked from her to the paper and back to her.

"Doesn't make much sense." Dan couldn't think of more to add.

Randi leaned over and put her hand on Dan's leg. "Dan?" The feel of her hand seemed to send electric shock waves up and down his leg. His thoughts were swirling, but nothing made sense to say. He put his hand on top of hers on his leg and looked down at their hands together.

"Dan, look at me."

When Dan looked up, Randi's face was very close. He could smell a mellow perfume. He could see the deep crevice between her breasts, which heaved with each breath. Her lips were slightly apart in an unspoken invitation. She leaned closer and put her hand on the back of his neck. More electric shock waves. Dan had a fleeting thought wondering what was happening here. Her lips were on his and they were in a tight embrace.

Randi pressed her breasts into Dan's chest as they kissed. She made some little moans. She put her left leg across his lap and slid up sitting on him as they embraced. She was sitting right on that swelling in his jeans.

When their lips parted, Randi put her hands in Dan's hair and pushed his face down into her breasts. He hungrily sought her nipples as she moaned even louder. She switched to sitting straddling his lap, rubbing against him as she writhed.

"Dan, give me a minute and then come on back." She tossed her shirt off as she left and disappeared down the hall. Dan stood and felt dizzy. He looked toward the direction Randi had disappeared. The bedroom he supposed.

"Dan, come on back." It was hard to ignore that call. He went down the hall, stopped at the door and looked in. Randi was sitting on her bed leaning back against a pile of pillows at the head. A small lamp overhead lit the scene with pale light. Randi's long blond hair was around her shoulders. Her bare breasts stood out in the dim light. A tuft of sandy colored hair showed where she had one leg crossed over the other. Dan thought he was seeing a dream.

Randi reached out her hand toward Dan in a silent invitation.

As he walked into the room he was vaguely aware of shelves of stuffed animals to his right. He pulled at the bottom of his tee shirt taking it off over his head. He watched as Randi stared at him and her face began to redden.

Dan loosened his belt and dropped his jeans and underwear to the floor. He could feel his pulse beat in his full erection. He was taking lots of short breaths but somehow felt he wasn't getting enough air.

Randi seemed to be looking at his penis in some kind of a trance. Her mouth was partly open and she was breathing audibly. As Dan came closer to the bed she slowly parted her legs.

Dan was taking small steps, moving slowly closer. Her beauty was devastating. Perfect in every way. She was completely naked and holding out her hand to him. Dan's glance fell on a pair of tiger striped panties on the floor on top of the green shorts Randi had been wearing. Tiger stripes.

There's no way Molly Ann would ever wear tiger striped panties. Molly Ann. Molly Ann. God, what the hell am I doing? Dan, you idiot, wake up. Get the hell out of here.

Randi seemed to snap herself out of her trance. "Dan, are you all right?"

"No, Randi, I'm not all right." He turned and picked up his clothes. "I don't know what came over me. I'm sorry. I'll get my stuff and leave."

"Dan, you don't have to. I'm a big girl and it was my idea, too."

Dan stopped at the door and looked back at the scene that had been an unbelievable dream a moment before. "Randi, I know. I just can't. I can't do that to my family." He turned and walked down the hall.

When Randi came into the living room her clothes were back on and Dan was dressed and had gathered his papers into his briefcase.

"Dan, nothing happened here. I guess we just got a little out of hand. No harm, huh?"

"I guess not, Randi. I think we'd just better work at the capitol in the future. For both our sakes. No harm." He grinned and waved goodbye.

Chapter 37

Randi ran back to the bedroom and looked for the video camera between her stuffed bears on the second shelf. There it was just quietly doing its thing. She stopped it and hit rewind. The tiny viewer replay first showed her getting into bed. Then just after she raised her hand, Dan came into the picture. It clearly showed him taking his clothes off and walking slowly to her bed with that huge erection sticking way out. He didn't just get all the money, he got everything else too. Damn. She started to get excited again. Dan was naked and in good view as he got right next to the bed. She couldn't see what changed his mind, but she'd have to edit out the rest anyway. Even though she didn't have him romping in the sack with her, she still had plenty to get him.

The tape isn't quite enough, is it, you little slut? Randi put the camera on freeze frame showing Dan with full erection next to her in her bed. She fondled herself into a wracking climax, screaming as it exploded. They must have crossed him with a damned horse or something. Randi bet that would have been a good fuck.

Chapter 38

Butch Grange spent the second week of May on a tour of seven states due to hold key primaries in 2000. Traveling in the new, larger campaign plane, his road staff now numbered over thirty people. He had named Ann Terrance his campaign manager on advice from his friends at the national party headquarters.

His view on Ann had changed so much from his first encounters with her she hardly seemed the same person. Under her care he had developed a ready stump speech that covered his main points. Over the months Butch had tried enough variations that he now had it down almost like a recording.

The Detroit hotel they were staying in was in the suburbs and was convenient to the appearances Ann had arranged.

"Ladies and Gentlemen, I want you to know that it is now within our grasp to get this country back to the founders' values and on to the critical issues facing the greatest power in the world. I am prepared to lead this great nation into the next millennimum proud of our good people and determined to prevail against anybody in our path." The warm applause filled the sanctuary of the True Faith Church west of Detroit. "I assure you that soon the Christian faith of our forefathers will once again be front and center of governing under my presidency." Butch grinned widely at the warm reception he was getting. Now for the punch line. He had used this borrowed line to get audiences to give him a standing ovation and it had worked most times.

"I will not permit godless humanism do to us what godless Communism tried to do and failed."

All right, on their feet screaming. "Butch, Butch, Butch." It was music to his ears. He smiled and waved both hands over his head. Hell, even Ann was smiling. He thought he was getting the hang of this. He turned and smiled broadly at the bank of cameras from the national organizations. This was what it was all about.

Ann's cell phone rang during the limo ride out to a country club luncheon put on by party leaders.

"It's Lance for you, governor." Ann rolled her eyes back in a gesture of resignation as she handed Butch the phone.

"Yeah, Lance, boy. How is Austin these days? Everything going along OK?"

"I think so, governor, but I'm calling because I'm picking up some signals of trouble over the dereg bill. Some of the complaints, especially from the independent power business people, are starting to have impact even on Republicans. Some of the State Affairs members are starting to grumble." Butch watched the three story mansions passing outside the car.

"Well, Lance, you just have to reassure them that it is OK. Look, Son, I can't back off on that thirteen five now. I've already been getting the benefits and they are being spent."

"Governor, please." Lance sounded panicked. "Don't you remember what we talked about issues and cell phones?"

"Oh, yeah. I just keep forgetting we can't talk about the deal. Sorry. Well, what do you want me to do, Lance?" Ann was giving Butch a worried look.

"I think you need to wind up your road trip as soon as possible and get down here to keep the pressure on for votes for the dereg bill. We only have a one-vote margin in the committee and the final hearing is coming up next week."

"Well, now I don't know. We've made commitments to meet people in Pennsylvania and New York. Those are two biggies and I just can't cut out and head back to Texas."

Ann reached out and took the phone. "Now, look here, Lance, what's this all about? You've known about this trip for weeks. We can't have you worrying Butch with nit picking stuff when he's got bigger issues to deal with. You just handle it and stop bothering us."

Butch watched as Ann's expression turned its familiar white-hot. Whatever Lance was telling her wasn't going over well.

After several tries she finally interrupted Lance. "Well, from what we saw of that committee, nothing is going to happen very fast. We'll be back in Texas at the end of the weekend. If you haven't got this fixed by then there's still time for Butch and me to save you."

He could hear Lance shouting on the phone even over the car noise.

"You don't need to get nasty, Lance. Just do what you can and we'll be back Sunday." She waited, listening. "OK, I'll hand you back to the governor." Ann handed him the phone.

"I'm here, Lance. You're not saying our deal is in trouble, are you?"

"No, Governor, I'm just saying to be sure it doesn't get in trouble we need our whole team focused for these last days of the session. That emphatically means you here to lead the team. I'd like to set up a meeting to discuss the whole business of traveling all over the country when the legislature is approaching a critical action on your bill."

"A meeting? A meeting? Sure we can set that up right away. Just call my scheduler over at the Cadillac Regency hotel." No response. "Lance, boy, did you get that?"

"Yes, Governor, I got it. I was just thinking how me and my work here in Austin on your legislation is relegated to standing in line just to talk to you."

"Now, now, it's not all that bad. We just need to operate by the plan and everything will work out." Ann beamed at him as he repeated one of her lines to Lance.

"Right, Governor, by the plan. I'll tell those rebellious legislators they need to operate by the plan. They'll probably tell me to stick the plan in my ass."

"OK, boy, I hear you. Let's talk Sunday."

Lance's down mood affected Butch for the first part of his meeting with party and church officials, but he was soon back on track. Looking around the room at all his fond admirers he couldn't think of anything worse than being back in Austin mired in that awful, boring legislative process. He knew it was just three more weeks and it'd be over and he'd be free to roam the country in his own plane. President Grange. It had a nice ring to it every time he heard it. It also came with a damn sight bigger and nicer plane. He'd go for it.

Chapter 39

Billy Gibson had informed all the committee chairs that May fourteenth would be the last Friday off and the legislature would start five-day weeks, then go seven days for the last week. Sam Turpin had called that Thursday morning with an urgent need to meet with Dan. Dan set it up for the afternoon in his capitol office to try and avoid the crowd that seemed to be always outside the State Affairs Office. Randi was getting good at handling them, but it still was a hassle. Dan now had a capitol security officer stationed full time outside his capitol office.

Sam came in at two and asked to meet Dan without Paula. He looked to Dan like he'd been on an all night drunk.

"Damn, Sam, are you letting this stuff get to you? You look like hell warmed over."

"It's all my bosses. They want me to assure them that they'll get what they want and I wind up working days here at the capitol and nearly all night doing what it takes to stay on top of all this."

Dan grinned at him. "That's why they pay you the big bucks, Sam. Hell I'm going through some of the same shit you are and I'm only making six hundred a month. You don't have much to complain about. You make more in a month than I do in a year."

That seemed to break the ice. Sam laughed and said, "OK, Mr. Chairman. As usual, you get the last word on the subject."

"So what is it now? You boys raising that thirteen bil figure again?"

"Hell no, I'm busting my balls to try and get the thirteen five. That's what I needed to talk to you about. I'm pretty sure we're going to lose our swing vote from Campo. He's been under tremendous pressure and I think he might cave. If he does, that would give us a tie and we'd need your vote."

"Oh, the cheese starts to bind. Are the rest of your votes firm?"

"About as firm as we can get them. I've got a pretty solid seven but number eight is shaky. Dan, you know I asked you about this when we were hunting. Have you had time to work it out how you'd vote?"

Dan had been hoping to avoid this, but he knew he couldn't show hesitancy. He was now totally dependent on his poison pills. No surprise.

"Sam, you know that it will be tough as hell for me to vote that way. Hell, the co-op my grandfather founded is lobbying me hard on this. I'll probably be in the dark at home if I go along on this. But I know how Billy's lined up on the bill. If you need my tie-breaker, you'll have it. I need more than you've given me so far to try and justify it. I'll have hell to pay." Dan tilted back in his chair and looked up at the ceiling of his office. "Shit, this is ugly."

"Dan, I was hoping I could count on you. I'll get you all the back-up material. You won't regret it. You'll see a lot of our folks solidly behind you next election. You can take my word on it." Sam stood and offered a handshake.

As the two men shook hands, Sam suddenly seemed to remember something. "Oh, Dan, by the way, what the hell did you do to that girl you were with down there in the valley? I can't get her to work any more and she's one of the best lookers."

Dan walked around the desk and looked squarely at him. "Sam, you've just got my commitment on one of the toughest votes I'll ever have to make. You'd better quit while you're ahead." A questioning look flashed across Sam's face, but he shrugged.

"OK, Dan. I hear you. But good whores are hard to . . ." Sam seemed to see something in Dan's expression that stopped him. "No problem. I have to go." He turned and left the office in a hurry.

When Sam was gone, Dan sat reflecting on the conversation. So she won't work anymore. Good for her.

But you know that slime Sam was wrong. He just extracted a commitment for a vote from Dan against everything Carbs have stood for for five generations. He thought good whores are not hard to find. If you think about it Sam just created one. The only thing between Dan and a red light over the door was his poison pills. He'd have to be triply sure they were in place and deadly.

But Dan realized that with all their last minute maneuvering and pressure it might create the excuse he needed for the Calendars Committee delay. Yeah, that's it. He'd use their own greed to nail down the number three pill. It was like walking a tightrope. Everything had to work just right or it was curtains. He needed to set up a meeting with Andy to go over everything again to be sure.

Chapter 40

Dan wanted to meet with Andy that weekend and away from Austin, but Andy's schedule wouldn't permit. They finally decided on a meeting the following Wednesday night at a little Mexican restaurant Andy and Dan's dad had discovered off the main road in Taylor. It was far enough off the beaten path that the capitol crowd likely hadn't discovered it.

Besides, Andy said they served the best fajitas east of San Angelo. They drove separate cars to minimize a chance they'd be spotted and arrived at the little adobe restaurant around seven. Dan noticed that there were only two vehicles in the parking lot and they looked like dusty work trucks.

Over a sizzling plate of beef, peppers and onions Dan laid out the work he had in place.

"Andy, I don't think anybody had a clue on the wrong signature for the number one pill or the misdated hearing minutes for two. Those are in place and ready for Rieger."

Andy took a large bite of his rolled fajita. "OK, Dan, but realize that those are the two weakest ones in the scheme. The killer is that rule that Calendars has to move a bill within seventy-two hours during the last ten days of the session. That's the sure kill."

"I know, Andy." Dan swigged his Carta Blanca beer. "I've got the timing all planned. The sub-committee hearing is set for next week. It's been delayed at the utilities' request while they try to get the votes for their thirteen billion deal. That puts it clearly in the ten day window."

"Yes, but you still have to get it delayed after it's referred to Calendars. Do you know how you are going to do that?"

"Andy, that's where the utilities' own greed is going to help me. They've pushed this money grab so high they're not just losing votes in the committee. They're losing them on the floor too. I can already picture them asking for delays while they try to get a majority of the House to vote their way. I don't think I'll have to do anything fancy to bust the seventy-two hours." Dan had lowered his voice as two men wearing suits came into the restaurant. He and Andy looked them over and didn't recognize any Austin connections.

"Now, Dan, you have to be sure that Billy isn't going to mess this up. From what I hear he's sold out completely to Butch and the utilities. He's just liable to be watching you on this."

Dan worked up his courage to confess to Andy about his tie-breaker vote. "Well, Andy, you'll find out anyway. I committed to Sam to vote their way if I have to break a tie on the committee." Dan looked down at the table.

"Don't worry about that, Dan. The good news is that they think it will be that close. Hell you can explain that kind of vote to the folks back home. Your dad had to make several of those. People understand."

"I don't know, Andy. This is a real stinker. But it will give me good cover with Billy. The folks just might not forgive me but you give me hope. Now I want to stay in touch with you when we get into the thick of things, but we probably shouldn't meet again. I don't want to contaminate you with this unnecessarily."

"Don't worry even a second about that. My hide's as thick as shoe leather. We can just meet in my office if you want to." They both grinned big and clinked their beer bottles together.

Riding back, Dan thought how powerful is was to have Andy on his side. Just the thought of taking on the whole Republican and utility establishments alone made Dan shiver. And Ann Terrance was likely to turn rabid over this. But it was coming down to a few days left and so far everything was lined up.

He and Randi had had some tough days right after the incident in her apartment, but it was soon forgotten and the two of them were back working in precision lockstep. Randi made it clear that she really liked her job and seemed to want some assurance that she hadn't jeopardized her position. Dan still held the view that he had the best staff of any committee in the House and he told Randi so.

As he went to sleep in his apartment, Dan remembered he was supposed to talk to Molly Ann. Too late tonight. That would be for tomorrow.

Chapter 41

Butch and Ann spent most of the week he returned from New York in strategy sessions with several campaign advisors laying out moves to get ready for the spring primaries. Lance had been pressing him to get more involved with the fight over the deregulation bill, but Butch was much more interested in the campaign planning and had spent only little time with Lance.

By Thursday, Lance was getting insistent. "Governor, I really need for you to call this list of Representatives. I've begged and promised about as far as I can go. They are getting heat from several sides and are starting to waver. And we have to have their votes."

"Hell, Lance, when I left, this deal was going along smoothly. What the hell happened?"

"Yes, Lance. We left you in charge and we come back to all this panic." Butch noticed that Ann Terrance was aiming her school marm comments to Lance instead of him these days.

Lance sounded to Butch like he was stung and spoke with an edge in his voice. "I'll tell you exactly what the hell happened. After we agreed with the utilities to back raising their compensation from ten billion to thirteen and a half billion, they started to work the House members on the higher number."

"Yeah, Son. That's what we agreed to. Those boys had a good explanation for the bigger number."

"Well, the other side got wind of the thirteen billion number and cranked up the pressure against it. They've pulled out all the stops. The independent power people are all solid business types so they have a lot of reach to our votes and they are having impact. And you see, Governor, with you gone for the whole week I didn't have your clout with the members to keep our votes in line. The utilities are in a panic."

"Damn, we can't have those boys getting worried. They're sort of putting the gas in my the tank, if you get my drift."

Ann Terrance spoke up. "Well, if we had the votes at ten billion, why don't we just go back to that number and quit all this fuss?"

Butch sucked his breath between his teeth. "Nooo, no, Miss Ann. We can't back off of that, right, Lance? We're already spending the money."

"What money? What the hell are you talking about, governor? This is a piece of proposed legislation, not some budget or something."

When Lance spoke he lowered his voice even though the three of them were alone in the governor's office. "You don't want to go into that, Ann. Just trust us that the thirteen billion has to stick. Going back to ten is not an option."

"I'll never understand this legislative system. It must have been designed when those old boys were into their second fifth of rot gut."

"Well, anyway," Lance said, "this whole mess raises the question of Butch taking long trips out of the state with the legislature at a critical stage. There is a major hearing next week and a big fight shaping up over deregulation with only ten days left of the session. I have to have Butch here to keep our thin edge on the bill. I've had to explain things to a different group of reps every day and they are starting to ask why they haven't seen Butch on this issue."

"Lance, you can't go making demands on the governor's calendar like that. We've got meetings set with big national players. You'll just have to handle it. Aren't you the legislative coordinator or something?"

"Look, Ann, what you don't know about the Texas Legislature would fill several books. A lot of decisions are made on the personal political level. Butch, if you expect to get this deregulation bill passed, you are going to have to stay here in Austin and work the members yourself. It's probably going to come down to one or two votes and there is going to be unbelievable pressure on our guys."

Ann got out a large planning book and opened it to the campaign's May schedule. "Just look at the appointments we have set next week. Do you want us to call Washington and tell all those senators that Butch is too busy to talk to them? That's ridiculous."

"The alternative is to watch the dereg bill go up in smoke and, Governor, I don't think you can afford to let that happen."

Butch looked from Lance to the schedule then to Ann. Lance represented that boring, awful legislative process and the schedule contained the cheering crowds and clamoring press he loved so much. But he had to have that dereg bill. The campaign was a nice show, but it was dead without the cash that was flowing in from all those thousand dollar checks from utility managers. He didn't know which way to jump.

"You folks are supposed to be advisors. Advise. Which way do we go?"

Both Ann and Lance started to talk at once. "You go ahead, Ann. I'd like to see you handle this one." Lance sat back, his arms folded across his chest.

For one of the first times ever Ann seemed to Butch to be at a momentary loss for words. "Now let me get this straight. Governor, you say you have to have this bill passed for reasons I shouldn't ask about. And Lance you're saying that while we got a good vote in that committee last month, the bill is now in trouble. It won't pass on its merits and you have to have Butch in personal contact with the representatives. And we've got firm appointments with twelve top US Senators and a whole list of church and business leaders next week in Washington. Also the press corps already knows about our planned trip next week. It's sounds like either way we go, it's going to make trouble."

"Ann, there's one thing you left out of your litany of the choices. Those senators and church leaders will still be in Washington in June and you can meet with them then. The legislature closes up shop a week from Monday and that dereg bill dies if it's not passed by the midnight deadline. I think that makes the choice clear."

Butch looked from one to the other. Neither seemed ready to budge. He was starting to feel a little sick in the pit of his stomach. "Well, can we wait and decide later? Maybe it will get easier to decide."

Ann sounded somber, like she knew she had to give in. "If you're going to break the Washington appointments, you'd better decide now, Governor. We have to have their support and we don't want to start off by jacking their calendars around. You're going to look bad enough in the press having to stay down here to take care of your own legislature. Don't add to the problem by delaying until the day before our meetings."

The sick feeling in Butch's stomach was getting worse. "Well, dammit Lance, this is a fine mess. How the hell do we get started to fix it?"

"Governor, I'll get Sam in here right away. He's got a rundown on every representative in the House and where they are on the bill. You'll need to start on the State Affairs members because they vote on Tuesday night. That's when the thirteen billion amendment will have to go on. After that it's the floor with all one hundred fifty of them. By Sam's last count the committee would have to have Dan Carb's tie-breaker to have any hope of passing the amendment so one vote is all it will take to lose in committee. The floor vote is less certain but Sam thinks its within a vote or two."

Ann stood and walked toward the door. "Governor, I'd better get with our staff and come up with some story for canceling the DC trip. I'll have that back to you by noon. You'll have to get on the phone to the senators and explain we're not coming. I'll talk to the other groups. But we first have to get our story straight."

Ann sounded quieter than Butch had ever heard. Depressing.

Lance stood as well and said, "And I have to get Sam over here. How about one o'clock?"

"Fine, fine, Lance. Do whatever you have to do."

When they had gone, Butch walked over and plopped into the big leather chair behind his desk. Just when everything was going great this shit had to happen. He had never had any love for the legislating that Lance always handled for him. Now he was having to give up what he loved to do in order to do what he hated. It just wasn't fair. He decided he was going to give that damned Sam a piece of his mind for messing up like this. He was so damned sure of this bigger deal. Shit, he should have known better. Butch thought maybe he could squeeze Sam for more money since he'd messed up so badly. He wished his stomach would stop hurting.

Chapter 42

Dave came over to Randi's apartment around eight Saturday night and they started drinking. He was drinking beer as usual and she had a pitcher of margaritas mixed.

"Dave, you won't believe what I've got to show you. It's going to blow your cork." Randi had been teasing Dave all week with hints of something big, but she wanted to wait until they could spend some time together before showing him. She had her little video camera in her purse.

"Come on, Randi, enough of this shit. You've been acting like a kid at Christmas all week. What the hell are you talking about?"

Randi had taken the video disk to a friend of hers who had a bank of electronic equipment and had her cut out the rest of the scene when Dan turned away from her bed. Her friend wanted to know the name of the guy with the big dick in the video, but Randi had convinced her it would be better if she didn't find out. Now she had the show ready for Dave and she could hardly wait for him to see it. But she wanted to do it just right.

"OK, Dave, I'm finally ready for you to see this, but not here. Let's go out."

"Go out? What the hell? What's wrong with here. Is what you've got to show me here or is it somewhere else?" Dave was on his fourth beer and sounding a little peeved with her.

"Just trust me Davie. I'm going to put my margaritas in a thermos and you put that other six-pack in the cooler and we'll go out. I want to go up to Town Lake and park in our favorite spot. I think you'll want to hoot and holler when you see this and I don't want to stir up the neighbors. Come on, let's go."

They found a parking place at a spot on the south side of the lake just off the jogging trail where they used to make out before Randi got her apartment. Randi finished her third drink on the way and poured another when they got there. They sat on the hood of Dave's pickup looking out at the reflections of the city lights on the lake. It was a cool evening and Randi could see stars showing through the tree leaves.

"Now, come on, Randi. What gives?"

"Dave, this is the hottest thing in Austin, Texas right now and you're going to be only the second person to see it." She reached into her purse and pulled out the video camera.

"Oh, shit, Randi. Did you do it with big Dan? Don't tell me you actually went through with it."

"I went through with it all right. As you'll see he chickened out some, but I've got him, don't worry. I'm going to make him the laughing stock of this town." She flipped the review screen out on the camera. "OK, you just watch. This is in my bedroom." She started the tape.

"Whoeee, Randi, you look good there. kid. Are you sure you want to..." Dave's mouth dropped open as the video showed Randi raise her hand. Dan Carb came into view. "Oh, shit, it is him." Dave watched in silence.

"Just keep watching, Dave. You'll have something to live up to."

Dave took a big swig of beer and stared at the little screen. "Oh, oh, he's taking off his shirt. He's dropping his drawers. Hell fire, would you look at that zipper buster?"

Randi laughed and poked Dave on the shoulder. "Live up to that, big boy."

"Randi, is he getting into bed with you? Damn you're something else. Whoa, he stopped. Hey, what the hell happened? Did you stop the camera before he jumped on?"

"No, Dave. You saw I was in bed. Something came over him and he turned back, put his clothes on and left. He never made it into bed."

"You're shitting me. Hell, you looked like a panting bitch in heat and, he was primed to sock it to you. Don't give me that dressed and left shit. Ha."

"Well that's what he did, but Dave, it doesn't matter. What I've got here is a tape of the mighty Dan Carb naked with a hard on getting into bed with me. I think that is more than enough to ruin him and that's what I'm gonna do. I want him to suffer as much pain and humiliation as I can give him. You watch. When this stuff breaks, Dan Carb won't be able to show his face in Austin."

"You're really sick, Randi. But you're letting your feelings about Dan Carb get in the way of good sense."

"How's that? Showing this on the ten o'clock news makes perfect sense to me."

"Listen, Randi, you're sitting on top of a gold mine and don't seem to know it. How much money did you say he was probably worth?"

"I don't know exactly, but somewhere around five million. I know he's got enough so that lousy thousand a month he's sending to my old lady is only pocket change to him. But what does that have to do with anything?"

"Randi, instead of putting that tape on the ten o'clock news, why not show it to him and see how much he'd pay you not to put on it on TV. I'd bet he'd pay a bunch. Maybe a mil or more."

Randi slid off the hood and stood directly in front of Dave. "Now, look, buster, get this straight. I'm not doing all this for his lousy money. I'm going to publish the fact that I'm his illegitimate sister, the tape showing him with his pants down and his dick up and I'm going to expose what he'd plotting to do to the gov's little electric bill. I'm going to be sure he doesn't have a shred of decent reputation about him when I get through." Randi was punching Dave's leg with her index finger as she talked.

Dave slid off the hood of the truck and stood facing her. "Now just a minute here. I've been helping out with all this shit. I should get some say in what we do. I think we should get enough money out of Carb to be set for life. Think about it Randi. A million dollars. We'd never have to work again for our whole lives."

Randi pushed both hands into Dave's chest, shoving him backwards. "Look, smart ass, I'm not doing this for a damned penny of his fucking money. I'm going to get him and do it before the session is over. And don't you try to pull some shit about you helping me. You know damn good and well I'm the one who set this up. It's going to play out my way."

Dave back-handed Randi across the face. "Don't go pushing me too far, Randi. I'm not going to pass up a cool million just to help with your hang-ups."

Randi screamed, then responded by slapping Dave right back. "You hit me, you son of a bitch. You know better than that. Hell, I think you loosened a tooth." Randi was rubbing her cheek. She could feel the rage building inside. The bastard was trying to screw up her deal. "You mess with me and I'll cut you completely out of this deal. I can handle it by myself and I know what I want to do. And it doesn't involve any money. You got that, dirt bag?" The last she said in a near screech.

Dave grabbed Randi by the shoulders and started shaking her. "I'll show you something about cutting people out of a deal." He reached for her throat.

Randi grabbed his hand and bit down hard, making Dave scream out. She broke free and pushed him down. She watched as he got shakily to his feet.

"I'll show you, bitch."

Randi walked over to him as he stooped down to pick up the large rock at his feet. As he stood to full height, Randi took a swing at him with her fist, hitting him right across his nose. Dave staggered backward two steps, his nose bleeding profusely. He still held the rock in his hands. When he tried to stop his foot struck another rock and he stumbled backwards down the ten-foot embankment and splashed into the lake.

"Ha, you dumb shit. I'll show you to mess with little Randi. Come on, ass hole, get back up here and take it like a man." She looked down the embankment but couldn't see much in the dark. "Hey, stupid, let go of that damned rock so you can float." No response.

Randi went back to the truck and got the flashlight out of his glove compartment and shined it where he fell into the lake. "Damn, Dave, stop fucking around. Where the hell are you?" Randi walked each direction, shining the flashlight but couldn't see him anywhere. She felt a twinge of panic.

"Shit, what the hell has he done now? Dave. Dave." She could hear the fear in her own voice.

Two joggers, who looked like frat boys, came over and asked Randi if she needed some help.

"No, it's OK. My boyfriend is just joking around. He went for a swim and he's hiding to fool me." She hoped that her light explanation was true. It seemed to satisfy the joggers as they went on their way.

More quietly, she called out, "Dave. Dave. That's enough. Come on up here." Randi started pacing between the lake edge and the truck. She knew something was wrong, but she didn't know what to do about it. Maybe she should call for help. Then she remembered the video. She didn't want a bunch of cops milling around finding her video. Damn, what the hell should she do?

She got into the driver's seat of the truck, started it and backed around to leave. She'd just take the camera back to her apartment. When she got back Dave would probably be standing around laughing at her, but she couldn't take any chances.

The five-minute trip to her apartment seemed to Randi to take an hour. She put the camera safely away in her dresser drawer, went to the bathroom and ran back down to the truck. When she got back to the lake, she called several times more, but got no answer. The flashlight showed no sign of Dave.

With her hands shaking badly, she dialed 911 on her cell phone and reported a possible drowning in Town Lake, giving their location. Within ten minutes there was an ambulance and two cop cars shining powerful spotlights all around the water.

A uniformed policeman came up to Randi. "Are you the party who called in this drowning?"

"Yes, Officer. Dave and I had been here talking and he started fooling around over there close to the lake. He fell in and I thought he was fooling with me. But when I called and he didn't answer, I got afraid something had happened to him." Randi started to cry.

"Now don't be upset, little lady. We're looking for him. You're sure he went into the water?"

"Oh, yeah. I heard a big splash and I didn't see him any more. I looked with a flashlight and still didn't see him. I thought he might be fooling me at first. But he didn't answer when I called him, so I dialed 911."

"OK, you just sit tight. We'll find him."

Randi sat on the hood of Dave's truck for half an hour listening to the officers calling back and forth. They had brought in a boat and were searching the edge of the lake. She thought back to the fight with Dave. Damn him for coming on so strong. This was her deal. But the bastard didn't have to go and drown on her. Her margaritas were starting to wear off and she felt slightly sick, either from hangover or losing Dave. Losing Dave. That's a helluva a thought. He might even be gone.

The officer who had been talking to her earlier came over. "Little lady, we can't find any sign of him. It may be just because it's dark. We're satisfied that he's not swimming out there. We'll come back and search more when it gets light in the morning. Sometimes it takes a couple days . . ." He cut off his explanation, looking at Randi. "I mean we will be able to tell a lot better in the daylight. I've got your name and number. If we have any questions we'll get in touch with you. In the meantime why don't you call it a night. You don't look so good. Are you able to drive?"

The officer appeared blurry to her as she looked up at him, but she said, "Sure, I'm OK. I'll just go on home."

She got into Dave's truck and drove home. She wondered what to do about his truck. She decided to just park it at her apartment.

She sank onto her couch, her head spinning. He couldn't be gone. Not Dave. She didn't have another friend in the world. Dave, dammit, you can't just leave me alone like this.

Chapter 43

On what was supposed to be his last Sunday off before the push of the final week of the session, Dan got a panic call from Billy Gibson as they were dressing for church.

"Dan, I'm glad I caught you. All hell's breaking loose over your dereg hearing Tuesday. Sam's not sure he's got the votes he needs and he's got Lance and Butch all in an uproar."

"Billy, those turkeys have been pussyfooting around for the last three weeks. All this shit is their own doing. What the hell do they want now?"

"Now, Dan, you know how much importance Butch is putting on this deal. He somehow has this linked in his mind with his whole presidential thing and every time there's a close vote, they get all shook up. Anyway, can you get away to come to town tonight? They want to get together out at Lance's again to get some help with a couple of your committee members before the vote Tuesday night."

"Damn, Billy, why can't it wait until Monday? I have plans with the family this afternoon."

"I hate to do this to you, Boy, but we've almost got this thing done. Is there any way you can change your plans? It'd mean a lot to me." Billy's pleading was something Dan had trouble resisting.

Dan paced in his bedroom with the portable phone. He knew he'd have to do, but he hated to ruin his last weekend before ten full days in Austin.

He knew he sounded as resigned as he felt. "OK, Billy, I guess I can mess with the family one more time for the cause. What time is Lance opening up shop?"

"I knew I could count on you, Dan. Lance said to be there around six. Maybe that'll let you get to church before heading over here."

"Yeah, I guess. Who else is going to be there? Are Sam and his henchmen coming?" Dan had made it clear to Billy that he didn't like some of Sam's tactics after the dove hunt weekend.

"No, it'll just be you and me and Lance and Butch."

"Butch is coming? Damn. That means that the wildcat will be there too, since Butch doesn't even fart these days without orders from her."

"Oh, yeah, I guess Ann will be there too. Hell, she's mellowing a little."

"Has she got that eye patch off yet? That made her look as mean as she acts."

"Now, come on, Dan. She's not all bad and besides she's got old Butch toeing the line like never before."

Dan took his mom and eldest daughter to church, returned home and had lunch with the family before packing and heading west to Austin. The fishing trip he'd promised his girls would have to wait until after the session. They said they understood, but Dan could hear the disappointment in their voices.

Now, driving up to Lance-a-lot's house, he was dreading the meeting. The only consolation he had was that all this fretting and worry over this bill was really for nothing. Dan was sure he had it killed anyway. That might make the night bearable.

Dan noticed from the cars in front that both Billy and Butch were already there. Either they were anxious or there was a pre-meeting before he was scheduled. Hmmm.

Lance met him at the door and ushered him into the living room. Billy, Ann and Butch were seated facing each other on the white couches in front of the fireplace.

Butch got up out of his chair and strode over to Dan. "Hi there, Dan boy. Good to see you again. Is everything OK over there in east Texas?"

Dan got a strong smell of whiskey on Butch's breath when they shook hands. "We'll be fine over there, Governor, if we can get a little more rain."

Dan shook hands around the circle of people on the snow white couches. It was obvious that they had been meeting for some time before Dan got there. When he shook hands with Billy, Dan raised his eyebrows in an unspoken question, but Billy gave no hint. An ominous sign.

Lance and Billy were dressed casually, but Ann Terrance wore a red pants suit and Butch had on a blue suit and tie. Dan didn't feel any regret over his jeans and white dress shirt.

Lance said, "Come in and have a seat, Dan. I hope we won't keep you too long, but we've got some important concerns to cover. Folks are a little worried about the dereg bill."

Dan took a seat in a chair close to the mantle. Lance's wife Nellie brought Dan a beer and disappeared, unsmilingly, into the kitchen. "Well, Lance, the hearing is already posted for Tuesday. Billy, I hope we're not talking about postponing that. Hell, there's not much session left."

Lance and Ann both started to speak at once. To Dan's surprise, Ann defferred to Lance. "Dan, I hope it doesn't come to that. We've been talking to all fourteen of your committee members. With the thirteen billion language in we think we've got a shaky seven-seven tie. We met with the last two members Saturday I think they have been satisfied and are voting for passage."

"Well, if you've got your seven votes committed, what's the problem?"

"Sam said you had told him you would cast the tie-breaker for the bill, but still had questions about the language tying them to continuing service after deregulation."

Dan and Randi had just reviewed a study by the Legislative Council lawyers on the several different versions of the continuing service provision that committed the utilities to be the supplier of last resort if a customer had no other alternative. They could plainly see that it was the utilities plan to take their money and run, leaving their customers to be served by an undercapitalized shell company that could fold at the first sign of trouble. The different versions of the bill only tried various ways to hide the risk of losing power after the deregulation was in place.

Dan looked squarely at Lance. "Lance, you know good and well the utilities have changed that service language so many times they can't keep up with the latest language themselves. Do you know what version we'll have to vote on Tuesday?"

Billy spoke for the first time. Dan thought he had been awfully quiet, keeping to himself. "Sam told me they had settled on the version you and I looked at Friday before you left. That's still good isn't it, Lance?"

"No," Ann said adamantly. "We had to make some minor changes to that section to get the last two votes on Saturday."

"Miss Ann, we who?" Dan noticed that she still showed a small white scar below her left eye from her encounter with Randi. Randi was full of surprises.

"That's really not your concern, Mr. Carb. We've been working to get a consensus and we think we have the votes we need." Back to the 'in command' voice.

"That's comforting to hear, Miss Ann, but by my calculation, you need my vote to pass this and I haven't seen the latest 'final' version." Dan's voice was dripping with sarcasm. "Or have you figured a way to do it without my vote."

Everybody but Dan looked at Billy. Billy cleared his throat loudly. When he spoke he sounded very hesitant. "Now, Dan boy, you know how important Butch sees this dereg bill. Right?"

Butch came to life. "Yeah, Dan, this is the most important piece of legislation of the whole session. I'm really counting on you for this deal to work. We've already been all over it."

"That's fine, Governor. And I gave my commitment on the bill some time back, but now Miss Ann here says that the language has been changed again. And it's the language that gives some assurance that the lights will stay on in Texas after we do this deal." Turning to Billy, Dan said, "Mr. Speaker, you're not asking me to sign a blank check, are you?" He watched as Billy squirmed in his chair. Billy took a long drink of his Jack Daniels.

"No, Son, I would never do that. Lance, don't you have a copy of that new language to show Dan what he'd be going for?"

Lance rubbed sweat off his bald head. He looked a little trapped. "Well, well, actually I'm not sure I have the actual language here. But, Dan, it's similar to the versions we've been passing around."

"Lance, don't give me that shit. Sure I've seen more than a dozen versions floated in the last two weeks. And they go all the way from the utilities taking no responsibility for the shell they plan to leave to keep the power flowing to them still on the hook for some of the performance. Where did this supposedly final version land on that question?"

Ann Terrance stood and moved to stand in front of Dan's chair. "Now, see here, Mr. Carb. You're not going to go into another of your tours into detail language like it was in that earlier hearing, I hope. This is pretty simple stuff. The governor needs this bill passed and the language we have now is what it takes to get the votes we need."

Dan stood, towering over her by a foot and a half. "All right, Ma'am, if you have the votes you need then you don't need me. I don't see why you had me ruin my family Sunday to come over here for you to tell me you don't need me." Dan took several steps toward the door. "Nice seeing all of you and thanks for the beer, Lance."

Lance jumped up and said, "Now, wait, Dan. She didn't mean it that way. You know we have to have your tie-breaker vote. We have to have you on board."

Dan stopped and looked pointedly at Billy but spoke to Lance. "Lance, the way this all sounds to me is that you folks had been working on this for a while before I got here. And you have me over here to tell me I have to vote for the bill, regardless of what it says or what it does to Texas."

Billy was having a hard time facing Dan's stare. He shifted nervously in his chair.

"It's not exactly that, Dan." Lance sounded uncertain and was checking faces around the room. "It's just that we have so much riding on this."

"Then why the hell, if it's that damned important, can't you just let me look at the service language? I can read it and tell you if I have any problems."

Ann spoke still standing. "You see, Mr. Carb, that's just the problem. If you have changes to make in the language we may not have time to check your changes with everybody. For all the hoop-la and hurry up, this bill is getting down to the wire for passage."

Dan finally addressed Billy directly. "Billy, am I expected to sign on to a pig in a poke?"

"No, Dan." To Lance he said, "Lance surely you have a copy of the language. Dan's right. We can't expect him to sign off on language he's never seen."

Ann walked over to her seat and looked in her little black briefcase. She pulled out a sheaf of papers and took several pages over to where Lance was standing. She spoke to Lance in a low voice, but Dan could clearly hear at one point, "Which one is it again?"

What a bunch of clowns, Dan thought. He'd already decided that he was going to go along with whatever they had on their final version. There was no way he could jeopardize his poison pills by resisting too strongly. He just needed to play hard to get to set up his final plan.

"Here it is, Dan. Ann had a copy with her." Lance gave Dan a legal sized paper with the familiar double spaced typing of legislative language with numbered lines.

Dan quickly scanned the amendment. As he expected it was a version that gave the utilities minimum responsibility after they got their payoff. Dan pretended to struggle with the language. He was aware that everybody else in the room was watching his every expression. When he looked up it seemed that they were all leaning forward, waiting for his response.

Dan grinned widely. "Hell, what's all the fuss about, folks? I've seen this version before. I'm OK to vote for it."

There was a collective sigh in the room. Butch jumped up and came over to Dan, pulled Dan's head toward him and kissed Dan on both cheeks. Dan had heard of this Butch gesture but had never experienced it. Dan was sure he was red with embarrassment.

Butch said, "I knew I could count on you to make the deal go, Dan. I'm real glad to have you on board. Yessir."

Everybody stood and Lance said, "I propose a toast to the end of regulation and the birth of a free market for electric power in Texas. This is truly a great day."

Drinks were raised and clinked together. Billy was still avoiding looking directly at Dan. Since Billy had apparently sold out so completely that he'd participate in this kind of force play on Dan's vote, Dan knew he was now completely on his own and at maximum risk. He swigged his beer.

Hell, that's why they paid him that big six hundred bucks a month, to take the high risks like this.

It was obvious that the meeting was now over. Butch and Ann were gathering up their stuff to leave. Dan was determined to talk to Billy so he stayed to walk out with him. They stood next to Billy's Mercedes.

"Mr. Speaker, what the hell was that all about? You bust up my family Sunday to get me over here for what? To have my arm twisted. What the hell would have happened if I'd said I couldn't go with their language?"

"I know, Dan. I'm sorry for doing you that way, but they called me after midnight last night just about to go out of their minds. Hell, I hated being part of that as much as you did. It's just that...." Billy looked far off into the night. "Well, Butch has a huge stake in getting this bill passed. Lance and Ann are on my ass full time worrying about this one damned bill. You'd think there wasn't anything else to do in the session."

"So have you given them clear run to jack the legislature around like I was tonight to get that one bill passed? Damn, Billy, you are starting to sound just like old Lance. Like a whipped dog with his tail between his legs. Is that Miss Ann pulling your strings, too?"

"Now, just a damned minute, Dan. It's not like that at all. I'm just under a lot of pressure." Billy's expression showed he was hiding more about this than he was saying.

"Well, Billy, I can tell you that even if they get the bill through my committee, they are going to have hell on the floor with that language. It's way over to the utilities' side of the balance and their opponents are going to have a field day with it."

"I know, Dan. I tried to tell them they were going too far, but they didn't want to hear that. Lance said that Sam has a plan to get the votes he needs once it gets to the floor. But I think it's close."

"Well, we're set up for the hearing Tuesday night. We'll get it past that hurdle and deal with the next one then. It's getting down to the wire."

Dan noticed that Billy looked unusually strained. His familiar smile was nowhere to be seen. Dan didn't know how much he'd been drinking before but Billy had downed two double Jack Daniels while Dan was there.

"Hey, Boss, are you all right to drive? You were hitting the Jack pretty hard in there."

"Oh, I'm OK. I'll take it slow." Billy managed a half smile finally and he turned and opened the door of his Mercedes coupe.

As Dan drove to his apartment, he reflected on how bad Billy looked. He was reminded of how his dad had looked in his last days in the legislature. He decided that this damned place was enough to drive you to drink or worse.

Chapter 44

As Butch's state trooper drove him to the capitol on Monday he thought about the pressure he was beginning to feel from more quarters than he could count. Lance and Ann were struggling to dominate his interaction with the Legislature and it seemed to Butch that one was running it one day and the other the next. But Butch's worst worry now was pressure he was getting from the religion-driven senators and state representatives. While they would support him tremendously on most of his legislative priorities, they wanted to extract a price of having some religious provision in every bill.

"What the hell does religion have to do with utility regulation, anyway?"

The officer who was just driving up to the front entrance of the capitol asked, "What's that, Governor?"

"Oh, nothing, Officer. I guess I was just thinking out loud."

Butch settled into the huge chair behind his desk after getting a schedule briefing from his chief of staff. He had put in a slot for a thirty minute meeting with the Speaker and his staffer would call to set up the time.

He looked at the stacks of correspondence and legislation his staff had put in front of him. "All this shit when I'd be a damn site happier in that plane flying around on the campaign trail," he muttered. He looked idly at some of the paperwork, none of which made any sense to him.

"Governor, the Speaker said he can meet with you at eleven before the House convenes."

Butch shuffled through the papers on his desk for half an hour getting more and more frustrated at not being able to understand the significance of most of what he read.

"Good morning, Governor," Billy said when he came in at eleven. "Looks like things are all lined up for the dereg hearing tomorrow night. Dan Carb's a good trooper. He'll bring it off OK, I'm sure."

"Yeah, that went well last night. Ann thought it was going to be a lot tougher, but Dan lined right up. I guess that's your work on him, huh?"

"Oh, Dan can read the writing on the wall and he'll do right most of the time. Governor, what do we need to cover this morning? Is it more on the dereg bill?"

"Well, sort of on that bill, but more in general. Hell, Billy you know that we Republicans have more than our share of religious crazies. Those guys want to put something religious into every bill we pass. Even the electric dereg bill. They won't take no for an answer and I don't know what the hell to do about it."

Butch noticed that Billy fidgeted in his chair. "Yeah, those guys can be a pain in the butt all right. So how can I help?"

"Well, Billy, here's the thing. You've got your share of religious nuts in the House too, but you don't seem to have too much problem with them. How do you do it? I need some help with that crowd."

"Now, Butch, that goes to the fundamental differences between your office and mine. You see, I've got almost total control over the flow and life of every piece of legislation the House deals with. Most of it is useless crap and that's why so few of the bills that get filed survive even to be discussed on the floor, much less become law. If I need to get somebody's attention, I can bottle up their whole legislative package until they start cooperating. But you see, you don't have that kind of stroke."

"Yeah, that's what I'm talking about. Those damned bible thumpers come over to me and pressure me to try and get provisions into bills, but hell, I don't have any say about that. And then they get all bent out of shape and start threatening to not support me." Butch stood and walked around to sit on the edge of his desk, facing Billy. He liked Old Billy, but didn't understand him much of the time. Billy was so steeped in the legislative processes that it was hard for someone from the outside to even follow his conversation.

"Well, Governor, that's sorta' the hand the constitution drafters dealt you. Officially about all you can do is veto passed legislation and usually by that time, it's too late to do much about most of the bill's provisions. But look, maybe I can help you. Who specifically are you having trouble with now and what's their problem?"

"It's the dereg bill for instance. I don't understand it all, but they want some special provision for churches over a certain size. I think they figure they can get a special deal or something. I don't know how to stop them and they're risking the main bill I need out of this session."

"Are these House members? Who the hell is it?" Butch noticed that Billy was getting red in the face.

"Yeah, it's some of those boys in the House all right. Collier and Burnes for starters. And I don't know any way to stop them."

"Governor, you're talking to the man who can stop them. I've got their names and I'll take it from here. I can guarantee you that nothing moves in the House without my letting it move. I know damn good and well that Collier has his main reelection bill due up tomorrow. I'll talk to them and I can bottle up every one of their bills if they won't get off this shit. Hell, I know that dereg bill is critical."

Butch grinned widely and went over to Billy's chair. "Mr. Speaker, you're something else. I was hoping to just get some advice and you're offering to fix the problem." Billy stood and the two of them shook hands. "I'd be forever grateful if you could put a stop to their messing with this bill."

"No problem, Butch. You should've spoken up earlier."

"You know, Billy, I hate to say it, but Texas is kinda screwed up on this. I'm the one voted on by the whole state. You're elected by just one hundred and fifty House members. But here you're the one that can deal with legislation while it's being formed and all I can do is veto it after it's passed, if it gets passed."

"But, Butch, you have the ear of the press and the people. That's the way you get to exert leadership."

"Yeah, leadership. What the hell is that anyway? I can't very well go attacking the churches on TV. I listen to all my advisors, I try to say the right things in speeches, but in the end it's guys like you that have all the power. I just get to sign your work after it's all done."

Butch sat reflecting on his talk with Billy for a long time after the Speaker left. He thought back to Ann getting so upset at the term 'weak governor'. This was a clear demonstration of being a weak governor. If he didn't have deals cut with the House Speaker, he'd be up shit creek trying to stop those crazies. Butch reflected on how the Texas governor got plenty of blame but had little to do with how state government ran and laws got made. That probably was good enough reason to make the try for the presidential thing. At least he'd get to make some decisions.

But he still faced the final eight days of the legislative session and the prospect made his stomach begin to hurt.

Chapter 45

The State Affairs Committee meeting on Tuesday night was once again taking place in a circus atmosphere. The room was mobbed and there was a second room with a TV set monitoring the hearing for the overflow crowd.

Dan and Randi had a brief meeting on the hearing in the afternoon but Randi was so experienced by now that Dan had very few suggestions. He reflected that the two of them were working smoothly as if nothing had ever happened in her apartment. Dan was still embarrassed at how far it had gone before he stopped it. Even now, with Randi behind his chair set to conduct the hearing on the dereg bill, he could smell her musky perfume and noticed his own reaction to her being so close. *Get your mind on business, you horny bastard.* He told himself. *You're facing a potential legislative buzz saw.*

Dan surveyed the room. Butch sat on the front row with Lance and Ann on either side. Dan still worked mostly with Lance, trying to keep the governor straight, but occasionally he had to deal with Ann. She had actually mellowed some, but she would still drop into that command mode occasionally and was really tough to deal with.

For the first time this session Betsy Pertny , the utilities busty lobbiest, was in the room. Andy told Dan that Betsy had been spending her time lobbying the bill in the Senate where she had the best connections. It was clear to Dan that the utilities must be worried and had their whole team focused on tonight's hearing. Somehow the pressure Dan felt was so high that nothing could really raise it.

Jim Clower, the House Republican leader and chair of the dereg subcommittee, presented their work to open the hearing.

"Mr. Chairman, I believe that with the changes we've made in subcommittee that this bill is poised to take its place among historic legislation here in the great state of Texas."

Dan thought that Jim always made way too much of things, but this time he was almost right. Except for a certain set of poison pills.

"All right, Representative Clower. Members, the subcommittee report is in front of you. Does anybody have any amendments or are we ready to vote?"

Representative Jones, the African-American Democrat from Houston, spoke first and gave an eloquent rendering of how the utilities had lobbied their financial package from an already outrageous ten billion to now over thirteen billion. He introduced an amendment cutting the package down to eight billion.

Dan watched Butch squirm during Jones' speech. Butch, Lance and Ann were in a huddled conference by the time Jones' amendment was formally introduced.

As Dan expected, the vote on the amendment was a seven to seven tie. The whole room looked expectantly at him. He felt awful about doing what he needed to do, but if he was going to really kill that piece of garbage, he'd have to let it pass this hurdle.

"Show the Chairman voting no." The room burst into a loud buzz, which took Dan several gavel bangs to quiet. "Look, folks, I know all of you feel strongly about this, but if you can't control your outbursts, I'll be forced to clear the room and conduct this hearing without you." The room got ghostly quiet.

Dan noticed that Sam was in the back corner making notes on the speeches and vote. Sam winked and nodded at Dan when their eyes met after Dan's first tiebreaker vote. Dan decided he'd need a barf bag to get through the rest of the hearing.

After five votes on changes to the subcommittee report, all of which failed by eight to seven votes, the report was finally adopted for sending to the House by the same vote. Dan felt like a real heel voting to save the utilities position every time. The only thing that got him through it was the certainty that the bill was doomed once it got to the floor.

As the hearing broke up, Butch came over to thank Dan. "Mr. Chairman, that was a masterful piece of work. Just what we wanted."

"Well, Governor, three of those amendments were offered to set up the floor fight on the bill. This battle is a long way from over, so don't congratulate yourself too early."

"Oh, I'm sure we're going to do OK, Boy. I feel it in my gut. We've got God on our side."

That last from Butch almost literally made Dan nauseous. The looks Dan was getting from all of the consumer and independent power folks were blistering. Dan decided he'd better set up a meeting with Andy soon. He was treading in dangerous political waters.

Chapter 46

"Randi, with no amendments, we can just send the subcommittee report directly to printing for the Calendars committee." Dan and Randi were meeting in his committee office after the hearing. "That should save a few steps."

"OK, Dan, but it's still getting close. The Calendars committee plate is already overflowing and they've told me I'd have to wait my turn."

"I'll talk to the chairman. There's no way this one gets delayed."

Randi wondered why Dan was pushing this bill in Calendars so strongly. From the conversation she'd overheard between Dan and Andy, she expected them to delay it in Calendars. She'd have to watch Dan's every move so she'd know when to move against him. She thought it was getting close to time, but still didn't want to make her move too early.

"Well, I can get the subcommittee report over to Calendars tonight if you want me to. They're already on their twenty-four hour schedule so it would get right into the queue."

Randi watched as Dan thought about getting the report in tonight. He seemed to be struggling with which way to go.

"OK, Randi," Dan said at last, "go ahead and bring it over tonight. I'll talk to the Calendars chairman in the morning to let him know this one has priority and it'll already be in his system."

Randi spent thirty minutes assembling the package to get to Calendars. She logged it in to the committee just after eleven and headed home.

Randi had thought that the bill's arrival at Calendars was the right time for her to confront Dan. She was getting nervous and was already missing talking her plans out with Dave. Dave. Poor bastard. They had dredged his body out of Town Lake on Sunday. His family came and got his truck and emptied his apartment yesterday. Dave's funeral was set in Dallas this Thursday, but Randi wasn't planning to go.

But, thinking back, Dave wasn't all that smart about this legislative plan. He would have gone for the money, when getting Dan Carb was the real reason for all this.

Chapter 47

Randi felt really tired when she climbed the stairs to the balcony at her apartment. She knew it was nervousness because her plans were coming to a head.

The man who approached her as she inserted her door key was dressed in blue trousers and a light gray sports coat.

"Miss Crendall?"

"Yes, can I help you?"

He took out a leather badge holder and said, "I'm Lieutenant Jerry Borton with the Austin police department. If you have a few minutes, we're just wrapping up that drowning in Town Lake and we need a couple things from you."

Randi panicked. She hoped she wasn't showing her feelings to him. "Well, Officer, it's late and I'm dog tired from working a legislative hearing. Can't this wait?"

"Oh, I won't be more than a couple minutes. Can I come in?"

Randi open her door. "Well, I guess if you won't be long." She turned on the light and put her briefcase down, pointing to her couch.

"Miss Crendall, as you know we're required to investigate any death that happens like this one. Can you tell me how long you'd known Mr. Treston?"

"I met Dave when I started working at the capitol three years ago. We dated off and on over that time."

"And you were on a date the night he drowned?"

"Yeah, I guess. We were mostly just sitting and talking. That was a favorite place for us." Randi watched the officer write on his little note pad.

"I understand. Now you told the officers you had been sitting on the front of his truck talking and Dave got up and was walking around. Is that right?"

"Right. We'd been talking and we both got up and were walking around in front of the truck."

"Now that put you between the truck and the lake, is that right?"

"Yes. We were talking and walking around. Like I told the officer that night, Dave started clowning around and slipped down the bank into the lake."

"Did you call for help?"

"No, at first I thought he was fooling around with me and hiding. Then when he wouldn't answer my calls, I got worried."

"So you called the police, is that right."

"Right. When he wouldn't answer, I called and the officers came out and looked for him using their boat. But they couldn't find him."

"And about what time was all this? Your call came to our dispatch at eleven thirty."

"I'm afraid I wasn't paying any attention to the time. All I know is I made it home after midnight when the officer told me they would pick up on the search again when it got light."

"OK, I think I've got most of what I need. In summary, you and he were parked talking and got outside the truck and were walking around. He got to clowning around and fell in the lake and when you couldn't find him, you called 911. Is that about it?"

"That's about right. Is there something wrong?"

"No, you know, just routine reports we have to fill out anytime there's a death. Do you think there's something wrong?"

Randi felt the panic again. With her voice higher than she wanted it she said, "No, no. I was just wondering why you came to see me so late at night."

"Oh, we tried at other times, but you capitol types keep odd hours. No, my report was due and I needed to get this final information down."

Randi relaxed. "Well, I hope I've helped." She stood and he stood too.

"Thank you for your help, Miss Crendall. We'll get in touch if we need anything else."

Randi showed him out the door, locking it and putting on the chain. She almost collapsed onto the floor in relief. *Just what the hell I need when I'm already uptight as a cheap banjo. Damn, nothing is ever simple.*

Chapter 48

Dan spent most of Wednesday working on some of his own bills and being sure they were headed for House floor action. He had watched as the utilities cranked up their lobbying effort. He concluded that the four big utilities had over fifty lobbyists working House members by Wednesday afternoon. The pressure was on and the clock was ticking.

Dan read the *Austin American Statesman* in his apartment Thursday morning and the local reporters had picked up on the push on the utility bill. There was a good background analysis of the bill's provisions plus descriptions of member office waiting areas packed with lobbyists on both sides of the dereg bill. Dan got a good laugh at the picture with the story. It showed a young lobbyist from Texas Utilities in intense conversation with a member from Texarkana who Dan knew would never vote for the bill. He guessed they break the new lobbyists in on the tough ones.

Dan planned to spend another day working on his own bills before the Chairmen's meeting with the Speaker in the afternoon. He was dressed for the capitol by seven and just about to leave when his phone rang. Damned early call. He hoped it wasn't the ranch.

"Hello."

"Dan, this is Randi. I didn't wake you up, did I?"

"No, Randi. I've been up and read the paper already. I was just about to head out. What's up?" Dan had never known Randi to be an early riser. She usually got to the capitol around ten in the morning.

"Dan, we need to talk and it needs to be away from the capitol. It won't take too long. I can meet you right away."

"Randi, this sure is mysterious. What's so serious that we have to talk now and not at work?"

"I'll explain when I see you. Do you know Eastwoods Park just north of the UT campus? It's just off 26th Street."

"Sure, I know it. Is that where you want to meet?"

"Yeah. There are a few parking places there and we can talk without being interrupted."

"Without being interrupted? Damn, Randi, what's this all about?"

"You'll understand when I explain, Dan. I can be there by seven forty-five. That work?"

Dan looked at his watch. He'd have time for another cup of coffee before heading out. "Sure, Randi, I can do that but I'd sure like to know what this is all about."

"Just trust me, Dan. You'll understand when we talk."

Dan drove through the morning traffic watching university students walking to eight o'clock classes. Eastwoods Park was a small grassed area with a few scrub trees, a small stream and some well-worn playground equipment. The park itself was empty this early Thursday morning and he had his choice of parking spaces for the crew cab truck. Randi pulled her old Datsun in a few minutes behind him.

Dan waved Randi over to his truck and she got in the passenger door.

"Hey, Randi, right on time. Come on in."

"Thanks, Dan. I know this is kinda unusual for a meeting, but I needed some privacy without everybody jamming us like at the capitol."

"Well, I've got almost an hour before my first meeting. What's up?" Randi was dressed in her dark suit for work and looked rather nervous.

"What's up? Well, Dan, I'll give you this little warning. This is going to surprise and shock you, but everything is set now and there's nothing that can stop it. Dan, there's a side of me that you don't know. I'll start at the beginning. When your dad was still in the House he hired my mother to work in his office. That was twenty-five years ago."

"What? Your mother worked for my dad in the House?"

"Right. She started working for him in the House and moved over with him to the Senate. But that jumps ahead. Here's the first of the shock I mentioned. Your dad and my mother had an affair while she worked for him." Randi paused, looking intently at Dan. When she spoke she put spaced pauses between her words. "Dan, I am your half sister from that affair. We have the same father."

Dan had the idea he had somehow stepped into the plot of a cheap movie. He couldn't comprehend what he was hearing. "Wh-what? You . . We're . . God, Randi, what the hell are you talking about?" They were sitting facing each other across the cab of the truck. Dan looked at Randi's face, fully expecting her to say this was a joke or something.

"Dan, what I am talking about is that you and I have the same father all right, but you got the gold mine and I got the shaft. You're a multimillionaire from dear old dad and I was raised in a junk trailer park in east Austin, scrapping for everything I've ever gotten. And, Dan, also what I'm really talking about is payback time."

Dan rubbed his face with both hands. She had to be making this up or she's gone crazy. "Randi, what is this shit? Are you making up some bizarre story or something? I mean a mystery meeting in a public park and a story that sounds like it comes out of a bad drug trip or something."

"You don't believe me, I guess. OK, Dan, have you ever heard of the Madison Development Company?"

Dan sucked in breath and felt a twinge in his stomach. Madison Development Company. A thousand dollars a month old Fendley said was to pay for oil production support in Austin. Austin? He realized he hadn't answered her.

"I've heard of it, yes. How do you know about it?"

"Dan, your dad – our dad – set up a thousand dollars a month to go to my mother to help her raise their illegitimate kid – me. That's what the hell Madison Development Company is. At least that's what I've come to understand it is. The only connection to a father I never had." A tear started down Randi's face and she wiped it with her hand.

Dan's head was spinning. The damned thousand a month. That fucking Fendley was lying to me. But Randi . .

"Randi, do you mean that you and I are brother and sister? I can hardly believe it."

Randi reached into her purse and pulled out several folded sheets of paper. She unfolded them and handed them to Dan. "I knew you wouldn't believe me so I brought some proof."

Dan looked over the copies of six one thousand dollar checks made out to a Norma Crendall at an address he recognized as the one that had been on Randi's application when he hired her. They were Madison Development checks and there was old Fendley's signature right at the bottom. That lying bastard. I'll kill the son-of-a-bitch. Dan looked from the checks to Randi and back at the checks. What Randi said was starting to soak in.

"Randi, this is a hell of a shock. You and I are brother and sister? How the hell did you come to work for me if you knew this all the time?"

"Dan, I didn't know all this when I started to work for you. My mother confessed it to me in January after a big fight. Don't mistake this meeting for some kind of a mushy family reunion. I've suffered every day of my life because I was the unwanted result of my mom and our dad fucking around. And it's now payback time." Randi stared at Dan, unblinking. "And Dan, since dear old dad is under the ground, the payback comes from you."

"What the hell are you talking about payback time? Randi, you're sounding crazy."

"I just may be crazy, Dan. I have been setting you up for the last four months and now I've got you and you're going to pay big time."

"You know, you are crazy. How the hell are you going to make me pay?"

"Well, first, I plan to go public with our little family secret. That'll look real good on Austin TV and I'll guarantee it'll make the Madisonville paper. But that's the last step. The real fun happens before that hits. Dan, I'm sure you remember that little get together we almost had in my apartment."

"Oh, I'm still embar... Randi, what the hell was that all about? If, as you say, you knew we were brother and sister, what the hell were you doing?" Dan was aware he was sounding confused as all this landed on him.

Randi laughed in a way Dan had never heard her before. The laughter had an almost horrific tinge to it. She stared straight at him, her arms crossed over her chest. "Well, brother of mine, there're all kinds of things you can do these days with those marvelous little video cameras. That nice bonus you gave me went to buy the best digital video camera I could find." Here she laughed even louder and harsher. "It was right there among my teddy bears. I have got the most wonderful clip of Big Dan Carb stark naked with his dick sticking right out in front of him and me stripped naked in my bed." She raised her hands in a mock camera-panning sweep and pulled a small computer disk from her pocket. "Can't you see it when it makes the ten o'clock news?" More laughter, now almost hysterical.

Dan shook his head, trying to clear his senses. "You videotaped us in your bedroom? God damn it, Randi, you're some kind of monster." Dan was sweating and turned on the ignition to open the truck windows. He could clearly hear a mocking bird singing in a willow tree down by the creek. He hoped this wasn't happening.

"Yeah, I'm going to trash you all right, but there's still more. When I get through you won't be able to show your face anywhere in Texas if I have anything to do with it." Randi's voice now had a raspy shrill tone and she sounded ominous.

"But, why, Randi? Why are you doing all this to me? I've tried to treat you well and I think I have."

"Dan, you don't even know how to begin to understand where I'm coming from. I'm going to make you pay for the shit life I've had up to now. Yeah, I've scratched my way up to halfway respectability, but that's a few years of doing better after twenty years of full-time suffering and pain. Look, you don't even have a clue about having to wear your damned underwear until it falls off in shreds because your drunken mother can't even keep enough money around to buy fucking underwear. And when she blew the thousand old daddy sent on a binge in Laredo, I had to handle my entire first period with toilet paper in my underwear. You don't even have a con-

cept of underwear stuffed with toilet paper, Dan. You've always had everything you needed and probably everything you wanted. Well, Brother, now
you've got little Randi and a shit load you aren't going to want."

"Randi, do you hate me that much?" Dan could feel his throat con-
stricted with tension.

"You know, Dan, that's the interesting part. Over the last few months
I've actually come to like you. You're a straight sort of person as far as I can
tell. Hell, you even backed out of my bedroom rather than cheat on your
wife when I was hotter than a two-dollar pistol. That says something about
you. But all I have to do is remember the first twenty years of my life and I
know why I'm using what I've learned about you and damn well why I'm
now going to gut you. Dan, you represent everything that has been wrong
with my life and you're about to get a taste of the dark side. From the look
on your face it's already started and I'm loving every minute of it."

Dan stared out the window. A tall, skinny student was walking by with
his girlfriend. He was wearing a heavily loaded backpack and leaned forward with the load. The girl was short, blonde and led a cocker spaniel on
a leash. That looks like ordinary life out there. What's going on in here?

Dan was beginning to wear through his initial shock and was trying to
think what to do about what he heard. "Well, Randi, if you're short of
money . ." He stopped. He could tell by her expression that he had just
made a big mistake.

"Ha," she said like she was spitting out something that tasted bad, "like
father like son. Throw a little money at it and it'll go away. Look, Brother,
your damned money is not going to buy your way out of this mess. The
fact that I'm the daughter of the great Senator Carb and the video of you
and me in the raw in my bedroom is already in the works. And hey, you
haven't even heard the third part of my little plan. Dan, I've been perfect-
ing a crosshair rifle shot for you and you're now sitting right at dead center.
That devastated look on your face is just the down payment on what I get
out of this. No, I don't want your god damned money. I want your reputation, your good name, your family status and your standing in the town
you live in and all over the state. I want you to know the feeling that I've
lived all my life with; that you're a worthless piece of shit and nobody cares
one damned thing about you."

Dan felt tears starting in his eyes. He didn't even know what to say.
"You said something about a third thing. What the hell could be worse
than this?"

"Oh, I don't know if it's worse, but it'll cook your goose at the Capitol.
I know that for sure. And it's the one that's called for us to meet this morning. It's on a tight clock."

Dan looked at her, his thoughts mush. He knew his mouth was open but he couldn't think of anything to say. He just groaned.

"Oh, the cat's got your tongue? Well, let me tell you about my little coup in the legislature. You see I know what you're up to on the dereg bill. You're going to delay it past the seventy-two hours in the Calendars Committee and then feed that to old Rieger so he can kill the governor's big utility deal. But little Randi is gonna rat on you and get your ass roasted with the Speaker and the Gov. They won't even trust you to get their coffee when I get through with you."

Dan blinked and shook his head trying to take in what he was hearing. "But, how . ."

"I've got my ways. I listened in on you and Andy plotting to kill that bill. I don't really give a shit whether the bill gets passed or not. I'm just going to be sure the word leaks out that you're plotting against the bill and you'll be in trouble with Billy, the governor and the press. And I'm going to warn them about the other two ways you're planning to kill the bill. How about that for a nice cherry on top of the cake?"

"But, Randi, how could you have worked beside me all these months feeling the way you obviously do about me? I just can't make any sense out of it all."

"Dan, you don't have to make sense out of it. Just sit back and watch me work. By nightfall the word will be out on your bill killing plans. I'm saving the stories about us being related for later and I think the video is last. I'm still working it out, but that's the plan for now." She sounded matter of fact, like she was planning a picnic or something.

Dan started to feel claustrophobic in the truck. He opened the door and walked toward the back of the truck. Randi got out and came around to face him. He could hardly stand to look at her.

"Randi, this is more that I can comprehend. Isn't there some way we can talk about this more later? Surely there must be another way."

"Dan, I guess I owe you something for being nice since I've been working for you. I've given you pretty much the whole blast here. I haven't gone public with any of it yet. I frankly wanted to enjoy watching you hear it first. As far as I'm concerned I've still got a day's work ahead of me and if you haven't fired me already I'll be in the State Affairs office. You take a couple hours to think about all this and we can get back together. But don't mistake this little respite as any hint of me backing off. This is the culmination of everything I have been working for. There's no stopping this and there's no turning back."

Dan tried to think of something reconciling to say but couldn't come up with anything. "OK, Randi, let's go on up to the Capitol. I've got a meeting at nine this morning then a break before the session starts." His watch showed eight-thirty. Had he only been here forty-five minutes? It seemed like hours. "I'll see you before ten."

"I'll be waiting." Randi started toward her car and stopped half way and turned around. "And, Dan, have a nice day." She laughed another of those hideous sounding laughs and got in her car. She started it and drove off toward 26th Street.

Dan knew he needed to get to his first meeting in the governor's office, but it was almost like his feet were in concrete. *Wake up, Son, and get going. You've got a helluva a row to hoe today.* He didn't even remember the drive down from Eastwoods Park, but he parked in the underground and headed to his Capitol office, seeing the surroundings like he'd never been there before. He would have sworn that when one of the pages greeted him as "Mr. Chairman," there was scorn in her voice, but he knew it was his imagination.

His walk through the rotunda and up to his office happened in a daze. He recognized his surroundings and even spoke to folks, but it was like he was walking in some kind of dream. A nightmare. That kind of dream.

Chapter 49

"There should be a law against fucking eight thirty meetings." Butch swore as he sat in the back seat of the black Suburban heading toward the capitol.

"Beg your pardon, Sir?"

"Oh, nothing, Officer. Just complaining about incompetent staff and early meetings."

"Oh, yessir. It's hard to get good help, isn't it?"

Butch laughed and patted the state trooper on the shoulder as he got out in front of the capitol. There were few people around the entry and he spoke to a state senator also heading in the front door.

When he walked into his office, Lance and Ann were already there like they'd been meeting for some time before he got there.

"Good morning, folks. How are we looking this morning?"

"Not very well, Governor. Good morning to you." Lance sounded to Butch like he was talking through clinched teeth. Never a good sign.

"Good morning, Governor. It sounds like the electrical deregulation bill is in trouble. That's why we asked for the early meeting. We need to work out how we attack the problem today." Ann was dressed in a black pants suit with a ribbon bow at the neck. Her face was flushed like she was in a strain.

"Well, well, I thought we had that deal put to bed. Lance, what's happening?"

"Governor, I think we're probably four or five votes short of floor passage. We've lost some key support over the last two days. We're going to have to scare up more votes if we expect to pass it. Let's sit down and sort out the details." Lance moved over to one of the overstuffed leather couches. Butch noticed there was already a pile of papers on the coffee table in front of the couch.

Ann sat in a straight chair facing Butch and Lance on the couch. She spoke, pointing to the document on top of the pile. "Now, Governor, according to Sam and the rest of the utility people, if the bill came to a vote today, it would fail by a seventy-seven to seventy-two margin. The opposition, mostly the independent power people, have turned five votes in the last two days. It's time for us to switch to hardball with those five votes."

Lance spoke up as soon as Ann stopped. "And that's where Ann and I disagree. Butch, as you know, those House members can get real independent. I think we need to try and persuade them, but not get tough right away."

"Now, wait a minute, who the hell are we talking about anyway? I mean I know lots of those boys. Whose votes have we lost?" Butch asked, looking at the list marked in three different color highlights.

"Governor, two of the five votes that turned are Republicans. Just give me five minutes with them and they'll get straight, I promise." Ann sounded like some kind of hoodlum.

"And that's where you misread Texans, Ann. We need to start off with how the bill will benefit them and their district. If you start off beating them over the head, they'll just get more opposed."

"Dammit, Lance, what kind of party discipline do you have here? You mean we have to bargain and persuade to get Republican votes for something the governor wants? I can't believe that." Butch turned to watch Lance's reply.

"Ann, you just haven't learned anything about Texas these last several months. Sure they'll listen to our arguments, but the reason they switched votes is because they were convinced that the added three and a half billion was wasting state money. They're objecting on fiscal terms. If we don't convince them it's smart spending we'll never get their votes. And anyway, we still need three Democrats to be sure of passage."

Butch looked from one to the other. "Well, what the hell are we supposed to do? We have to have that bill passed. I've already spent the money."

"Governor, please. Remember you're not supposed to be making that connection. I know we need the bill and we'll get it somehow." Lance looked at his watch. "The Speaker and Dan Carb are due any minute. Let's get their perspective on all this."

Ann looked at her watch. "Well, gentlemen, we'd better be ready to get those votes whatever it takes. I say there's no time to pussyfoot around with it." She got up and started pacing around the office.

"Well, Governor, how do you say we handle it?"

Butch looked from Lance sitting in front of him to Ann pacing around the room. He couldn't think of a thing to add to the argument. "Let's just see what Billy has to say. He knows this stuff best." Just then his secretary came in and announced that they were in the waiting area. "Show 'em in, Miz Kelly."

Butch noticed that when his secretary, Mrs. Kelly, came into the room, Ann stopped her pacing and stood almost at military attention. With all the people Ann had intimidated during her stay in Austin, Mrs. Kelly, a gray-haired, wiry seventy-year-old had instead intimidated Ann. The elderly lady spoke to Ann like she was a misbehaving daughter and Ann never voiced one of her tart comebacks. Who was to know?

"Come on in, Mr. Speaker, Dan boy. Have a seat and lets see if we can settle this latest storm." Billy still showed the strain Butch had seen on Sunday at Lance's house. Carb looked like he was sleepwalking.

Billy looked at Lance. "So we may be a few votes short on the dereg bill, Lance?"

"Yeah, Billy. The independent power folks made some headway the last few days. We even lost two R's. Sam says we're five votes short."

"Damn. Which Repubs?"

Ann spoke up cutting off Lance's answer. "Mr. Gibson, you don't have to worry about the Republican votes we need. I'll take care of them."

"Well, now, Miss Ann, you'd better walk a little carefully on that. Some of those boys can get a little hard headed."

Ann waved her hand to show her disdain. "I know how to bust their balls, Mr. Gibson, and I'm not afraid to do it when it counts like this."

Billy looked at Lance with raised eyebrows. Lance leaned back on the couch, arms folded, and said nothing.

Butch decided he'd better step in. "Well, we've still got three more votes we need. Billy, you can help with some of those other boys."

"Hell, yes, Butch. Look everybody gets real nervous right here at the end of the session. It happens every time. Folks get concerned about all their own bills and get real uptight." He paused and looked at Dan Carb. "Dan, the bill is already in Calendars isn't it?" No response. Dan was looking blankly out the window. "Dan," Billy repeated.

"Oh, sorry, Mr. Speaker. What did you say?"

"The dereg bill. It's in Calendars isn't it?"

"Yeah. We sent it over Tuesday night."

Butch decided that Dan must be really hung over. He looked like he was in a fog.

"Well, we will have to watch the times, but we've got all day today. Lance, just give Dan and me the names and we'll take it from here."

Butch marveled at how calmly Billy handled what had been a big fight between Lance and Ann. To Butch, Billy sounded like this was a matter of routine business. In ten minutes the names were parceled out and every-body knew who they had to talk to. Lance insisted on talking to the Re-publicans with Ann. Butch thought that was probably a good thing the way Ann was talking about ball breaking.

When they had gone, Butch talked Mrs. Kelly into taking the pile of papers off his desk and putting them into a file cabinet. She asked him sternly, like a school marm, if he'd taken care of them. He told her he'd get to them later. Damned complicated papers anyway.

Chapter 50

After Dan and Billy parted outside the Governor's office, Dan suddenly remembered something from that long-ago orientation when he was first elected to the House. There's a small chapel on the second floor of the capitol. He'd never been back there since that first tour, but somehow that seemed to be where he needed to go.

He spent long minutes alone in the dim light trying to get his thoughts collected. He thought about the ranch and Molly Ann and the girls. And what about his Mom? The pain and shock they were in for was too much to comprehend. He knew he had to talk to Molly Ann. But before any of that he had to talk to Randi. He had to try to get her to back off if he could. When he thought back to their talk in the park it seemed like something that happened to someone else far, far away. But it kept coming back to him. He had to face her again.

When Dan walked into the State Affairs office everything looked perfectly normal. Randi was at her desk going through a thick pile of bills from the morning mail. Their young intern was on the phone. Dan signaled for her interrupt her call.

"Randi and I have to go over something in my office. No calls and no visitors. OK?"

"Yes sir, Mr. Chairman. I'll guard the door," she said smiling.

Dan looked at Randi, nodding his head toward his office. She picked up a steno pad and followed him, closing the door behind her.

"Randi, Randi. Where to begin? I mostly want to know if I had a very bad dream or did we actually have that talk in the park."

"No, Dan, it wasn't a bad dream. Actually, for me, this is the end of a bad dream. I guess here in the familiar surrounds of the office it seems grossly out of place, but I'm feeling good about my plans. You wanted to talk. Go ahead."

"Well, I guess I'm really having a hard time believing this is really happening. Are you sure you're going through with it?" He could hear the tension he felt weakening his voice.

"I've never been more certain of anything in my life. I've worked my ass off to get to this day. Nothing or nobody is going to stop me now."

Dan heard the same almost fanatic tone in Randi's words as he'd heard that morning. But maybe he could salvage something from this hell fire.

"OK, Randi, I've got that you're determined to gut me. I guess my reputation is gone here and at home. Your illegitimacy and the damned video will just get aired. It's shitty, but if that's what you want, so be it. There's one thing, though, you might want to think about. That's your plan to expose my plot against the dereg bill."

"Oh, no, you're not going to wheel and deal over this one, Brother. I'm going to gut you all the way around."

"Randi, I'm not trying to bargain with you. The way you've got this rigged, I don't have anything to bargain with. But think about what you're doing if you ruin my dereg plan. The governor has already gotten two million dollars for his presidential campaign, based on the passage of that bill. If it passes at the new $13.5 billion he gets another three million."

"Dan, that doesn't mean jack shit to me. I'm after your ass, not that damned bill."

"I know. I know. But just realize that Butch's campaign has already spent all of that five million and if you save that bill for them you'll save Ann Terrance's ass in the bargain. She drove Butch to spend the money before he had it and if that money doesn't come through, she'll get canned."

Randi sat back in her chair. Dan could see he'd given her something to think about. He needed to press his case.

"And, Randi, with the other two things you're doing to me, I won't be able to show my face anywhere in Texas, especially here at the capitol. Think about it. You could be rescuing Ann Terrance with overkill on me." Dan could hardly believe he was actually bargaining over his own reputation. He seemed to watching a bizarre scene played out by two strangers.

Randi looked like she was lost in thought for long moments. "You just might have something there, Dan. I'd sure hate to do anything to help that yankee bitch. I'll think about that. I'll let you know. By the way, do I still have a job?"

"Uh, I guess so. The way things are heading I really don't give a damn. Sure, just hang out. It doesn't matter to me anymore." Dan could feel his thoughts drifting back to his time in the chapel. Randi said something to him as she got up to leave, but he didn't catch it. He sat and stared at his closed office door.

At just after eleven, his committee intern timidly knocked on the door. "Mr. Chairman, they're calling for you on the floor. The session has started." She offered him his floor packet, a five-inch thick folder with the day's legislation and analysis.

He managed to smile a weak thanks to her, took the packet and left the office. He didn't think Randi was at her desk, but he wasn't sure.

Chapter 51

As the session dragged on into the afternoon, Dan knew he wasn't wholly there. He had been in several conversations about bills that were on the calendar, but he couldn't remember anything of them.

Billy called him up to the podium to follow up on the meeting in the governor's office. They talked during long speeches supporting a loosening of hunting regulations, a favorite topic of legislators.

"OK, Dan, I think that Ann has already slammed the two R's that switched on dereg. They've both been to see me this morning and they looked like ground meat. They're back on board."

"Yeah, she's a bitch all right." Dan was pleased he'd managed to say something on subject.

"Now, we need to figure out the best way to get the other three. Any ideas?"

Dan struggled to get engaged enough to make some sense, but he found he didn't have the energy to do so. "I don't know, boss. This is a tough one." At least a platitude.

"Dan, what's wrong with you? At Butch's office this morning and again now you seem to be out of it. Are you coming down with something?"

"I might be, Billy. I haven't been doing well lately. Look, maybe you'd better talk to the other three votes we need. I'm not sure I'm the best one to do it right now."

Billy looked hard at Dan. Dan could tell he was genuinely puzzled. "Damn, Boy, did you get into some bad whiskey or something? You don't look good at all."

"Yeah, maybe that was it. I might just head up to the office and rest for a while. Maybe that'll help."

Dan left the floor and started toward his capitol office but remembered that Paula would be there with a list of things for him to do and maybe a waiting area full of people lobbying both ways on the dereg bill. He couldn't face it. He stopped on the second floor rotunda balcony and looked down at the crowd of mostly tourists on the first floor. He knew what he needed to do.

Chapter 52

Randi had dealt all afternoon with competing lobbyists trying to get an edge in what seemed to be a huge looming fight over the dereg bill. Word was apparently out that some votes were being turned back in favor of the bill and the consumer groups and independent power people were sounding desperate.

She thought back to Dan's proposal to let him go ahead and kill the bill. She could almost see Ann Terrance's face if it failed. Maybe she could let that part of her plan go. It'd be fun to watch that bitch fry.

When three more lobbyists burst into the State Affairs office demanding to see some more files on the bill, Randi just smiled at them and turned them over to the intern. If Big Dan didn't give a shit, why should she?

Leaving the intern with the room full of shouting suits, Randi excused herself to the rest room, but instead headed down to the parking lot.

Outside the liquor store near her apartment she poured enough chilled margarita mix from the gallon jug to make room for the fifth of tequila. She shook the jug and took a swig before heading out.

"Wasting Away in Margaritaville," she sang as she pulled into her apartment parking space.

Sitting on her couch with a large tea glass of the iced green drink, she thought back over her day. "Yep, I think little Randi deserves a toast. You cut big Dan Carb down to size and from the looks of him, he ain't recovered yet. You go, Girl!" The room started to swim with the effects of the drink.

"That little old video is gonna play big for you. Hell it might even make one of those slimy national TV shows." She leaned dreamily back on the couch. "Yes, Oper, Big Dan and his big dick really make quite a show, don't' they? Ha, ha, heh, ha. They make them dicks big down in Texas. Whoooeee!"

As she finished her third glass of margarita, Randi's thinking started to drift back to the night Dan was in her bedroom. She started to get aroused. Probably would've been a good fuck. Too bad. The glass slipped out of her hand, the drink spilled onto the carpet.

Chapter 53

Dan tossed his floor packet onto the back seat of the crew cab and pulled out of the capitol parking lot. He didn't know where he was going. He was just going.

He drove through Austin toward the river and took 7th Street toward the Interstate. He knew that it was time for the four o'clock Chairman's meeting in Billy's office, but he couldn't bring himself to go. He just drifted.

Dan was almost to the Austin airport when he realized he was heading toward LaGrange on his normal way home. No, he couldn't go home and face Molly Ann in this shape.

At LaGrange he pulled into a roadside beer joint, removed his coat and tie and sat at the bar sipping a beer. The place faced onto Highway 73 and had three garage type doors open to the front. There were only three other patrons and the graying man behind the bar seemed lost in his afternoon soaps.

Dan tried to get his bearings with all that the day had brought. There was no doubt now that Randi was going ahead with her plans to ruin his public reputation. He'd have to find a way to face Molly Ann with that news. But what about him? Here he was at forty-seven a successful and respected state leader about to be dragged into the gutter by an illegitimate half-sister he'd never known. His career as a public official would go up in flames.

Hell, wait a minute, he thought. He didn't start off to be a damned politician. He could just go back to the ranch and be with his family and his mom.

Mom. God, Randi was about to reveal daddy's sleeping around and a daughter none of us knew about. And on TV, no less. And me, buck naked. Dan tried to picture his mother getting that news and trying to face the people in Madisonville or at their church. "Shit," Dan said out loud.

"What's the problem, bud?" the bartender asked, looking over from his focus on the television.

"Oh, sorry, I was just thinking about something." Dan felt foolish.

"You want another beer or something?"

"No, I'll just pay my tab. I've got to get going."

Dan pulled out onto the highway still heading south. At the turnoff of Texas 21, which would have taken him toward home, he just kept going south on 73 toward Columbus. He couldn't stop thinking about what Randi's scheme would do to his mother.

Dan almost ran off the highway when his next thought hit. Hell, what about Molly Ann? Me with my dick out in Randi's bedroom. Poor Molly Ann has enough to worry about without me showing my dumb ass on TV. Dammit. How many ways can you mess things up, Boy.

He stopped at a little grocery store and bought a six pack of beer, a small ice chest and a bag of ice. Dan knew he was risking a ticket driving after having the beers, but he couldn't stop himself. Hell, he couldn't go back to Austin and he couldn't go home. Where the hell could he go?

At Columbus the signs for Interstate 10 showed one way for San Antonio and the other for Houston. He thought about going to see the Alamo, where the fight for Texas had cost the lives of all those brave men. No survivors. Then he thought of the battle of San Jacinto where Texans had routed an army many times their size and won the day and the war. Did he need to head for 'no survivors' or 'win the day'?

It was after seven and getting dark when he turned east toward Houston. He ate seafood at the San Jacinto Inn and afterwards wandered along the park road looking at the lighted spire and the park grounds. Dan tried to picture the day of the battle with a ragged band of Texans sneaking up on the sleeping larger army and taking it by surprise. Kinda the way Randi was taking him by surprise. That line of thought just made Dan's mood darker and darker.

He needed to find some way to cope for himself and try and save face for Molly Ann and his mom. Not to say his girls. Maybe if they moved out of the county. No, dammit. His family had been on that land for four generations. He was not going to let this run them off now. But he still didn't have a way out of the box Randi had built him into.

Chapter 54

Billy had called Butch and wanted to meet that night at seven to give him a rundown on the dereg vote situation. Butch was tired and set the meeting up at the mansion so he could get away from Ann and Lance's constant badgering.

When they were seated with glasses of bourbon in front of them, Billy said, "Governor, this is proving to be a tough one. I think those utility boys went to sleep after that bill cleared committee, thinking it was a cakewalk."

"Hell, Billy, they said they had kept up the pressure. I think those independent power boys took to lying about this."

Butch watched as Billy squirmed in his chair. "No, I think they just worked harder and smarter. I think they're more desperate and it shows. The damn capitol is running thick and fast with utility lobbyists now, but they're having to try and play catch-up."

"Well, Billy, what about the votes you were working on? I thought you were pretty confident this morning." Butch was wondering if he'd put too much confidence in Billy. He wasn't looking very sure of himself.

"Butch, let me speak plainly. There was a lot of work put into passing dereg at $10 billion. It's that move up to thirteen five that has some people getting nervous. Hell those two R's are from strong districts, but they'll attract an opponent in their own primary if they are seen as giving away the state treasury."

"Now, don't go talking like that. This dereg should be a good deal for Texas."

"Governor, it's not me talking like that. That's the talk I'm getting from Democrats and Republicans alike. I think the big U's just got a little too greedy for their own good. Hell, this deal was raising eyebrows at $10 billion."

"But, Billy, can't you pressure them to go along?"

"Sure, I can, but I'll pay a helluva a price if I do. Just from the members

I talked to this afternoon, they are asking for a whole lot to vote with you. And I don't know what Miss Ann told those two R's but they acted like they had been rode hard and put up wet."

"Tell me the bottom line, Billy. You have to have some way to get those votes. Hell, it's only three or four."

"Butch, I'm going to be frank with you. I've had to ask members to make some tough votes before and I've done it because I thought it was good for Texas. I'm just having trouble making that case this time. I think the utilities screwed up when they only asked for ten in the first place."

Butch looked at the forlorn expression on Billy's face. For the first time he considered the possibility the dereg bill might not pass. Then he remembered again. It couldn't fail. The damned money was already gone. They had to pass the damn bill.

"We have to pass this bill. Tell me what else I or anybody else can do. We have to have it."

"Now, that's a dangerous statement. Don't let anybody else hear you say that. We won't be able to find pockets deep enough if that word gets out. I haven't given up by any means. I just wanted you to know that it's going to be hard to get our majority. If I can't do anything else, I'll try to get some of the 'no' votes to take a walk. Hell, Governor, I've got two no votes that are in the National Guard. You might be thinking about some reason to activate their units to get them out of the capitol."

Butch sucked in breath. "Damn, Billy, I'd have hell doing that. Are you serious?"

Billy grinned widely and took a long sip of his drink. "No, not really. At least not yet." Billy stood, drained his drink, and put the glass down. "Look, I'm meeting with two more members tonight. I'd better get going."

"When can we talk in the morning? I want to get this settled." Butch could hear panic in his own voice.

"I'll be in my office by seven. By eight I'll have the new count and you can call me. I also may have some names for you to work. It's getting down to the wire and we'll have to pull out all the stops."

Butch stood and the two men shook hands. "Billy, you know I've got a lot riding on this. If you pull this off, I'll be forever in your debt. You call me for anything – anything – and it's yours."

"OK, Butch. Try and get some sleep. We've got a tough old Friday tomorrow."

Butch poured himself another drink. Sleep, hell. Who could sleep with five million dollars uncovered. Hell, he'd damn near have to drop out of the race if he couldn't come up with that money. Hmmm, drop out of the race. That might be tempting.

Chapter 55

The lights in the Houston malls were dimmed and only the clubs were still lit up as Dan headed northwest on US-290 out of Houston. It was just after midnight. Dan still didn't know where he was going for sure or what he needed to do.

He was focused on the possibility that Randi would let him go ahead and kill the dereg bill. She'd seemed interested and that was the only part of her blasted plot she showed even the slightest hint of flexibility. He probably should get back to Austin.

Back to do what? Billy would be pissed over him bailing out yesterday. His calls would be stacked three inches thick on his desk. Did he really want to get back into that?

He watched the lights of isolated houses and ranches drift by as the truck went along on cruise control. He thought he'd be sleepy by now, but his nerves were rattled and sleep was the farthest thing from his mind.

The lower speed limit through Hempstead slowed him as he passed at two in the morning. A lot of the small town police worked the highways after midnight figuring to ticket the late speeders. Dan knew from bitter experience that his State Official plates meant nothing to them. He'd learned during his first term how little the city police thought of his State Representative status. He'd been stopped for speeding in Caldwell on his way to the capitol. When the policeman came up to him, standing next to his truck, Dan had handed him his State Rep ID along with his driver's license.

"What is this? A joke?" the officer asked looking at Dan's State Official card.

"No, officer, it's a threat," Dan had said with a smirky smile.

Dan had to call his staff to come get him as the officer had kept his truck and driver's license. His dad pulled strings all over to get him out of that one. He'd learned his lesson well.

Back up to speed, Dan again tried to figure out what to do. From somewhere came the idea to go home and talk to Molly Ann. He'd been feeling a strong need to talk to her to try to soften the blow. Hell, it would be nice to see the ranch. Maybe get in the jeep and ride the pastures.

Then he had a scary thought. What if Billy called Molly Ann trying to find him. It would scare the hell out of her. He'd better get back to Austin and see what the mess looked like now. But he didn't want to go.

Dan stopped at an all night grocery and got a cup of coffee. The clerk behind the counter seemed to be in a talkative mood. Dan spent over an hour talking about how the prices on cattle were heading for a low they hadn't seen in twenty years and that meant bad times in ranch country.

"Yep, I've heard of five ranchers giving up and selling out in the last couple months. Some of them were fourth generation on their land." He spoke with a drawl that reminded Dan more of Georgia than Texas.

"Well, my family's been on our place over by Madisonville for several generations too. Who are they selling the land to?"

"I think it's developers. They'll probably build subdivisions and stores."

"It's a waste of good land if you ask me. Well, I'd better be getting on down the road. Big doings in Austin." Dan thought it was a strange conversation to have at four in the morning, but it made him feel better talking about something familiar and not quite so ominous. The big doings in Austin were a big, horrible mess, but Dan knew he had to face the music.

With a cup of coffee for the road he headed up 290 toward Austin. The sun was just beginning to lighten the eastern horizon when he got to Texas 21, his usual way to Austin. He pulled off considering whether to take that route. He looked at his watch. Four thirty. He'd just go on up 290 to see some different road for a change.

The growing light to his right lit some patchy ground fog that was forming in some of the fields. Dan pulled off the road beside a field with round hay bales scattered across it where the baler had dumped them. The sunrise behind the field gave a ghostly glow to the ground fog and the huge bales. He sat in the truck, sipping coffee and watching the sunrise go from pale white to red then pink. He thought about the peaceful collection of sculptures and mists in front of him. He pictured himself in the peaceful scene. This was much closer to the center of what was important to him than all that shit in Austin. There were probably views much like this on his ranch. Far away from the killer life of Austin. Far away from Randi and her vicious hatred. Dan was sure she hated him or at least what he represented. He was everything she'd always wanted, but couldn't have.

Then he thought about his dad. All those years of deceit. Dan had always considered his dad distant. He spent much of the time away from home, supposedly on state or legal business. He obviously spent some of it in bed with a woman who worked for him. "You pious bastard," he said to himself. "You damn well were ready to get in bed with Randi, weren't you? What had she said? Like father like son."

Dan had second thoughts about that. All the chances he'd had to run around on Molly Ann and never done it. Randi set him up out of hate. Shit. He'd been suckered. But there was no getting around the fact that she could do just about whatever she wanted.

Dan started the truck and pulled out onto the road. He'd decided that his situation was neither the Alamo nor San Jacinto. His was more like Grandfather Carbach, surrounded by Comanches and outgunned. Time to hunker down and save whatever there was to save from the situation and try to live to fight another day.

He didn't know what living to fight another day would look like after Randi did her worst, but he would have to stay with what had brought him this far. As the Austin skyline emerged in the sunlight in front of him, his sense of dread returned but at least there was some determination to get on with it. He'd have to hope that Molly Ann, his daughters and his mother could find a way to forgive him. May be more than I should try and deal with right now.

When he got out of the truck at his apartment, he felt stiff and his clothes were sticking to him. He probably smelled as bad as he looked. He had to get the show going.

Chapter 56

When Dan had showered and shaved he started feeling better, but he knew as unaccustomed as he was to staying awake all night, he'd be running on empty today. The tight feeling in his stomach he associated with the tension Randi had put there yesterday. Was that only twenty-four hours ago? Surely it was sometime last month.

Dan called Andy at home just before seven.

"Andy, sorry to be calling you so early but I need to talk. I've got trouble."

"It's OK Son. When you get my age you'll get a whole new notion of getting up early. I've been up since the paper boy dropped off the "Statesman" at four this morning. What's up?"

"You won't believe it when I tell you. We need to meet somewhere where we won't be interrupted."

"Sounds bad, boy. Why don't you come on over here. I've got the coffee on and I was about to put on some eggs. I'll add a couple for you."

"Andy, you're a gem. I'll be there in ten minutes."

Dan drove the short distance to Andy's apartment over on Burnett. It was an older complex with much more stable residents than Dan's apartment. Trimmed with huge white Greek columns, the dark red brick gave the buildings a look of class and decorum. Dan had spent a lot of his first session at Andy's while the senator taught him the ropes of succeeding in the legislature. As he knocked on Andy's door, Dan hoped he wouldn't think all his teaching had gone for nothing after Randi gutted him.

"Come on in, Son. You look a little ragged. You sick or something?"

"No, Sir, I wish I was sick. I'm afraid I didn't sleep any last night. I've been riding around trying to see if I could figure a way out of the mess I'm in." The smell of breakfast cooking filled the room and Dan felt hungry.

"Come on over to the table. I just turned the eggs out. Sit down and tell me what it is has you looking like a whipped dog. Nothing can be as bad as you sound."

Dan fixed his coffee and took a sip. "I don't know, Andy. This is pretty bad. I'll start where it started with me about this time yesterday morning. Fasten your seatbelt. You know Randi Crendall, my State Affairs staffer?"

"Sure, and she'd been a good one, hasn't she?"

"Oh, it's not her work. Andy, she asked me to meet her in a park yesterday morning. She had a shitload to hit me with. Andy, do you remember a Crendall woman that worked for dad?"

"Sure, she was with him in the House and for some of his time in the Senate. She quit after a while, though. I haven't seen her is a long time. Crendall. Crendall. Same name as your aide. I hadn't put that together before. What did she have to say?"

"What she had to say was that she is my half-sister. From her mom and my dad when Dad was still in the house."

Andy shook his head, like he was trying to clear his thoughts. "What the hell? That can't be. Hell, I was there the whole time. I never saw anything like that. She must be lying."

"No, Andy, she has the goods. Dad's old lawyer in Madisonville has been sending a thousand dollars a month to her mom for years. She showed me copies of the checks with Findley's signature written on the Madison Development Company. Hell, I asked that old bastard about those checks and he told me it was for help in Austin. But he didn't really explain it."

"Dan, you mean that Randi who is working for you is your dad's daughter by another woman? What she doing working for you?"

"Andy she said she'd been raised up Austin trailer trash by a drunk of a mom and I'd gotten all the fame and the money. She's out to ruin me as payback for the life she's led compared to the one I've led. That's why she got herself in my confidence. And, Andy, she's got stuff to do it, I'm afraid."

"Like what?"

"The first thing is the fact of dad's having an illegitimate child and secretly sending money all these years. The next thing is she's been listening to our plans about killing the dereg bill. She's already got it going to out me on that to ruin me in the House. Billy will have a fit and the damned dereg bill will get though when he finds out about my poison pills."

"Damn. She's really got a bee in her bonnet. Hell, Dan, you can't be responsible for what your dad did, however bad it was."

"You know what the press will do with that. It'll be all over the state and my name will be toast. But I haven't told you the worst."

"Worse than this? What the hell?"

"Well, she set up a meeting back in April on the dereg bill at her apartment supposedly so we could get away from the lobby frenzy."

"Dan. Don't tell me."

"There's no excuse, I know, but with Molly Ann sick and all . . ."

"Dan Carb. Are you telling me you screwed your own sister?"

"No, I stopped it before that, but she showed me a lot of hide and, well, I got, well, worked up. The deal is that she had a video camera in her apartment. We didn't actually get in bed together, but she's got some compromising videotape." Dan wiped sweat off his forehead. "She says now that she set it up and it proves that I'm as bad as our dad. Like father like son is what she says." Dan could feel tears coming into his eyes.

"So she's really out to get you? Did you try to talk her out of it?"

"Oh, yeah, I managed to make her madder than she already was by asking if she needed money. Andy, she says she found out who her daddy was back in January and she's been angling to get even with the Carbs ever since. She sounds crazy when she talks about it." Dan wondered if all this made any sense to Andy. "The only thing I've been able to get her to consider is letting me go ahead and kill the dereg bill. And that's only to get back at Ann Terrance. That's not for sure. She's supposed to let me know. The rest hits the papers in a few days. I'm afraid I'm toast, Andy. If I'm lucky Molly Ann won't kick me out. And what about Mom? And the girls. God, what a mess. I won't be able to show my face in Madison County."

"Boy, you're right. That's a mess all right. But don't go thinking your family will drop you. You'll have to 'fess up and take your medicine. But from what I know of that family of yours, this will cause a storm, but you'll stick together in the end."

"I hope you're right. After dad and I both get trashed, I don't know. Let's hope. Well, thanks for the breakfast and for listening to me, Andy. You're the best friend I've ever had and there's nobody else in the world I could have talked to about this. And, thank you for helping me get my courage up to face it. Well, I'd better get up to the capitol. I played hookey yesterday and Billy's probably after my ass."

"I don't know if I've offered much help with this one, Boy. 'Sounds like you're in the clutches of one determined woman. It also sounds like you're hoping to do in the dereg giveaway as a parting shot. If she'll let us do it, it'll make a fitting exit for you. And look, if she's going to ruin you anyway, what's to lose if you catch heat for killing Butch's money bill."

"Yeah, I guess. I'll let you know where Randi is on killing the bill."

Dan arrived at the capitol just before eight o'clock. Paula was already in his office on the second floor. Dan ducked her questions about the day before. It seems that Billy had security out looking for Dan.

His message pile was towering on one corner of his desk. Dan had no stomach for the messages. He would call Molly Ann and let her know that the session was heading toward a crazy close and he'd be in touch. He thought about telling about Randi's plans but didn't have the courage when it came to actually telling her. Later and face to face.

Chapter 57

Dan had played off Billy's idea that he'd been sick on Thursday afternoon and made an excuse for missing the afternoon.

"Shit, Dan, I've got a hornet's nest on my hands with this damned dereg bill. If the word gets out what I gave to get the last two votes, I'll probably lose more 'cause I'm running out of things to give away."

"Old Butch is getting desperate. Did you get the votes?"

"I've still got two more to get. I'm not going to bring the bill up if it's going to fail. I'm trying for at least a vote or two pad."

Dan thought Billy looked almost as bad as he, himself, felt. Dan knew it would be a blessing when he killed it.

"Well, I'm back now. Is there anything I can do?"

"Hell, I don't know. These guys are playing serious hardball. I'll work them a while today and let you know. Just don't go disappearing again. This is getting serious. Remind me to tell any future governor who wants to run for president to go bungee jumping instead. It's a lot safer."

"OK, Boss. I'll be around and on the floor today. Just holler."

Dan walked down to the annex and opened the door to the State Affairs office with some trepidation. He wasn't sure if it was the likely lobbyist crunch or Randi that had him nervous.

"Mr. Chairman," ten people seemed to say at once.

"Just hold on, boys. I've got to meet with my staff and get some things set, then I'll get to you."

He dashed into his office leaving the outer office in disarray. He managed to nod to Randi on his way. She came in and took a chair across the desk. Dan decided that the two of them could place high in a ratty looking contest.

"Well, Dan, I've been thinking about what you said yesterday."

"Hell, Randi, I've spent the whole night thinking about what you said yesterday." Dan thought he'd try some humor. She grinned in spite of trying to keep a serious expression. "I haven't pulled an all-nighter in twenty years."

Randi shifted to a blank look. "Dan, I'm never going to be happy until you're trash around here and everywhere I can make it that way. But, I've been thinking that letting you kill that bill and watching Bitch Ann roast might just be a bonus. Go ahead. I won't rat you out on that."

Dan knew his grin back at her was big.

"But, don't you mistake for one minute that I'm not just as determined to get you. Ann is an asshole, but she's not responsible for my whole life of misery. That's your and daddy's position." She said the word 'daddy' like she was spitting out a fly she'd gotten into her mouth.

Dan reconsidered mentioning his thought about his dad and her life of misery. "OK, Randi, I thank you for thinking about the dereg deal. If it passes everybody in Texas will be paying through the nose for a long, long time."

"Do you need my help on the bill?"

Dan got a flash of his old sense of Randi as the competent staffer. He realized his 'old sense' was still good just yesterday morning.

"No, it's playing out just fine. Ann and Lance are thinking about delaying the bill in Calendars without any help from me. I'm working them and in the end it'll get delayed beyond today, passed on second reading tomorrow, then killed it Sunday before the third reading vote."

"Won't they try to put a blanket procedural amendment on second reading to cover the Calendar's problem?"

"If that happens that'll trigger Rieger and the whole show right there on Saturday. It will be messier for me but what the heck. We'll be ready to go whatever."

Randi started to get up to go. Dan asked, "Randi, it really pains me that you hate me like you seem to. That's never happened to me before. That's why I couldn't sleep last night. I'm not handling that well."

"I don't know what you expect me to say. I've been scheming for months to cook your goose and now it's happening. I'm getting even for a life of misery. I guess maybe it's not personal. It's family. Yeah, that's it, Big Dan. It's family."

With that Randi gave another of her laughs that seemed to come from a horror movie and left, closing the door behind her.

Dan spent an hour listening to people gripe about the way the bill was being worked behind the scenes. The two lobbyists from Reliant and Texas Utilities came in together and thanked Dan for his support and vowed to help him to explain how this was good for Texas. Dan decided that would be the trick of the decade.

The sound of the bell calling the session meeting saved him from the rest of the parade of complaints. Dan felt like a heel taking heat while knowing that his kill was back on track. He decided he was heading into being first a hero then a slimy low-life. The fun of being a public official. All the glory and six hundred dollars a month to boot.

Chapter 58

By noon Randi's head was hurting so badly that she was feeling nauseous. There had been a steady parade of people demanding something about the dereg bill and she was about fed up with them.

The office intern looked shocked when Randi told her she was going out for lunch. Randi ignored the pleading look on her face and headed for her car. Maybe just a short nap will fix me up.

Lieutenant Jerry Borton stepped up to her as she was unlocking her apartment door.

"Howdy, Ma'am. I need to talk to you."

Randi almost felt like fainting, but she knew she needed to stay in control.

"Uh, er, you need to talk to me? I thought you – we'd talked last time." She could feel her stomach turning flips. She hoped she didn't barf right on the spot. It would look like hell.

"I know we'd talked before, but some other questions have come up. I was wondering if we could visit some more. There's just some more information we need."

Panic. Randi was seriously afraid she'd mess in her pants. "Officer, I just came home from work because I wasn't feeling well. Is this something we need to do right now?"

"Yes, ma'am, I really need to talk to you. I don't think it's a big deal. I'm just trying to close out the file on your boyfriend's accident."

Accident. Accident. That sounded better to Randi. "I guess you could come in and I'll try to help. But I need to make a stop. Come on in and have a seat. I'll just be a couple minutes."

Randi opened her door and headed into her bathroom. She noticed that Borton stood just inside the closed front door.

She washed her face in cold water and tried to think what he could want. Hell, he'd been in the ground over a month by now. Surely this was over. Randi took a swig of Pepto Bismal to try to calm her gut, brushed her hair and opened the door to face the policeman.

"OK, Officer, thanks. Let's sit down."

When they were seated on the couch he said, "I've been piecing together the situation at the lake that night and a couple of things still don't quite make sense."

He paused and Randi didn't know how to respond. Her head was hurting badly and she hoped this wouldn't last too long. "Like what?" she finally asked.

"Tell me again the sequence of how things happened that night. I want to hear it from you again."

"Well, like I said, Dave and I were parked at the lake sitting on the hood of his truck talking. He got to clowning around at the edge of the bank and slipped into the water. I thought he was fooling around at first."

Borton referred to some notes on a small pad. "Right, that's what you said. And after he fell in what did you do?"

"I tried calling to him, but he didn't answer. That's when I called 911 and all the police showed up."

"Well, Miss Crendall, do you remember talking to some joggers that night after Dave fell into the lake?"

Randi thought back again. "Oh, yeah, two college boys stopped and asked if I needed help. I'd forgotten that." Randi's stomach felt like it might cramp with strain.

"OK, so they asked if you needed help and you told them no. What did they do then?"

"What did they do? I don't know. They just jogged off down the path, I think. Why?"

Randi decided that Borton was good at his job. His expression didn't show anything about what he was thinking.

He looked back at his notes. "And you stayed there until you called the emergency number and the police arrived."

Randi remembered the trip back to her apartment to stash the video camera. She didn't want to bring that up. She worried that she'd hesitated too long to answer. "Yeah, yeah, that's right. I tried calling Dave some more, but he didn't answer. Why?"

He closed his notebook. His look at her was stern. "Ma'am, we interviewed those two joggers. They confirm what you said about them asking if you needed help and them jogging off when you said 'no'."

"Great. So what's your problem?"

"Those two boys continued jogging around the lake and passed by again. They told us that you and the truck were gone when they passed again.

And that was before the police arrived. You're lying about what happened out there. What's going on, Miss Crendall?" He was staring at her with that same, blank expression.

Randi was sure she was about to throw up. She struggled to keep calm and try to answer him. "I, I . . .I just took a little ride. That's all. I needed to clear my head."

"Now come on, Miss Crendall. Don't make your situation worse. You see, we've been handling this as a routine accidental drowning, but with your story not checking out and the way you're acting now, you raise our suspicions. Just tell me the truth. It'll go a lot easier for you."

"Well, I had to go back to my apartment for something. Honest, that's where I went. I went to the bathroom at my apartment and came back. Right away."

Borton was slowly shaking his head. "Your boyfriend was in the lake, possibly drowning and you drove off to go the bathroom and then came back to call for help. Now what kind of bullshit is that?"

Randi shifted on the couch. She was beginning to feel very uncomfortable.

He continued. "Miss Crendall, I had hoped to get this report closed by the end of the month, but the way you're acting, you're making it tough. You didn't tell us about the joggers. Now you're saying you left your friend drowning in the lake to go take a piss. What else are you hiding?"

Randi's thoughts were spinning. She had to get him happy so he'd get off this damned case. She tried to sound as sincere she could. "Officer Borton, I promise you, you've got the whole story now. I had forgotten the joggers coming by. I'm sorry. And Dave and I had been drinking and I was afraid that if I called the police they'd arrest me for being drunk." Randi was amazed at how this story was flowing out. "I went five minutes to my apartment, went to the bathroom, washed my face and took some Pepto. I wasn't gone fifteen minutes. Hell, I didn't do anything wrong. Dave was probably already drowned by then. He wouldn't answer me."

He looked skeptically back at her. "OK, Miss Crendall, I guess that will do for now. But I can tell you I'm not through with this case. I think that more than what you've told me went on at the side of the lake that night." He looked down at Randi's hand. "One more thing for now and I'll take off. I want you to let me borrow that ring you're wearing. We need to get a wax impression of it for comparison."

Randi looked down at the Hopi good fortune ring on her right hand. "A comparison of what? Am I being charged or something?"

"Oh, no, you're not charged with anything. It's just to complete our files."

Randi knew that the impression she had made so far wasn't good. She thought maybe if she gave him the ring it might show some better cooperation. If that ring was ever to bring me good fortune, it had better be now. "Sure, here it is," she said taking off the ring and handing it to him. "Anything I can do to help. I'm ready to close that whole night out too." Randi cursed herself inside for the shakiness of her hand as she passed him the ring.

As he was walking out to leave Borton said, "We'll get you your ring back right away."

She managed a weak smile and closed the door behind him. Randi went to the kitchen, ate the dozen donuts she'd gotten the day before and then passed out exhausted, lying sideways across her bed.

Chapter 59

Dan got through the Friday session on autopilot. There was a parade of bills with fervent supporters and opponents, but he couldn't stir up any real interest.

Billy called him up to the podium around three when the calendar was almost done. "Well, Dan, I'm still scratching for another vote or two. I've got a supplemental calendar all ready to go to vote today, but it's too close. I need you to talk to Calendars. Make up some story and delay it to tomorrow morning."

"We're liable to run out of time, Billy. Are you sure you've got this deal done?"

Billy wiped sweat off his forehead. It probably wasn't the temperature. He tried one of his patented grins, but it came off a little crooked. "Oh, we'll come out OK. I may not have a damned chit left when I get done, but I'll get it somehow." Billy stepped away to gavel a bill passage and put a new one on the floor.

When Billy stepped back, Dan tried to lighten the conversation. "Why the hell are you sacrificing everything on this one damn bill? Did Butch promise you a night with Ann or something?" Both of them broke out laughing so loudly that the representative at the front mike turned around to look before continuing his impassioned speech.

"I guess we'd better behave back here. And no, Butch just made me some nice promises for this bill."

"OK, I'll go talk to Calendars and get it on tomorrow. I'll blame it on my incompetent committee staff or something."

Gerald Hanes, the Republican chair of the Calendars Committee, was one of Dan's best friends in the Legislature. He represented a district in West Texas and was a rancher like Dan. The two of them had worked together tirelessly to get the Speaker's group of committee chairs really working as a team. Dan felt like a heel, not being honest with Gerald about the delay, but there was no way he could risk his pills. At this point, all Dan could think about was his own desperation and how his whole life was about to be wrecked.

Dan left the capitol shortly after the session was over. He was headed for an early bedtime. He called Andy on his cell phone as he drove to his apartment and told him that the kill was still on.

Dan lay in his bed thinking about his miserable situation. But that didn't last long. Fatigue overtook him and he went soundly to sleep.

Chapter 60

Since she'd gone to bed so early, Randi woke up at three in the morning, fixed a pot of coffee and sat in the living room. The visit from Borton still had her confused. If she wasn't charged with anything why keep questioning her? She suspected that Borton was up to something, but she hadn't a clue what it was.

The fitful sleep she got between five and nine left her dragging as she dressed for the capitol. Saturdays were normally a day off, but not at the end of the session. With only three days left until adjournment, every day would be busy.

Randi also wondered at herself still going in to work with all she had planned for Dan Carb. He had to know she didn't give a damn about what went on in the State Affairs office. But she had told Dan she'd go along with the poison pill on dereg. There might be work to do on that.

Randi could tell that Dan was suffering from her attack on him. He just didn't have the same confidence he usually did when he was at work. If Dan only knew the Austin cops were still bugging her about Dave. He'd have something to throw back at her. Shit! The thought hit Randi like a ton of bricks. She almost ran over a car in the right lane as she pulled to the curb on Congress a few blocks from the capitol.

Randi was raging. That's it. That fucking Dan Carb is the one who's set the Austin cops on me. Hell, he's still got the pull to do it. That's why that fucking Borton couldn't tell her anything. The son-of-a-bitch was fishing for something to pin on her. She pulled out into the traffic to the accompaniment of screeching tires and blaring horns. I'll go public on the bastard right now. I'll show him to fight back at me.

By the time she parked in the underground lot, Randi had cooled down a bit. She told herself she needed to think this through. If Dan was trying to get her to back off, why didn't Borton come out with something on that?

Anyway, if Dan pressed her he should know she'd just talk and it would all be out.

But what the hell was Borton up to? Randi thought back over that night with Dave at the lake as she walked toward the elevator. Dave had gotten pissed at her because she wouldn't hold Dan up for money. He'd slapped her and then she had slapped him and he had fallen down. When he started to get up he'd picked up a rock and threatened to hit Randi with it. That's when she slugged him and bloodied his nose.

Randi tried to picture that night again. Hit his nose. I hit him in the nose with my fist. My fist with my Hopi ring on it. Borton wanted to make a wax impression of my ring. Oh, God. He's trying to prove I hit Dave and caused him to drown. Is that murder?

Randi's first instinct was to run away. But that would make her look guilty. She needed to calmly think this through. Borton was probably still fishing. Why the hell did she give him her ring?

It was obvious from the empty waiting area in State Affairs that the action and interests had shifted to the floor. Dan's poison pill was falling into place. Randi was glad to have a break so she could sit at her desk and try to figure out what to do about Borton.

Chapter 61

When Butch hadn't heard anything from Billy on the dereg bill by eleven Saturday morning, he went over to the Speaker's Office to check on progress.

"Well, Governor, I didn't call because I've been working my ass off all last night and this morning. But you can relax. I just got the last vote I needed for passage and the bill is on a supplemental calendar."

Butch heaved a sigh of relief. "Damn, Boy, that's cutting it close. Are you sure you've got the votes?"

"Well, with it this close, we'll have to wait and see how it goes. There are still some wavering votes, but I think we've got it now. I'll bring it up after lunch and we'll just have to fight it out. If it looks shaky during the debate, I can always table it and bring it back up. But I don't think I'll have to do that. It's close but I think it will pass by one or two votes."

"Damn, Billy, that is close. How did we go from being sure two weeks ago to this close now? Hell, this should be a popular bill." Butch was starting to doubt the confidence he'd placed in Billy. This was too important to be resting on one or two votes.

"Butch, let me be plain. Two weeks ago the bill was for a ten billion dollar settlement with the utilities. I think if it was still ten billion today we'd have a nice vote pad for passage. When you cut the deal to raise it up to over thirteen billion, you let the utilities greed kick in and that gave the other side all the ammunition they needed. I think Sam and his henchmen caused all this trouble. I've made commitments to get these votes I never thought I'd have to make. My ass is out a mile and we still don't know if it's going to pass."

"Now, Billy, you know that I'm going to take care of you. Just get out there and get us those votes and everything will be all right. This is going to be the deal of a lifetime." Butch knew Billy was right on the thirteen billion being the problem. But hell, he needed that additional three million to keep his competition quiet. As he walked back over to his office, Butch decided he'd make a good free enterprise president, with the risks he was taking to get there.

Chapter 62

Dan sat his desk on the House floor for most of the morning only passively monitoring the progress of bills becoming law on third reading. He couldn't muster interest in any of them. He'd eaten lunch in the Speaker's conference room with several other committee chairs. The Speaker buying lunch showed how badly he wanted to keep the members in the House working. There was some grumbling, but everyone was used to the end of session push. So far this one was calmer than some. So far, Dan thought, so far.

Billy brought up the supplemental calendar with the dereg bill on second reading around two in the afternoon. When Jim Clower, the senior Republican, took the front mike a hush fell over the House and gallery.

"Mr. Speaker and members, the bill before you is one that I know has been thoroughly discussed and not without some disagreement. But let me tell you that this is one of the most important bills to come before you this session. This legislation will put Texas in the forefront of competition for the supply of electricity and you and your constituents back home will see your power bills drop as a result of your action to pass this bill today."

Dan thought he might be sick. It was bad enough to put up with the travesty of this damned bill, but to have Clower claiming it was the most important bill of the decade was almost more that he could stand.

But his kill strategy gave him comfort. With the bill coming up on Saturday, it was well past the seventy-two hour limit in Calendars. Dan wanted to wait to see if it would fail of it's own weight before getting Rieger onto it.

The arguments and amendments went on for most of the afternoon. Most of the killing amendments were failing by three or four votes but the make-up of the majority kept shifting, depending the issue. Dan couldn't tell how a final vote on the bill would go, but he needed to stay with his vote for passage to set up the certainty of the poison pill. If the bill failed on Saturday, there would still be time for them to make adjustments and bring it up for possible passage. If it passed today and came up on Sunday for third and final reading, the kill then would be fatal.

The string of amendments finally played out around six in the evening and Billy called for a vote on passage. The buzz of conversations in the House and gallery was so loud the Billy had to gavel for quiet.

All eyes were on the voting panels at the front of the Chamber. Green lights indicated a vote for passage and red ones a vote against. The boards looked like Christmas tree decorations with red and green lights as the last few votes were registered.

"Have all members voted? Have all members voted?" Billy banged the gavel. "By a vote of seventy-five to seventy-three, House Bill One has passed second reading." The roar that broke out was deafening. Billy's incessant gaveling had no effect. He screamed a thirty-minute recess into the mike and left the podium.

Dan looked around at members standing stunned at their desks. Everyone knew that one vote the other way would have done the bill in and they were all shocked by how close it was. The press was diving for the door to get on their cell phones. The six o'clock newscasts would get interrupted.

Dan watched closely as Representative Rieger slowly got up and headed toward the member's lounge. Dan needed to talk to him, but not such a public place. Dan walked over to intercept him.

"Mr. Rieger, I need to catch you for a minute some time. Just some information I thought you could use."

"Sure, Dan. That damned HB-1 argument went on so long, I've got to get to the restroom. I'll see you in the lounge."

"How about we meet at your office. I need to get something and I'll see you there in fifteen minutes."

"Sure. Whatever. I'll bet this recess goes longer than thirty minutes anyway."

Dan went to his office and got copies of HB-1 with the date and time stamps on it. He also got a copy of the bill as it went to the floor. That was all he needed for Rieger.

Rieger's office was in the annex and the old gentleman was seated at his desk when Dan walked in.

"Mr. Rieger, it's HB-1 I wanted to talk to you about. It'll be coming up on third reading tomorrow, but it's got a big problem."

Rieger's expression brightened. "My kind of big problem? Damn, Dan, what are you up to? Here, let me see it."

Dan handed the copies over the desk and sat watching Rieger go over the bill copies. He finally looked at Dan over his horn-rimmed glasses. "The seventy-two hour rule. It's over by more than fourteen hours. That's a killer."

"Well, as usual, you didn't hear this from me. But when it comes up on third tomorrow, it would be good if you could ask the question."

Rieger grinned. Dan knew he enjoyed his role as the rules stickler in the House. Rieger looked like a kid at Christmas. He rubbed his hands together and looked at the bill copies again.

"Dan Carb, this is about as big a bill as I've ever had a shot at. It just may bring down the roof of the chamber when I kill this one. And on third reading two days out. I hope you've got your reasons. I didn't like the damned thing much myself and that's why I voted against it. It'll be a pleasure."

The two men shook hands and Dan headed over to the State Affairs Office, hoping no one had seen him in Rieger's office. What the hell? After Randi goes public it won't matter anyway.

Chapter 63

When Dan came into the State Affairs office after the vote, he seemed to Randi to be walking with a spring in his step. Almost playful.

"Hi, Randi. Great day, huh? Come on in and let's talk about how it went."

She went in and sat down. She was having trouble believing Dan's sunny behavior given what she was planning for him.

"So, it passed second reading, huh? Are they popping champagne in the gov's office?"

"No, it's too early for that. I guess you heard it passed by only one vote."

"Yeah, a close one. You voted for it I take it." Randi watched as Dan leaned back in his chair and seemed relaxed.

"Oh, sure. I want it to get to third reading tomorrow. And I just talked to Rieger. He's like a kid in a candy store. Thinks this is the biggest bill he ever had a shot at killing. Yeah, the stage is set for the big fireworks tomorrow. And, Randi, with all the other stuff you have against me, I'm glad you let this one go through."

Randi felt a slight twinge of guilt, but it didn't last. "I'll want to be where I can see the Bitch when Rieger blasts it tomorrow. And, yes, Dan, I'm still going through with my plans for you. I'm putting everything into motion Monday for the news to break on Tuesday. And before you ask, no second thoughts. It's going down."

"Oh, I know you're going to do it, Randi. I'm even coming to be at peace about losing all this." Dan made a gesture pointing around the whole room. "I tell you one thing. It sure frees me up to kill the dereg bill with no concerns."

Randi didn't like to hear Dan saying he was accepting his fate from her revelations. She wanted him to suffer. After he'd returned to the floor, Randi sat thinking about the conversation they'd just had. They say that death row inmates, when they know the end is coming, get a strange kind of peace and quiet about dying. Maybe that was it.

Chapter 64

Billy tried to recruit Dan to help keep his votes in line for the third reading of the dereg bill due up on Sunday morning, but Dan had begged off.

At his apartment, he had tried to recapture his sunny mood from the conversation with Randi that afternoon. Dan badly needed to let Molly Ann know what was about to land on him, but he hadn't found the courage to do that yet.

"Hi, Molly Ann. How are you feeling today, Love?" He'd reached her just after nine and knew she'd be tired and not in a mood to talk long.

"Oh, we're doing all right, I guess. Some of the cows got out of the pasture on the other side of the highway, but Ben and the hands got them all back in. Ben says we need to get them to better pasture to keep them from breaking the fence trying to get more grass."

"Good old Ben. Well, I'm just about wrapping up the session. Just two days to go. It's crazier than usual."

"Dan, you don't sound so good. What's wrong?" Dan rolled his eyes up at Molly Ann's ability to see through him even over a phone.

"Well, there's some possible trouble brewing over here." Dan wondered how much he should tell her. He decided to wait longer to break the horrible news. "I don't know. You're just liable to have to put up with me around the ranch after this one."

"Now, Dan Carb, don't be coy with me. It sounds a lot more serious than you're letting on. What's happening? You're not letting that crazy legislature get to you are you?" He could hear a thread of worry in her voice.

"No, hon, it's the usual only worse," Dan lied. "I'll get through it and I'll be home in a couple days and we'll have a long talk. Just a rough old session."

"OK, if you say so. The girls have only a few more days of school and they're itching to make up that fishing trip you canceled."

"Well, you tell them we'll get to that as soon as they're out of school.

We might even go over to Toledo Bend and go bass fishing. Tell them and that should hold them for a while."

After he hung up the phone, Dan tossed and turned in bed for over an hour. He knew that as soon as Rieger killed the bill there would be trouble. Maybe he could duck the heat, but Billy would see right through any way he tried to hide his part in the demise. Lying to his wife about how serious his trouble was and facing Billy's certain wrath tomorrow wasn't a very comforting thought to go to sleep on.

Chapter 65

Worried about his razor thin majority, Billy brought the dereg bill up just after the nine o'clock start of the session on Sunday morning. Billy laid the bill out before the House and Clower once again began heaping praise on the legislation.

There was a line of representatives at the back microphone waiting to speak on the bill. Dan noticed that Rieger was second in line. Perfect.

From the length of Clower's speech, Dan assumed that Billy must be having to offer more deals to keep his votes on the dereg bill. When Clower finally got to a stopping point, Billy recognized an Hispanic legislator from the valley who spoke strongly against the bill as a giveaway to the rich at the expense of the poor people in the state. It was a theme that had been thoroughly covered on the second reading and most of the members didn't seem to be listening.

When he finished, Rieger stepped to the microphone. "Mr. Speaker. I rise on a point of order on House Bill Number One," Rieger toned in his scratchy voice. The House went deadly silent. "I move to stop all further consideration of House Bill One under Section 4.135 of the Texas Constitution." All the air seemed to be sucked out of the huge chamber by the collective inhale.

"Mr. Rieger, bring your point of order forward." Billy looked and sounded like he was patronizing the old man. The Speaker stood with a fatherly grin watching Rieger make his way down the center aisle.

By the time Rieger made it up to the front podium there was a crowd of thirty or more legislators with him. Dan joined at the back of the crowd, listening as Rieger read the constitutional language and showed Billy the date and time stamped copies of the bill.

When Rieger finished there was an audible gasp among those gathered at the front. Other members left their desks and the crowd grew.

"Now, Mr. Rieger, let me consult the parliamentarian here." Billy scanned the crowd and caught Dan's eye. He jerked his head signaling Dan to come on up. Dan started through the crowd.

By the time Dan made it on to the dais, Billy was in heated conversation with the House parliamentarian and they were going over several thick books.

"I'm sorry, Mr. Speaker," the parliamentarian said. "Rieger has this one dead to rights. It's all documented. The bill was well within the last seven days of the session and just as clearly spent over seventy-two hours in Calendars."

Billy looked at Dan with a blistering glare. "God damn it," he said in a hiss. "Keep trying to find a way around it. I'm going to try to stall for time."

Billy spoke to the crowd around the front podium in a hushed voice. "Members, it looks like Mr. Rieger might have a point here, but we're still researching it. Just be patient."

Several of the bill's supporters sprinted down the center aisle and out the back door. Dan knew they were off to let the utility lobbyists know what the trouble was. Dan also knew that all this was only delaying the inevitable because there was no way around the kill. And no way to get another bill in for consideration. He had to be careful not to let Billy see his satisfaction. The next several hours would be tough enough without getting caught gloating.

Billy walked over to Dan. "God damn it, Dan. What the hell is this all about?"

"Look, Billy, you know I tried to keep that damn bill moving. It was you and Butch that lost your votes and had to have more time."

"Don't give me that shit, Carb." Dan knew his cover was blown when Billy addressed him by his last name. "I know damn good and well we had to have the time. I'm talking about Rieger. How the hell did he find out in less than twenty-four hours?"

Dan was saved by someone at the rail calling out, "Mr. Speaker, Mr. Speaker."

As Billy got into a heated debate with several members on both sides of the point of order, Dan slowly stepped off the dais and headed back to his desk. He noticed Randi sitting in the gallery. Randi gave him a wink and a quick thumbs up sign.

Chapter 66

Randi had watched the line at the back microphone from a seat on one side of the gallery. From where she sat she could clearly see Ann Terrance sitting with several others from the Governor's staff. Everyone seemed very serious, the way Ann liked them to be. What a bitch.

Randi watched the little group get bored with the tirade about giving money to the rich. When Rieger stepped to the front of the line, Randi stared right at Ann.

"Mr. Speaker. I rise on a point of order on House Bill Number One."

There was a stir in Ann's tight little group but they stayed intent on watching the crowd gathered at the front of the chamber.

The debate about Rieger's point of order went on for over thirty minutes. At one point one of Sam's lobbyist henchmen came up into the gallery and whispered something to Ann. She spun around and barked orders to several staff members around her and they all took off running out the back door. Randi watched as Ann sat now surrounded by empty seats, steaming and looking down at the continuing debate.

Billy finally came to his microphone at the front. Randi knew what was coming. "Members, please step back. Mr. Rieger, your point of order is sustained." Billy looked and sounded like he was speaking at a wake. "House Bill One is pulled from further consideration based on Article 4.135 of the Constitution."

In the uproar that followed, Ann Terrance's face turned beet red and she slammed her notebook down on the floor beside her. Randi was treated to Ann alternately stomping and stumbling over seats as she tried to make her way out of the gallery. She was trying to scream people out of her way in the crunch, but wasn't having luck.

Dan was right. This was worth it.

Chapter 67

Billy turned the Speaker's gavel over to Representative Gerdy, the chairman of the Liquor Control Committee. A sure sign Billy wasn't much interested in whatever bills were going through after the failure of the dereg bill.

After Billy had been off the floor for about a half hour, Dan's desk phone rang. "Dan, it's Billy. Come on in the office. I think we may have a way out of this mess."

"Uh, OK, boss. I'll be right there."

"And, Dan, I don't know why you've done what you've done, but if you expect to stay a part of the leadership, you'd better be ready to help."

Dan heard an ominous tone in Billy's voice he'd never heard before. "I'm on my way."

Dan started toward the front of the chamber toward the Speaker's office. He knew he was in for an ass chewing, but he was ready. What the hell kind of fix could Billy have in mind? Oh, well, time to face the music.

Billy's secretary nodded Dan toward Billy's office door. When he walked in, the reception awaiting him included Lance, Ann, and Butch. Billy was sitting behind his huge desk. Dan thought a firing squad couldn't look more threatening.

"Come on in, Dan. Have a seat and let's see how bad this is." Billy got up and came around to sit on the front edge of his desk. Lance and Ann were sitting on one of the short couches and Butch was in an overstuffed chair facing them. Dan sat on the other couch and looked up at Billy.

Butch spoke first. "Dan, boy, this is a dark day for Texas. I sure hope you didn't have anything to do with that damned order point."

"That's a Point of Order, Governor. And any member of the House has the right at anytime to raise a point of order against any bill under consideration. Mr. Rieger has a long history of tracking the progress of bills on the lookout for procedural problems. He's done this dozens of times."

Ann Terrance spoke through clenched teeth. "What a stupid ass system. You mean that any jerk can come along and ruin months of work like that. No wonder Texas is such a fucked up place."

There were quick glances exchanged around the room over her language and the insults. Lance turned in his seat to face Ann. "Now, Ann, don't go talking like that. We're here to try and rescue the bill and you're not helping. Billy, do you have some idea of how we can recover from this?"

Ann started to respond hotly to Lance, but Billy cut her off. "Folks, in the last hour, we've looked at every precedent we could find and it doesn't look good." Billy fixed his gaze directly on Dan. "There's one slim possibility and it depends on what Dan is willing to do." Everybody in the room was now looking at Dan.

Billy continued. "Dan, right after your committee meeting your staffer, Randi, I think, took the bill on over to Calendars. I think it timed in just after eleven. If she'd waited until the next day we could stretch the time limits and set aside the Point of Order."

Dan spoke carefully. "But, Billy, I met with her that night. None of the amendments that were offered stuck so the Sub-Committee report went through just as it was submitted. We only had to put the State Affairs cover pages on it and it was good to go."

"Right, I understand, Dan. But it's possible that if you claimed now that your staffer didn't have your authority to submit the bill that night, we could claim that the bill wasn't officially submitted to Calendars until the next day. Hell, you could claim she acted without authority and fire her ass."

Dan thought of the irony of firing Randi for this made up charge when he had a damn site bigger reason to run her off.

"Then how do we explain that my signature is on the paperwork transmitting the bill to Calendars?"

Lance looked at his copies of the bill. "He's got a point, Billy. Dan's signature is right there on the bill. But the date is typed in. You could still claim she didn't have authority to do it and typed the wrong date."

Ann stood up and got in her command stance. "Mr. Carb, you don't seem to understand the gravity of this situation. You don't have any choice but to blame it on your staff person and get this bill back on track. Too much is at stake for you not to." She said the last while shaking her finger at Dan like a school marm.

Dan stood and walked right up to Ann, staring down at her. "I don't think you understand how an elected body works, Miss Ann. It's those of us who run for office and are elected who get to say what has or has not to be done." Dan turned to Billy. "Mr. Speaker, let's stop pussyfooting around here. You know already anyway. I'm the one that put Rieger on the Point of Order. It was this bunch that delayed the bill past seventy-two hours by not keeping your votes in line, but I watched you do it and even helped it some."

"Dan, be careful. You're treading on dangerous ground," Billy said, softening his earlier tone.

"No, Billy, it's time I faced the music. Governor, I know you need this bill to keep your presidential campaign afloat, but the price Texas will have to pay is way too much. Hell, I was opposed at ten billion, much less thirteen." Butch started to say something, but Dan kept talking. "The damned utilities saw a chance to make a killing for themselves and leave the state power system in a mess. They just played your campaign money needs to get what they wanted and I, for one, won't stand for it."

"Billy, you can do what ever you want to me, I'm not going to fire Randi or question the dates. Like it or not folks, your great venture with this rotten deal is over with. Yes, I set it up to fail and fail it has. You're just going to have to live or die with that." Dan could feel the heat on his face and neck. "And one more thing. Miss Ann, if you think that Texas is, as you put it, such a fucked up place, you should consider getting on the next plane out of here. The state will be better off when you're gone."

Ann took a step toward Dan and he moved to meet her. Dan decided he must have looked pretty fierce because she took two steps backward and sat back down on the couch.

"Now, now, don't let this get personal." Billy motioned toward the door. "Would you all please excuse us? I need to talk to Dan privately."

As he passed, Butch said to Dan, "I just can't believe it, Dan, boy. I thought you were in this deal from the start."

"Governor, I did what I thought was best for the state and my district. I'd do it again the same way."

Ann stepped carefully as she passed Dan. Her eyes were fixed on the floor.

As he went past Dan, Lance said, "It was an awful thing to do, Dan, and I hope you had good reasons. You're burning a brilliant legislative career."

Dan couldn't think of a response to that so he kept quiet.

When the door closed behind them, Billy went to his liquor cabinet and poured two glasses of bourbon. He handed one to Dan and they clinked glasses. "Here's to a great run, Dan. You know as well as I do that it's over. There'll be a million dollars for anybody who'll run against you. Why, Dan, why? And to not even to let me, your best friend in this place, know." Billy's look at Dan was forlorn, but not angry.

"That's the part I hated the most, Billy, but there was no way. I saw from that first meeting at Lance's the kind of pressure Butch was putting on you. There was no way I was going to subject you to what I knew I'd have to go through on this. I knew anybody associated with killing that bill would be toast. It was a job for a lone wolf and I'm it. Texas still needs you with that gavel. And, Billy, they won't have to put up a million to beat me. I won't even be in the race. You might say that killing the dereg giveaway is my parting shot. I'm hanging it up."

Billy walked over to his window and looked out at the front lawn of the capitol. For a long time he seemed to be lost in thought. When he finally spoke, it was in a hushed voice. "OK, Son, it sounds like you knew what you were in for. I hate to see it end like this, but you have to do what's right for you. I'm going to miss you."

When Billy moved toward Dan, Dan thought it was to shake his hand. Instead Billy put down his drink and the two of them hugged. Billy was almost teary when he again picked up his drink.

"Mr. Speaker, I'm going to miss all this too. But probably after I get to spend some time on my ranch and be with my family, I think I'll get over it. Billy, I'm going to miss you too. You've taught me a lot and I'll never forget it. And I'll be in touch some too. Anyway, I've still got a year and a half in this term, unless you think they'll impeach me." Dan grinned and it seemed to lighten the room. "Hell, you'll have to come over and shoot another buck some time." Dan knew they would not stay that close, but he needed to offer it for his own comfort.

Dan drained his drink, shook hands with Billy, stared long at him, and headed for the door.

He assumed he'd be the center of a storm for the rest of the next two days, but he thought he had already faced the toughest part and done right by what he believed. The rest was just static. That was until Randi goes public.

Chapter 68

Dan wasn't ready to face the other members on the House floor so he headed down the back hall and took the stairs down past the first floor to the capitol basement. He hoped to avoid anybody connected with the dereg bill. He needed to calm down after the session in Billy's office.

He walked the entire length of the capitol basement and took the stairs up to the first floor in the Senate wing. Dan was almost to Andy's office when Sam Turpin saw him and ran to catch him.

"Dan, Dan, we have to talk. There has to have been some misunderstanding."

Dan stopped and faced him. The two of them were standing close to the wall as public traffic passed both ways in the hallway.

"Sam, I don't think we have anything to talk about. I've already told Billy and Butch that I did what I thought I had to do. We can't unring that bell." Dan thought Sam looked like he'd been on a three day drunk. His eyes were lined with red and his collar and tie were loose around his neck.

"Look, Dan, we've invested our whole session to get this bill passed. We're not going to stand still while you go on some crazy tangent trying to kill it. Too many people have too much on the line to lose it now."

"Now, look, you know damn good and well the risks and safeties built into this process. You folks got too greedy and didn't pay attention to how the procedures were going. I just called your hand and you can't live with that. Tough."

Sam reached up and caught both of Dan's coat collars. "I'm sorry, Carb, that won't cut it."

Dan put both his fists between Sam's arms and knocked his hands off his coat. With his hand on Sam's throat, Dan pushed the lobbyist against the wall. "If you want to make this personal, Sam, we'll go to it, but I think you'll come out worse than you did on the House floor." Sam was gasping for breath and his face turned bright red.

A capitol policeman came over to the two men. "Representative Carb, is there any trouble?" Several tourists had stopped to watch the exchange.

Dan let go of Sam. "No, Officer, thanks. I was just explaining some things about the legislative process to Mr. Turpin here."

"Well, you boys ought to take this conversation into an office before you draw a crowd."

Sam straightened his coat and started to leave. In a hissing whisper, Sam said, "You haven't heard the last of this, Dan. You don't know what you're messing with."

Chapter 69

Randi had watched from the gallery as Dan headed toward the Speaker's office looking like he was going to his own hanging. A shame to ruin such a brave soul, but that's life.

She'd decided that the sooner she firmed up her plans to go public with her illegitimacy the better. Randi had made a date to meet a stringer she knew from the *Austin American Statesman* at a coffee shop on 15th Street. But when she pulled into a parking place at the restaurant a dark blue sedan stopped directly behind her car.

What the hell? Then she saw Borton get out of the car. Shit, he must have been following me. Randi tensed.

Borton came to the driver's window. "Miss Crendall, we need to talk. Can you get out of the car?" Randi noticed that another man in a dark suit had gotten out of the car and was standing at the back her parking place.

"What the hell is going on? Sure, I'll get out of the car. But tell me what's going on." Randi opened her door and stepped out. She halfway expected Borton to get handcuffs out the way he was acting. Randi was shaking all over.

"Now, don't misunderstand, but we need to talk and this time it needs to be down at the station. So I need to advise you of your rights." Borton took a worn index card out of his shirt pocket. "Miss Crendall, you have the right to remain silent. If you do not remain silent, anything you say may be used against you in a court . ."

Randi held her hand up. "I know the Miranda, Lieutenant. Am I being arrested?"

"No, this is not an arrest. But you need to come to the station with us. If we can clear up some matters you may be in the clear. If not," he gestured with both palms up, "who knows? Now are you ready to go with Officer Mallow and me?"

Randi looked at the other man, then at Borton. She had a fleeting thought of trying to tell the reporter she wouldn't be able to meet but dropped that idea. "It looks like I don't have much of a choice. I haven't done anything wrong. The sooner I can get your questions answered the better, as far as I'm concerned." Randi locked her car.

Borton turned and opened the back door of the sedan and the other officer helped Randi as she got into the back seat. It was only when she was seated and they were headed out of the parking lot that Randi realized that there were no door handles on the inside of the back seat. There was a heavy metal screen between her and the men in the front seat and doors were locked. The only way out was for them to open the doors from the outside. She didn't think she was claustrophobic, but the fidgeting panic she felt must be pretty close. The space seemed to shrink as they drove across Austin.

The Austin Police Station, with its heavy, tan stone exterior, looked more formidable to Randi than it had ever seemed. They went up the back stairs from the police parking lot with the two officers walking on either side of her.

The room they led Randi to was bare with only a small wooden table and three chairs. It looked like a set for *Law and Order*. They left a uniformed officer with her.

Borton came in with Mallow and the uniformed officer left.

"Miss Crendall. Randi. I think I have asked you now three times to tell me what happened at the lake between you and Dave. Every time I have asked I managed to pull a little more of the story out, but only when I confront you with evidence about it."

"Hell, Borton, I don't remember every little detail. I told you I was drunk. Dave was drunk too. Didn't your test prove that?"

"Yes, his blood alcohol level was elevated."

"Oh, another detail I left out. It was beer he was drinking. That's what got him drunk."

"Don't be a smart ass, Randi. Young lady, you might get out of this in the clear or you might be in trouble. You'd better figure out how to cooperate with us if you expect any help from us."

Randi decided she'd better calm down and listen. "OK, I'm sorry. What else do you need to know? I didn't do anything wrong."

"One more time, you and Dave were talking and drinking sitting on the hood of his truck. Was it an argument?"

"Well, yes, at times we were arguing. Dave was messing into my life and I wanted him to stop."

"Messing in your life, huh? And did he take kindly to you telling him to stop?"

Randi remembered Dave slapping her and hitting him back. "No. No, I guess he didn't. We got down off the truck and were arguing. He slapped me and I slapped him back."

"So that's another detail you left out. He hit you and you hit him back. As part of this argument about him messing in your life?"

"Yeah."

"How hard did you hit him back, Randi. You said you slapped him."

"Yeah, after he'd slapped me. He just wouldn't back off. Like he was going to hit me again."

"So you hit him in self-defense?"

"I guess so. We were just arguing."

"Now this is important. When you slapped him, did you hit him with your right hand or your left hand?"

Randi looked up at the ceiling and then back at Borton. "Hell, I can't remember. He hit me and I hit him back."

"Did you punch him or slap him?" Borton demonstrated the two ways with his right hand.

Randi suddenly thought back to her ring and the wax impression. That's what they're fishing for. Did I hit him hard enough for the ring to make a mark? Damn, I must have been really pissed. How the hell do I answer?

"It's a long time ago and, like I said, I'd had several margaritas. I may have backhanded him or I might have punched him with my fist. Hell, he picked up a rock and came at me. I thought he was going to bust my head open."

"Randi, it's important for you to try and remember. If you hit him hard enough to knock him out on his way into the water, this is a much more serious matter. Now, did you slap him or punch him?"

"I just slapped him. He was staggering around swearing at me. He hit me and I hit him back. Yeah, I think I slapped him."

Borton looked at Mallow with raised eyebrows.

"With your right hand, wearing the ring?"

"I guess so. I'm right handed. That's probably the hand I hit him with." Randi was trying to figure out from their reaction how this was going for her.

Borton reached into his pocket and took out Randi's ring. He handed it to her. "Randi, we still have to do some checking on this comparing the wax impression with the autopsy data. This is as far as we can go today, but I need to know how to get in touch with you over the next couple days."

"Well, unless I get fired, I'll still be up at the capitol working for Dan Carb in the State Affairs committee at least until midnight tomorrow night when the session ends. Either there or at my apartment. I'm not going anywhere if that's what you're asking. I didn't do anything wrong. I just defended myself and Dave fell drunk into the lake."

"That may well be the explanation of all the facts. We just need for you to be available if more questions come up."

They drove Randi back to her car on 15ᵗʰ Street and dropped her off. She assumed that her reporter was long gone. She sat in her car for long minutes trying to get the shakes under control. Randi had never felt so trapped as she did in the back of that police car. It wasn't a feeling she ever wanted again. I've got to get Dan Carb before they come at me again. Tomorrow is the Memorial Day holiday. Maybe they'll give it a rest.

Chapter 70

By the time Dan made it back to the House floor in mid-afternoon, it was obvious that the word about his role in killing the dereg bill was out. The bill's opponents kept coming by to congratulate him. They were jubilant and could not say enough about his sacrifice.

When Jim Clower came over to Dan's desk, Dan noticed that other members formed a circle several desks away as the two talked.

"That was a low down, dirty move, Carb. Why didn't you just come out and say you didn't like the bill?"

"Because if I had, you and Sam would have figured a way around my opposition. Those guys have bought off so many people, from the Governor on down, there was no way to publicly defeat this. And, Jim, I sincerely believe that this was bad legislation. Bad for business, for consumers, for competition. You were setting us up to be stuck with the same shell power supplier that California has. That is just asking for trouble."

"But, Dan, you could have influenced the bill to be better. You had a say in that, didn't you?"

"Let me tell you how much say I had in it. The day before the committee vote, I got called into a meeting and I had to make a big fuss even to see the language of the damned bill, much less to object to it. They told me they had the votes, they were out of time and I had to go along with it. Sure I told them I'd go along. Only because I knew I'd put in a sure kill."

Clower looked down at the desk and started fiddling with the buttons on Dan's console. "No changing your mind? What would it take?"

"Another bill with less than half the price tag and clear provision for supplier of last resort." Dan held up his hands, palms out. "And, I know, that's not in the cards. I've already tried."

Clower rubbed his chin. "You know we're going to come after you in 2000."

"No, Jim, you're not going to get that chance. This is my last session. You'll just have to go after somebody else."

Clower's jaw dropped at that news. He seemed to have run out of things to say. He reached out and the two men shook hands. Dan noticed that the members watching seemed to relax at their handshake.

Dan had just taken his seat when Lance Dunn came up to him. "Dan, the Governor wants to see you right away."

"Lance, you know I don't have anything else to say to Butch. I said it all in Billy's office."

"I know, Dan, but he wants to see you. We think there may be another way to look at this. Anyway, will you do us the courtesy of seeing Butch? He's waiting."

Dan pushed back from his desk and followed Lance out the back door of the House. They walked halfway around the rotunda at the second floor level and into the Governor's suite of offices.

Lance didn't wait to be let in. He just walked over to the double carved oak doors and opened them. Butch was seated behind the massive desk.

Dan turned around when he heard the door close behind him. Lance had gone out. Dan could not remember ever being in a room with Butch without someone from Butch's staff present.

"Come on in, Dan, boy. Let's sit over here on the couch and be comfortable. Can I get you a drink?"

"No, thanks, Governor. I'd better pass."

"OK, son. Now you just relax. I want to tell you a bit of a story. I don't want to pressure you on this deal. No, I just want you to have all the facts and then you make your decision."

"Well, Butch, I think I've already made my decision. I guess Billy told you."

"Yeah, he says you're thinking about retiring from politics. I know the temptation, but hear me out. You may have second thoughts."

Dan thought 'If you only knew'. Randi was now about twenty-four hours from ripping Dan and his family name to shreds. By the six o'clock news on Tuesday, Dan would be the butt of every late night comic in the business, not to mention a political liability on the scale of Monica. *OK, Governor, try to convince me you can overcome that.*

"I'm willing to listen. I'm skeptical, but I'll hear you out."

"I couldn't ask for more. Now what I'm about to tell you is in the strictest of confidence. You'll have to give me your word." Dan nodded. "You see, I've been working really hard on getting my presidential race going and it's going better than I ever expected. Now I know we're in different political parties, but my chances to wind up in the White House are really looking good. I've made a strong start and I don't think there's anybody who can catch me."

Dan settled back into his seat. This sounded like quite a show.

"So, I think you're a smart man and a good politician. You've always looked out for the farming and ranching interest in Texas and I applaud your efforts. In fact, I'll need to put some Democrats into my cabinet because the country is becoming more and more evenly split. I have to show some bipartisan spirit in order to get anything done as President. Don't you see how the deal might work?"

"I'm afraid I'm not following you, Governor."

"What I'm talking about is the possibility of Secretary of Agriculture in my cabinet in Washington. A position to impact farming and ranching across the whole United States, not just Texas."

"Now, Governor, I know you can't make that kind of offer."

"Right, right, Son. That was not an offer. That was just a possibility. But it isn't a possibility if that little ol' bill doesn't pass."

"How the hell does one bill in the Texas Legislature affect all those grand plans? It doesn't make any sense."

"Just trust me, Boy. It makes all the difference in the world. Now Billy tells me that you could get the point of order set aside just by running off that little girl working for you. Hell, I'll get her a fine job anywhere she wants with a raise in pay. She's the least of your problems."

If you only knew. Dan decided that he wouldn't help himself by turning down this illegal offer right away, but his situation left it completely hopeless. Just more medicine to take.

"Governor, as interesting as that sounds, I just don't think I can go for it. I really appreciate you thinking about me for a possible cabinet position, but I'm afraid I have to say no. You may not understand now, but wait a few days. It will become clearer to you."

Butch looked genuinely puzzled. "A few days? We don't have a few days, Son. We have to do this deal before midnight to save that bill if I understand it."

Dan stood up and Butch joined him. "Governor, as much as I wish I could help you, it's out of my hands. I wish you luck."

"Dammit, Carb, you're walking away from the deal of lifetime. I can really make it worth your while."

"Governor, it's not about money either. I've got more money than I need. It's something else that I can't explain."

Dan shook Butch's hand and left him with a confused look, staring down at the ornate coffee table where they'd been sitting.

Dan at least knew why Lance had left them alone. If the Governor was going to try to bribe Dan into dropping the poison pill, there had better not be any witnesses. Damn serious hardball.

Lance was waiting in the outer office. Dan answered Lance's raised eyebrows with a shrug and walked out into the hallway.

Chapter 71

Dan had tried to hide out in his capitol office, but the crush of press, lobbyist and members trying to get in to see him was too much. He'd given his staff the rest of Sunday night off and headed to the House floor. At least the capitol police could keep the public and press away from him.

That didn't help much either. There was the usual hectic pace of bill passage leading up the last twenty-four hours of the session. Lots of hopes and dreams were being trashed or fulfilled. But Dan had no interest whatsoever.

The old expression "If looks could kill" was more to the point. Dan was being shunned by members he'd served with for years. By seven-thirty Sunday night, with the session set to go all the way to midnight, Dan decided it would be best for him to leave. He wasn't doing anybody any good by staying. Billy couldn't even look at him.

As he walked through the underground annex parking lot, the raincoated man seemed to materialize out of nowhere. Dan's first response was to wonder when it had started raining. It was clear the last time he'd looked out.

"Representative Carb."

His east coast accent seemed to go with his black hair in a crew cut and the narrow, dark eyes.

"Yes, can I help you?" Dan stopped walking and faced the man who stood a good foot shorter.

"No, but I think that I can help you."

"What? I don't think I need any help."

"You need more than you realize. You have stepped off into a very serious area of national concern and you need to be very careful."

"Serious? National concern? I think you've got the wrong person." Dan started toward his truck again. The pull on his sleeve stopped him.

He turned to again face the smaller man. "Look, buddy, I don't know who the hell you think you are, but just keep your hands off me. And I don't know what the hell you're talking about."

"Here it is as plain as I can make it. We in the Agency don't take kindly to your messing around in national matters the way you're doing today. What you did when you killed that utility competition bill impacts national interests. You're placing yourself at personal risk. We just thought you ought to know. Might change your mind."

"Now wait just a damned minute. What Agency? 'We' who thought I ought to know? And are you threatening me?"

"You don't need to know the answers to those questions. All you need to know is that you have, probably innocently, strayed into a national issue in ways that place you in jeopardy. I'm going to be watching. If you straighten up and fly right, there'll be no trouble. We're not responsible for what happens if you don't get the message."

With that he turned on his heel and walked back toward the stairway to the annex.

Dan was flabbergasted. *That bastard just threatened me if I didn't drop the kill on dereg. Damn, these boys are serious. Agency? CIA? Well, Dan, boy, you've finally made it into the big leagues.*

As he started his truck, Dan wondered seriously what to do about that conversation. If he reported it, nobody would believe him. He'd have to find out what he meant about my "not getting the message."

Chapter 72

After the police left her at her car, Randi thought about going back to the capitol but didn't have the stomach to deal with the chaos of the session closing plus the mess the dereg fight had created. She figured that Borton must have something on her or he wouldn't keep coming back with more questions. Randi knew she should talk to a lawyer, but that prospect scared her even more. If the police were keeping tabs on her, her talking to a lawyer might make them think she was guilty.

She was on the way back to her apartment when she thought of Dee, a woman she'd worked with two sessions ago. The two of them had shared their hopes to go to law school some day, but Dee had actually enrolled. If Randi had it right, Dee would just be finishing her first year of law school. Yeah, I can ask Dee general questions and find out what kind of trouble I might be in.

Dee answered on the fifth ring and sounded tired.

"Hi, Dee, I'm glad I caught you. This is Randi."

"Hey, Randi. How's the wheeling and dealing going at the capitol? Sounds like you've been at the center of the big dereg fight that's all over the papers."

"Oh, that. Yep, that was a zoo all right, but it's only one more day and the session's over. Did law school treat you right?"

"Hell, girl, it's still treating me. I'm up to my ass in studying for finals. They try to kill off anybody that's not serious in the first year. I'm surviving so far, but just barely." Randi grimaced. She hoped Dee wasn't too busy to see her.

"Dee, I need to talk to you right away. I'm trying to help a buddy in another rep's office with a legal question and I thought you would have the quick answers."

"I don't know, Randi. I've just been at this a year and I'm more confused than certain about the stuff they are cramming in my head. Anyway, I'm jammed with two finals next week. Can't it wait?"

"No, they're in a hurry. Look, I'll just run by and you can tell fast if you can help or not. It'll just take a few minutes." Randi was pleading.

"Well, I guess. But don't come here. I haven't stopped studying to clean in two weeks. I'll meet you at that little coffee shop on Burnett. You remember, right down from my place."

"Sure. I'll be there in fifteen minutes."

Randi found herself checking the traffic behind her for any sign that Borton was having her followed. She didn't see anything, but the way they tracked her to the restaurant on 15th, she had to assume they were watching. Just meeting a friend for coffee shouldn't cause any problem.

Dee was waiting at a small table when Randi arrived. The little shop only seated about twenty people and this afternoon there were fewer than ten there. Most were dressed in shorts and tee shirts and looked like students.

Dee said, "Randi, you look a little ragged. Have you been overdoing it this session?"

"Oh, no, just the usual end-of-session crazies. I'm OK. Look, my buddy needs to know something about criminal law and I don't have a clue. She doesn't think there's any trouble, but she wants to check it out."

"Criminal law? I took a couple courses, but that's just the start. What's the problem she has?"

"Well, she was partying with some friends out at Lake Travis and things got a little rowdy. She and another girl got into an argument and slapped each other. Well, they had been drinking and the other girl actually fell down and broke her arm and is threatening to go to the police and file assault charges against her. My buddy wants to know if she has anything to worry about."

Dee wrinkled her brow. "Well, I think it depends. If they think the other girl fell because she was drunk, your buddy doesn't have anything to worry about. But if the fall was caused by an act your buddy did, then I think it gets fuzzier."

"What do you mean it gets fuzzier?"

"If I remember right, if your friend's hitting her actually caused the fall and broken arm, then she can be charged. Even if both parties were in the argument, if there was a positive action taken that directly resulted in the injury, then she's subject to being charged."

"But there was no intent to harm the other girl."

"Randi, that's not the point. You see there are lesser charges she might get caught on. Just like if someone does something and another person ends up dying. Your point about intent goes to whether the charge is murder."

Randi sucked in her breath.

"But with no intent to kill, there's manslaughter, reckless endangerment and I think a couple of others. They are lesser crimes, but still crimes. So in her case, there might be several levels of assault charges she might get caught on. It would all depend on how the story comes out to the police and how they interpret the incident. I'd tell her to hire herself a lawyer and get the straight story on it. It might be nothing or it might be trouble."

They parted outside the restaurant and Randi thanked Dee. They made plans to get together when the session and the semester were done. Randi had been hoping for comfort, but she didn't take much away from her meeting with Dee. Manslaughter. Reckless endangerment. Shit.

She made stops at the grocery store and the liquor store on the way to her apartment. She decided her luck was running a little better when there was no sign of Borton as she unlocked her door.

Randi poured a whole can of chocolate sauce over the key lime pie she'd bought and ate the whole thing, washing it down with a strong margarita in an iced tea glass. She poured herself another drink and sat on her bed.

To her audience of stuffed bears she said, "Well, guys, it looks like this might be it for little ol' Randi. That fucking cop is on my ass and he just might put me where the sun comes in stripes. Prison." Randi drew back in disgust at the sound of the word. She downed her drink and went to pour another.

"But Randi here is going out with a bang. Hah, hah. A bang. Get it? Me and big Dan Carb in the raw ready for a bang. Hell, you boys saw the whole thing. You can be my witnessesh. I'm going to bust Big Dan'sh ass on my way out." The room was starting to spin and Randi felt sick at her stomach. "Uh, oh," she shouted as she raced to the bathroom and threw up into the toilet.

She got up off her knees and staggered to the kitchen. The open tequila bottle was on the counter and she took a mouthful, swished around and spat it into the sink. The last thing Randi remembered was turning the bottle up to her mouth, draining the rest of the fifth straight.

Chapter 73

Dan could remember other sessions when they got to the last day and there was a sense of everything happening at such a pace there was no way anybody could keep up with it. That was part of the strategy of the Speaker to increase control and tighten his grip on what bills made it into law and the bigger number that got lost along the way. With more than five thousand bills filed in a typical session and only a few hundred making it into law, there was a lot of disappointment to go around.

But Dan somehow felt above all that this time. He knew as he walked into his office at nine on Monday morning that today would end more than just a session. Four terms in the House. Hell, almost forty years of having a Carb in either the House or Senate. And all because of Daddy's fucking around and Randi's abiding hatred. Randi. Dan couldn't remember seeing her after lunch on Sunday. He wondered where she was. Probably off planning his demise.

Paula tried to get Dan interested in two of his own bills that were up for final passage today. "Dan, we're still getting calls from the breeders associations about this bill on herd control and Mad Cow Disease. You don't expect any trouble on it do you?"

Dan felt as though he was watching this discussion on TV and not part of it. It wasn't fair to Paula after all her hard work. Dan hadn't told Paula about his planned retirement from the House. With her background, Dan knew she'd easily land a job in another office with more than a year to plan.

They somehow concluded the discussion of the day's bills and Dan answered the ten o'clock call to the floor, almost sleepwalking through the proceedings.

Several of the reporters at the back of the House chamber tried to get information from him about the dereg debacle, but Dan referred everybody to the Speaker. He wasn't about to compound his troubles with some press quotes. He'd just hide and let the process play out. Now just twelve hours to go.

The one thing Dan was concerned about was the damn little yankee in the raincoat. He hadn't counted on being threatened as part of his kill plan. Dan knew he could go to the DPS or to the capitol police but that would escalate into even more problems because it was sure to get to the press. Dan swore again at Texas' lack of a State Police department. With the constitutional ban coming out of the carpetbagger days of the civil war, county sheriffs were the highest level of police presence and this was not an issue Dan wanted to bring to the Travis County sheriff.

From the phone at his desk on the House floor, Dan placed a call he thought he'd never make. He had dealt with the Texas Rangers over cattle stealing rings before, but never for a criminal matter.

"Hi, Bill. It's Dan Carb." Lieutenant Bill Kerry was a career Ranger and operated out of his ranch in Hearne. They had worked together and put eight people in prison on a cattle stealing charge several years back and he and Dan had stayed in touch ever since.

"Hello, Dan. What you been up to?"

"Oh, not much. Or maybe really too much. Bill, this is kinda an official call. I'm in Austin at the capitol and the legislature is going to wind up the session tonight. If you're free, I need for you to come on over here and meet with me today. It's important."

"Don't tell me they're stealing cows at the capitol. What's going on, Dan?"

Dan wondered how much to tell him. He'd better be clear so Bill would come for sure. "Well, Bill, I've actually received a threat over some of my work here in the legislature and it . ."

Bill interrupted. "A threat? Dan, what the hell are you talking about? Are you in danger?" He sounded tense.

"I don't think so, but I'm not sure. That's why I wanted you to look into it."

"Hell, boy, that place is crawling with police. I'll come right away, but if you're in trouble, get one of them while I'm getting there."

"I don't think it's that urgent, Bill. But I'd be much obliged if you can get over here."

"Give me two hours. Where do I find you?"

"Just come to the House door on the second floor of the capitol and ask one of the House sergeants to get me off the floor. I'll stay here, out in the open until you get here."

"Damn, it sounds serious, Dan. Are you sure you're OK?"

"I'm fine, Bill. I'll see you shortly."

Dan sat at his desk, now largely ignored by everyone. It was like the members were afraid to get too close for fear of his troubles rubbing off on them. That suited Dan just fine. He sat there actually reading the bills in his packet, something he almost never did on bills not his own. It was a very strange feeling in a very familiar place.

Chapter 74

Butch Grange had not slept at all Sunday night. He had been looking forward for so long to the legislative session being over so he could get back to the campaign trail he loved so much. But now, here it was the last day of the session and instead of planning his next trip he was trying to figure out how to cover five million dollars of expenses he owed.

His daddy had given him a half million, about three hundred thousand had come in from the utility people and he'd pulled another half million out of the family business his son was running. But the family well was running low and he desperately needed the rest of the money Sam had committed. If he had to cancel his airplane and all the events Ann had scheduled for him, it would be a signal to the rest of the Republican candidates that Butch was faltering.

Maybe Dan Carb had reconsidered overnight. Maybe he'd seen the light. This thought was the only thing that got him going. By ten Monday morning Butch was at his desk. Lance and Ann were facing him.

Ann seemed so rattled that her usual take-charge aura was completely missing. "Governor, I've come up with an idea that might just get that point of order problem solved."

"Great, Ann. What is it? What is it?"

Lance's sounded skeptical. "Now just a minute, Ann. Butch, I think we have to be careful meddling into internal House workings."

"Oh, to hell with that, Lance. This is desperation time. Ann, what's your idea?"

"Well, we've all been focused on getting Dan Carb to say that that Crendall woman didn't have authority to bring the bill to the Calendars Committee. But Carb isn't budging, even with threats. I think we ought to approach the girl ourselves. She's young and for a few thousand dollars she'd probably say anything we asked."

"I'm not listening to this," Lance said, putting his hands over his ears. "I did not hear threats or bribes being discussed in the Governor's office."

Butch waved him off. "Do you think she'd go for it, Ann? Hell, we wouldn't need Carb then. She could just say she did it on her own and that might leave Billy room to move on the bill. It's a stroke of genius." Ann took off to put the plan in motion. Lance seemed to mope out of the office.

Butch never did figure out how the wire services got wind of his problems around the dereg bill, but around noon he started getting calls from Washington and New York asking about rumored trouble in his campaign. The press calls he had been relishing, now gave him fits.

"I'm not going to start responding to every rumor someone wants to start." This was his fifth call on the subject and the second from the Associated Press. "My plan to stay in Texas and look after business in the legislative session is going just fine. I'll have plenty of new initiatives to report when I'm back out on the campaign trail." He hung up the phone, clear that he shouldn't take any more calls.

"Whew, Mrs. Kelly, just put all those press calls through to the national campaign office. I can't talk to them any more." Mrs. Kelly had just come into his office and seemed to be in a bad mood this morning. Probably all this last minute rushing around.

"That's fine, Governor, but what about that crowd in the waiting area trying to get in to see you? They're like a pack of hungry dogs and I can't get rid of them."

"Oh, damn, are they in the office too? 'Sorry, I didn't mean to swear."

"Well, they nearly have me swearing, too. They all got the rumor that you're in some kind of trouble over the electrical matters and they look like they're ready to camp out until you answer them. It was up to fifteen reporters the last time I counted."

"Mrs. Kelly, I can't face that crowd now. We're still working out the issue. I need to get away."

"But where? They think they're on a hot trail and you won't get any peace, wherever you go. You need someplace to hide." Butch didn't like the idea of running away, but this situation was shaping up to be a major mess.

"But where?" he asked.

"Why not come over to my place? Nobody will think of looking for you there. And you can talk to Mr. Lance by phone to check on things. Governor, I can go get my car and bring it right up to the Senate wing door.

You put on a raincoat and one of those gimme caps and slip out through the staff offices. And don't dare smile at anybody. That's a dead giveaway."

"That sounds like a plan, Mrs. Kelly. You're a life-saver. I can just stay there until this heat blows over." Butch wondered why he wasn't supposed to smile.

It was nearly two when Lance pushed his way through the mob of reporters in the Governor's waiting room to find the Governor gone. The call to the DPS confirmed to him that they thought he was still in his office. There had been no trips out. The DPS captain quietly started a search of the capitol and mansion.

Chapter 75

The note from the sergeant that Bill Kelly was waiting to see him came in just after two. Somehow just Bill's name on the note made Dan feel better. He headed for the back door.

Bill was dressed in a checked shirt, nice tan slacks and he wore his signature white straw Stetson. His gray hair stuck out in tufts below his hat.

"Hey, Bill," Dan said, shaking his hand. "We need to make our way through that crowd out there and find a place to talk."

"Lead the way."

Dan had to fend off several reporters and two utility lobbyists but they made it out onto the balcony inside the capitol dome. Dan headed to the House library, a place he thought they could talk without too much interruption.

Dan and Bill went back into the rows of shelved books. It appeared that they were the only ones there beside the lonely librarian behind the front desk who seemed to ignore them.

"So, Dan, what's this all about?"

"Well, I killed a bill that a lot of the big power brokers around here were counting on passing. It's got me in deep shit with the Speaker and the Governor, but I'm sticking to my guns. It all broke yesterday and there's been uproar every since."

"They're not the ones threatening, are they?"

"No. At least I don't think so. Last night when I was heading down to my truck in the underground parking lot, this guy I've never seen came up to me and started telling me I was messing with national issues and I needed to back off. He mentioned something about 'the Agency' but he wouldn't identify himself. My guess is CIA. He said everything would be all right if I backed off killing the bill. Then he said he wouldn't be responsible for what happened to me if I didn't."

"Damn. That doesn't sound good. What did he look like?"

"A little short, dark-haired guy with a flattop. He's got brown eyes and yesterday he was wearing one of those tan raincoats with all the flaps. And it wasn't raining."

"Have you seen him since? Is he still hanging around?"

"I haven't seen him, but he seems to appear and disappear fairly easily. With that raincoat he's easy to spot. I assume since I haven't backed off on that bill he's still around here somewhere."

"OK, you just go back to work. I'll look around for him. I'll let you know."

Dan left Bill in the rotunda and went back onto the House floor. It was more of the same now with bills coming over from the Senate trying to get final approval.

Around four-thirty a sergeant brought Dan a note. It was from Bill. "Your guess on the agency was correct. Taking raincoat out for cleaning. We'll talk when I get back." Dan looked around the gallery but saw no sign of Bill or his raincoated friend. He looked back at the note and broke out laughing. It was the best he'd felt in two days. He couldn't imagine what Bill was up to and couldn't wait to hear.

Dan ate a dinner of cold sandwiches in the member's lounge, still mostly being treated as an outcast. He still hadn't heard from Randi and wondered what she was up to. He was afraid she'd do her thing at the last hours of the session and he'd be further humiliated. Oh, well. It can't get much worse.

Chapter 76

The first thing Randi saw was the underside of the kitchen cabinet. She couldn't figure out why she was on the floor, but her head hurt so badly she'd have to get up and find some aspirin. She rolled over on her side and tried to get up. It wasn't going to be easy. Just sitting up made her dizzy and sick to her stomach.

She waited for long minutes and finally was able to stand, holding onto the counter. The apartment was dark except for a little light coming in from the living room curtain. She walked unsteadily over to the front window and parted the curtain. Still dark. Maybe she just woke up early.

After she sat on the pot for a long time, almost falling back to sleep, she headed over to the nightstand to set her alarm. She wanted to get to the capitol by at least noon so she could get the reporters lined up.

She picked up the alarm and the clock said nine-thirty. She started to set the alarm but stopped. How the hell is it dark outside at nine o'clock in the morning? After checking to be sure she saw darkness outside she looked back at the clock. "Shit. It's nine o'clock at night. What the hell happened to Monday?"

When she saw the broken tequila bottle on the kitchen floor she suddenly remembered. "Dammit, Randi. You've almost blown it. Get your ass in gear."

Her face in the mirror looked to her like last week's leftovers. "Shower, wash my hair, make-up. I've got to look good for TV. Damn the time!"

Getting cleaned up and dressed seemed to take forever. She picked out a nice white blouse and a black ribbon tie to go with her black pants suit. Her hair was freshly washed and dried. The make-up didn't completely cover the wretched condition of her eyes, but it made them a lot better. Two big swigs of Pepto had her stomach better under control. She hoped she could hang on.

It was past ten-thirty when she pulled into her parking place in the annex lot. Randi had the little video disc of Dan in her bedroom in the pocket of her jacket. She tried running to the elevator, but couldn't keep it up. This must be the hangover of the century.

She checked by the State Affairs office and found it dark and locked. Just an hour left of the session. The staff would be preparing for the 'Sine Die' parties after the final gavel fell on the session. Randi hoped some of the reporters she was close to were still around. It depended if anything was still being debated.

When she got to the second floor her heart sank. The crowd outside the House door was mostly lobbyists and it wasn't much of a crowd at all. The session must be winding down peacefully. She didn't recognize either of the two people in the press room. Shit. She'd missed them.

On a gamble she went up the stairs to the House gallery. There were several dozen people watching as someone made a loud speech. It didn't help Randi's headache. Dan wasn't at his desk. Randi walked over to talk to one of the sergeants standing near a window. But as she passed the window, something outside caught Randi's eye. Borton's dark blue sedan and two Austin police cruisers were pulled up by the curb at the north door of the capitol. Borton stood talking to two uniformed officers showing them some papers.

Randi was sure she'd wet her pants. Her head and stomach took turns giving her ripping pain. He was coming to arrest her! Damn luck. She hadn't found her reporters yet and that bastard was going to arrest her. She had to run. But where?

Out on the third floor balcony Randi looked down and saw Borton and two of the uniformed policemen run across the seals heading for the stairs. They were coming to get her. Randi started to cry. She couldn't think which way to run. Her head was pulsing shots of pain. She sensed the walls closing in on her. The back of the cop car. Jail. She couldn't see for her tears. She heard footsteps pounding on the stairway below her. God. What should she I do? Then she saw her way to get out and get Dan Carb at the same time.

Chapter 77

The second note from Bill Kelly asked Dan to meet him in the DPS office on the first floor. With zero interest in the closing floor action, Dan headed to meet him.

Bill had arranged a private office for them to talk.

"Bill, that last note was a little cryptic. Where's our raincoat guy?"

"Oh, it turned out he was walking around with no identification on him. Probably meant he was up to no good. I found him lurking around over on the Senate side. Talking to some skinny, dark haired woman about a guy named Randy."

"Probably Ann Terrance. So what happened?"

"Oh I just followed him for a while and caught him downstairs in an empty hallway and asked him for his ID. He wasn't too interested in cooperating with this 'cowboy,' as he called me. A DPS buddy and I got him cuffed and took away all his Dick Tracy toys. They sure do give those boys a lot of things to play with."

Dan grinned big. "You cuffed him? Did you charge him or something?"

Bill looked a little coy. "Nah, nothing like that. He's just on a little trip out to west Texas in a DPS cruiser. Since he couldn't give us any idea who he was or why he was hanging around the capitol we took some precautions. He's gonna have about a twenty-five mile walk over some rough ground to the nearest phone when he gets dropped off about sunrise tomorrow. We told him we don't take kindly to his type messing around in Texas business."

"E-e-e-e-e-a-a-a-a-a-a-a-e-e-e-e-e-h." The blood-curdling scream rising in pitch came from the hallway outside the office where Bill and Dan were talking. They both jumped up and ran for the door.

Several people were running toward the center rotunda and they ran that way.

The scene Dan saw when he got to the rotunda was sickening. There was blood spattered all over the granite floor and the walls. When Dan recognized the bloodied body with the long blond hair in the pool of blood in the center of the room he almost fell backwards. Someone was saying that she had jumped from the third floor balcony. Dan looked up and saw people all along the railings looking down at the scene.

DPS and capitol police officers were moving people out of the rotunda. Dan walked toward the north door from which he had entered. He didn't see where Bill had gone. Just before he got to the door he noticed a small square sitting on the floor next to the wall. He reached down and picked up the tiny video disk. The label on the disk in Randi's flair handwriting simply said, "Big Dan". He put the disk in his inside coat pocket and went down the hall toward the north capitol door.

He stopped in the big carved doorway to the closed House Post Office. Randi. Randi. Poor devil. But why? What a helluva way to get at him, if that's what she was trying to do. Dan was shaking with shock and he tried to calm himself.

He headed up the stairs that led to the back hallway of the House chamber. The sister he'd just found was gone. And she hadn't gotten the word out that she was his sister. He stopped on the empty landing at the top of the stairs. Hey, he had her video. Her threat to ruin him was gone. He could stay in the House.

The picture of that foggy field full of hay bales and the feeling of being back on the ranch completely filled Dan's senses. He could smell the hay. He could hear the meadowlarks calling back and forth over the hills. He knew where he belonged. *Thank you, little sister, for that.*